EMBER
OF
Light

HANNAH JACKLIN

Cover Design: Getcovers.com
Inside Illustrations: Inda Ashes Art

First Edition: 2024

Ember of Light is a work of fiction. Names, characters, places, and incidents are the product of the author's imagination or are used fictitiously. Any resemblance to actual persons, living or dead, events, or locales is entirely coincidental.

ISBN 978-1-7381816-0-5

DEDICATION

To my love, Joseph

And to all of those who are kind enough to read.

Ember of Light

Born from the light in a flash so powerful it left the earth scorched, leaving evil to be born of the embers.

1

UNSEEN ARRIVAL

Dreams are figments of the imagination—mismatched images and tiny slivers of truth. That's what I thought, or at least that's what everyone else believed. What if dreams could contain something else, something truly real? A look into reality; past, present, or future.

I dreamed of him before I saw him, in the alley behind the old Western Apartments.

As I walked the worn path, a shiver crawled up my spine, the familiarity of the scene playing tricks on my senses. He appeared in front of me as if emerging from the fog of a half-forgotten dream. His hair, the color of darkness, fell forward, partially obscuring a tired face in its shadow.

His eyes swept over the dirt before halting at the ground by my feet.

I stood rooted in place, the tiny hairs on the nape of my

neck bristled, and my leg muscles tightened as they prepared to run. His eyes rose to meet mine, the color of sapphire.

Despite his presence in the usually quiet trail, I continued, gripping the single strap of the workbag that hugged my shoulder. My mind flicked between now and the dream, which meant nothing to me a few moments ago.

In the dream, the sky darkened suddenly, and the ground disappeared beneath a thick blanket of fog. I looked down at my hands, shuddering as I noticed the gray pallor of death settling into my skin.

His eyes held mine as his approach slowed. I scanned his tall form, stopping at his neck where a thin leather cord hugged his throat; a pendant sat neatly in its hollow. A delicate silver pattern, like that of an exploding sun, covered its surface.

I blinked heavily as I hurried past. The fog dissipated as I pulled myself out of the dream and back to the present, leaving the familiar stranger behind me.

"Small" was an understatement; "quaint" was the nice way to put it. Houses grew closer the nearer you got to the heart of Hayzun. A large bell tower with four clock faces acted as the center point on a town-sized compass.

School was in session, as autumn was well underway. As I got closer to the school building, I could hear the indistinguishable chatter from the open ground-floor windows.

I couldn't help but feel hard done by. I barely graduated. Money became tight after my father passed, and I took on every shift possible at the animal clinic. It left little time for education. My father was once the clinic's primary veterinarian and taught me many things over the years, enough to keep us afloat.

As I continued to walk, the path veered right, then widened. The earthy scent of pine trees enveloped my senses.

A movement caught my eye on the ground. A man knelt by the edge of a large wooden box, working the loose earth. From a plastic container, he plucked a purple flower, planting it in the dirt.

It's a bit late in the season for gardening, isn't it?

His balding head turned up at the sound of my approach. The garden was new, and so was he.

I moved forward, admiring his work. The friendly-looking man offered a slight smile as he plucked another flower from its pot.

The ground felt rough underfoot. Leaves and pine needles scattered across the dirt, softly crunching beneath the soles of my shoes as I hurried along.

Shades of red, yellow, and brown drifted from the sky, blanketing the earth in their vivid colors. A beautiful scene masked the reality of fall; death had once again plagued the trees of Hayzun.

A black shadow grazed my periphery. Glancing over, I saw an enormous bird screeching, extending its black wings. It flew from branch to branch high above, then landed on the uneven ground in front of me. Its beak opened and closed, emitting low whistles.

Small beady eyes watched me, eerily human-like, monitoring my movements. As I neared, it screeched one last time, fluttered its feathers, and pushed itself into the air, landing in a nearby tree. My eyes tracked its movements as it followed me, moving from tree to tree.

I finally left the bird behind, pushing the door open to

the clinic. In the distance, the bird cawed while a doorbell rang above, signaling my arrival to the clients and their human counterparts.

Today marked a late morning start for me, meaning everyone else's day was well underway. Upon entry, a bitter scent greeted me—the familiar yet foreign smell of antiseptic. My father always emphasized the clinic's importance in caring for those unable to care for themselves. Since his passing, I found that sentiment rather trivial. I had more important things to worry about like having enough money for food.

Mason emerged from the back hallway, his tattoo-clad arms contrasting with the clinic's subdued colors. His tall, lanky frame settled behind the front desk, a nod of acknowledgment passing between us. Bones, the senile office cat, left a trail of long white hairs against my scrubs as he rubbed against them.

While Mason called a patient to the front desk, I headed down the hall and to the left to stow my work bag in my locker. The gray paint had long since worn away from the tin, leaving patches of rust.

Returning down the hall, the white tile floor squeaked under my shoes as I re-entered the main office. The harsh fluorescent lights flickered to life as I turned them on, their dull buzz filling the small room and echoing off the large back window.

I pulled out the old chair at my desk and settled into the thick pile of papers that needed filing. Thin rays of sun slipped through the clouds, warming my back through the double-paned glass.

Minutes ticked by as I sat, the sun gradually lowering in the sky.

Closing the drawer, I spun around, accidentally dropping a handful of papers as the window cracked loudly. It wasn't the first time a bird had collided with it. It more than likely wouldn't be the last either.

Feathers stuck to the glass in clumps, coated in beads of a red sticky fluid. Cringing, I grabbed a garbage bag, gloves, paper towels, and window cleaner. Opening the back door, I glanced below the window to find a raven, wings spread, lying still amid the tangled grass.

My gut twisted at the sight. It resembled the cawing bird that had followed me earlier that morning.

Donning the gloves, I opened the bag and bent down to pick up the bird. Blood matted its slick feathers, coating my fingers and palms. Its beady, lifeless eyes seemed to follow me as I carefully placed its large body into the bag.

Inches from its destination, the bird wrenched itself sideways, pulling on its wings and twisting against my hold. Surprised, I let go and watched as it flew into a nearby tree, shocked it had survived.

Regaining composure, I grabbed the cleaner and a cloth. Wiping most of the blood from my gloves, I began working on the window, the bird still observing me from a distance.

Stuffing the stray feathers into the bag along with a wad of paper towels, I abruptly halted. An image vividly appeared in my mind, urging attention. It danced in my head, slightly blurred at the edges like a memory fading after a few hours. My feet led me back inside to the desk. There, I retrieved a blank sheet of paper and a pen. The image flowed from my mind through the pen and onto the paper.

I sketched the image on a blank sheet of paper, the lines flowing from my pen as if guided by an unseen force.

Hayzun was a small, sleepy land dotted with houses, farmland, and an immense number of pine trees. Maine is its home, nestled a few miles from the coast. Compared to other towns, it was minuscule, with a population of fewer than ten thousand people.

The most excitement it had ever seen was in the mid to late 1800s when it was a flourishing mining town. It still hosted a small wash plant at the far end of the gulch, and a coal mine had long been abandoned deep in the forest behind the old water tower.

Crime was low, even though the laws were lax due to the scarcity of people to commit it. Like most towns, cities, or neighboring counties, there were different types of people here. Those better off lived closer to the outskirts of town, marked southeast by a relic of a clock tower, while those worse-off resided closer to the town square, where the lots were smaller, and the houses were of lesser value.

Living southwest of town was not something to strive for, but I had no choice. Being an only child of a widowed mother, who was distant both maternally and physically, was bound to get you stuck in a sort of limbo—not poor, but not well-off.

My house was smaller and less structurally sound than those to the east, but it offered more safety than those to the north.

The town, a reflection of the waking world and the dreams seeping into reality emerged on the page.

As the ink journeyed along the paper, I felt a connection to something beyond my understanding as I etched markings from border to border. Lines, thick and thin, shades from black to white diverged against one another. The image held layers of meaning, like a puzzle waiting to be solved. It hinted at an intricate dance between light and shadows, a dance I found myself inexplicably drawn into.

Bold gates sat closed, perpendicular to a winding road. Just inside the gates sat a small brick building with a spire, surrounded by an unkindness of ravens flooding the surrounding trees.

I couldn't shake the feeling that my dreams, the things I was seeing held more than mere figments of imagination. There was a thread connecting them to reality, a thread I was just beginning to unravel.

SHATTERED MEMORIES

Creaking caught my attention as the office door swung open. I quickly hid my sketches under the pile of disorganized files beside me. Miles, a gray-eyed stout man, entered, his graying hair neatly combed back.

"Charlotte, there is someone in room three. Mason and I are busy with another client. He says he found the dog on the side of the road," he informed, and I nodded, pushing my chair back and standing as Miles hurried out.

Glancing at my drawing beneath the pile of papers, I paused for a moment before pushing my way through the door.

Room three awaited just down the hall. Swinging the door open, I stepped inside. On the metal table lay a medium-sized dog, dark fur matted and its body limp. I wasn't alone; a dark figure stood near the far wall, hands pocketed and back turned.

The dog flinched as I approached, prompting the stranger to face me. It was him—the unsettling figure from that morning.

I took a step back, uneasy under his scrutinizing gaze, then turned my attention to the injured dog.

"Do you know what happened?" I cringed as my voice echoed off the walls and the cold tile floor. It didn't sound like mine.

The stranger shook his head, joining me at the metal slab. It was a male dog, no collar, likely a stray. Patches of missing fur adorned his back leg, evidence of a possible collision on the road.

My dad had taught me the basics, so I knew what to do. It was one of the only things I was confident in because I had the best teacher.

The dog lay still, and despite the injuries, it seemed not to be in pain. Putting on gloves I moved to inspect the scratches on his back leg.

As I rounded the corner to examine the dog's face, it unexpectedly lurched forward, growling, and baring its teeth. Startled, I jumped back, a wave of heat creeping through my body. The dog whimpered in pain.

The stranger stepped forward, calming the animal with a touch. I tried again, this time successfully. Scratches lined his pink skin, beads of blood wetting his fur.

A sudden, firm grip on my wrist jolted me, causing me to startle. I looked up to meet the stranger's eyes. He flipped my arm over, revealing long scratches.

"What happened?" His inquiry sent a shiver down my spine along with his voice. It was the first time I heard him speak.

"A raven hit the window this morning. I thought it was dead, but it wasn't," I explained, feeling a deep connection between that incident and the scratches on my arm.

"Do you need help?" His concern was evident in his eyes. I hesitated, fingers trembling as I reached for bandages and alcohol.

Without a pause, he took them from my hands and took charge. As he tended to my wounds, he glanced at me through his lashes while pouring the alcohol. Expecting pain, I closed my eyes, bracing for the sting. Surprisingly, nothing happened. When I dared to peek, he was calmly wrapping a bandage around my arm, securing it in place with tape.

Turning from me, he went over to inspect the dog further, now comfortably asleep. His gentle touch on the dog's matted fur struck a chord within me. As he petted the animal, I gathered more bandages and ointment.

After cleaning the wounds and trimming away some of the hair, I gently wrapped them in gauze. The animal lay still, almost as if it understood I was trying to help after his earlier outburst. I glanced at the stranger and then back at the large animal.

Retrieving a set of forms from the cupboard and a pen from the drawer, I turned to the stranger and removed my gloves.

"Can I have your name for the paperwork?" I eyed him carefully. There was a moment's pause before he spoke.

"Jesse." His name reverberated in my ears, sounding oddly familiar.

"Last name?" Another pause, almost too long

"Carter." I nodded, jotting it down on the form. My

attention returned to the stray. I didn't want to see him end up at the shelter.

"Do you want to keep him if we can't find the owner?"

"If not, he'll go to the shelter." Jesse glanced at me, seeming to ponder the question.

"I'm only in town for a few days," he replied after a brief pause. A sinking feeling settled in my stomach. Was it for the dog or the stranger I saw in my dreams? I shook off the unsettling sensation.

"Would you mind carrying him to the kennels for me?" I asked. Jesse nodded, stepping forward and carefully lifting the dog against his chest. The dog winced softly as he was moved.

Guiding the way from exam room three to the back kennels, I opened an empty kennel. Jesse gently deposited the stray onto the mattress and secured the door.

As he turned to speak, a mix of voices interrupted us, resonating from the lobby. We hurried out to see what the commotion was about. Jesse followed closely behind. The volume of the conversation escalated with each step, echoing through the lobby of the clinic.

3

TANGLED THREADS

I rushed into the lobby to find a female officer speaking to Miles. Officer Gates wore a morose expression on her youthful face.

"They found him in his office this morning," she uttered, her gaze lingering on Miles.

"What's going on?" My voice came out harsh as everyone else fell silent. Mason stepped forward, pulling me aside. I felt Jesse move behind me. Mason eyed him up and down before clearing his throat, his attention returning to me, hands wringing.

"They found Miles's brother in his office this morning. He tried to hang himself." He paused, his words hitting me hard. "He's still alive, but in a coma." My eyes widened, my hand shooting to cover my mouth. Miles's brother, the mayor of Hayzun—why would he do something like this? The pit in my stomach grew, bile forcing its way into my throat. He had always been cheery and happy anytime I saw him. I guess you never truly know what is going on in someone's life.

"That's not the only thing." Mason's voice interrupted my thoughts. I looked back up to him, and Jesse stiffened behind me. Bones once again rubbed up against my legs. Mason noticed the cat's odd behavior, then his gaze shifted to my bandaged arm.

"What happened?" Mason gently took my arm in his hands.

"A bird hit the window and was still alive when I picked it up," I explained, pulling my arm back.

"Are you okay?" I nodded, sensing Jesse moving closer to me into my periphery. His features were rigid, his jaw set. Mason ignored him and continue to speak, "Irene Walker, has gone missing."

Irene Walker, previously from Falmouth, had gone missing on October third, presumably in the early morning. They discovered her car abandoned at Hayzun Memorial Hospital, where she worked nights.

Her black and white portrait stared at me from the posters on the desk, an oval face framed by what I imagined to be dark hair. The news hit me harder than expected, and a lump formed in my throat. It wasn't just the missing person's case or the attempted suicide; it was the convergence of all these events at once.

The last person to go missing in Hayzun was a young child who had been separated from his mother and was found hiding under the old weeping willow south of the clock tower. There weren't many places to hide here.

A ringing filled my ears, jolting me back to the reality of the small, stuffy office. The phone sat to my left, red lights signaling an incoming call. Picking up the receiver, I held it to my ear.

"Hayzun Animal Clinic." There was a breath on the other end, followed by a pause. "Hello?" The line went dead, sending an irritating beep tickling my ears. I replaced the corded phone on the receiver. Darkness flickered in the corner of my eyes, dissipating as I followed it to the corner of the room.

The image of the church I drew that morning flashed in my mind. The only church in Hayzun sat nestled between the Black Willow Hotel and a poorly maintained railway.

I turned, peering out the window behind me where I could make out pieces of the wrought iron fencing that bordered the church's graveyard. A shiver of sadness rolled down my spine as I remembered walking through the lines of headstones. Many were old, some new, and far too many marked lives that ended too quickly. It was almost two years ago that I attended my father's funeral there. A knot formed in my throat as I turned around, thinking of that day. The day I stood in front of a casket-sized pit that was soon to house the only person who cared about me.

The sun began to lower in the sky, casting a pink hue that filled the small office. Another day was coming to an end.

A knock at the door jerked my attention. Mason stood there; his face framed by raven-colored hair. The tattoo on his left arm coiled like a serpent from his wrist to his bicep.

"Do you want a ride home?" He stood waiting for a

response as I shuffled papers. Mason started working at the clinic almost a year ago. He had always been kind to me, which, for some reason, was just as unnerving. I suppose my trust had dwindled to an almost nonexistent level over the years.

"No, it's okay." I wrung my hands before wiping them on my pants. "I can walk."

"Are you sure?" I nodded. "I don't mind," Mason added.

"I could use the walk." I smiled, standing, heading to the back room to gather my things. Minutes later, I was retracing my steps home, passing through the schoolyard, gravel alleyway, and down the sidewalk to an empty house.

Walking up the steps to my front porch, I pulled a key from the front pocket of my workbag. The worn-out wood creaked under my weight, setting a rhythmic tune with each step. I was about to insert the key into the rusted deadbolt when my eyes caught a flicker of movement near the corner of the house. A gasp escaped my lips, and in my surprise, the key slipped from my fingers. I watched it tumble, a glint of metal catching the dim light, as it fell through a crack in the wooden porch, landing softly on the damp soil below. The figure stepped into the wash of light produced by a blinking spotlight above the door—it was Jesse.

"How did you even find me?" I asked.

"It's a small town," he replied with a shrug.

"I still don't understand what you're doing here." I felt unease creeping into the pit of my stomach.

"I just wanted to make sure you made it home, okay?" He tucked his hands into the pockets of his jeans.

"Why wouldn't I have made it okay?" The feeling in my stomach persisted. I shook my head. "Well, I'm fine, so you can go now." When he didn't move, I took a cautious step back.

There was a spare key tucked away, a secret known only to me, hidden in a broken bulb above the door inside the light fixture. I hesitated, not wanting him to discover my hiding spot.

I felt Jesse's scrutinizing gaze as I wrung my hands. My fingers brushed over the pearl-colored scars that adorned my wrists—puckered and raised. My mind wandered to the origin of those scars—the day of my father's funeral. It was then that I crossed the Rainbow Bridge for the first time, a multicolored expanse spanning one side of the gulch to the other. It marked my first venture beyond the town's limits.

Dressed in a deep navy-blue dress, tears staining my cheeks, I yearned for an escape. It was a choice that would haunt me. The further I wandered, the more distant I felt from the sadness waiting for me back home.

I walked until the sun lowered in the sky and stars began to form, my mind wandering just as far. The screeching of tires pulled up beside me, jolting me back to the cracked walkway lining the winding roads.

In hindsight, I shouldn't have been out so late, and for a long time, I blamed myself. I blamed myself for how quickly they pulled me into the vehicle—an old, weathered van. I blamed myself for how easily the dress made it for them to violate me and leave me bleeding on the concrete. I think my mother blamed me too. When I called her crying from a nearby phone booth, she sounded irritated when I needed her to come get me.

It pushed me over the edge. Losing my father, then that. Only when the pain seared my wrists and stained the water in the porcelain tub did she take me to the hospital. Any ounce of care she had mustered for me died with my father.

I shook my head, bringing me back to the porch, back to the stranger. His features softened.

In the harsh light of the porch fixture, I noticed small, pale lines on his forearms. Tattoos? Scars, maybe?

Catching me looking, he cleared his throat. Rude, considering he was, in fact, on my porch and not the other way around. He seemed to realize this and adjusted his hands in his pockets.

I took a step back, feeling a sudden chill as the wind rustled through the trees, sending a shiver down my spine. Jesse shifted, his eyes briefly meeting mine before he averted his gaze, focusing on a distant point in the darkness.

"Look, I didn't mean to startle you," he said, his voice carrying unexpected vulnerability.

I hesitated, unsure of what to make of his sudden appearance. I wanted him gone, yet a strange unease tethered me to his presence.

His attention wavered as he abruptly turned and headed down the front steps, leaving me confused.

Once he was far enough away, I reached up and pulled the spare key from the bulb, careful not to cut myself on the glass. The metal was cool between my fingers.

Hearing the deadbolt click, I pushed the door open and stepped inside. The air was cool, carrying the faint scent of aged wood and dust, yet it held a comforting familiarity. Or as homey as an empty house could be. After my dad passed, Mom took up a job a couple of towns over. I hadn't seen her in months, nor did I expect to. I was always closer to my father.

I closed the door and flipped the light switch. It engaged with a soft click, but the room stayed dark. Again, I flicked it, and again, nothing. I peered out of the glass panel that lined the door. The lights were on in the houses that flanked the street. Streetlights were on. It was just my house that was out of power. Had Mother forgotten to pay the bills? It wouldn't have been the first time.

4

WHISPERS IN THE DARK

I walked from post to post, the crisp autumn breeze rustled the flyers in my hands as I taped them carefully to storefronts and benches.

The young woman's gaze stared blankly at me from the black and white rendition affixed to a staple-ridden pole. A vivid dream from the night before lingered in my mind, conjuring its own version of her fate. In it she wasn't just missing, she was dead.

Starting from home, I wove a careful path northeast to the clock tower, the cobblestone streets beneath my worn-out sneakers telling tales of the town's history. Then, I headed northwest, ending up outside the sushi bar across the street from work.

Miles gave me the morning off to post flyers for the missing woman. Flashes of light blinked off in the distance, catching my attention. They seemed to emanate from behind the church. My vision blurred momentarily as an image of yesterday's drawing flashed in my mind. I still had time before Miles was expecting me.

The church stood just up the road, and it took me only minutes to reach there. Massive gates lay open in front of the hoary building, connecting to an iron fence that stretched out on both sides. My shoes crunched over the gravel driveway as I hurried ahead. Voices echoed off the stone walls, and I allowed them to guide my way.

Rounding the side of the building, I spotted the origin of the lights. A towering angel statue stood amid the tombstones, and an unsettling sensation grew as I neared the ambulance and police cars. A stretcher lay beside the ambulance, surrounded by attendants with somber expressions.

Among the figures, a dark mass occupied the space on the stretcher. Moving closer, I noticed the yellow tape sectioning off an area to the left. My gaze returned to the mound on the stretcher. My stomach churned as the reality hit me: a body bag, and it wasn't empty.

Questions raced through my mind. The missing girl? How had this happened? My legs carried me forward until halted by the yellow tape, marking the cordon around a part of the gulch. Barricades lined the edge where bystanders gathered, attempting to catch a glimpse.

Amid the crowd, one familiar figure stood out—Gates. Her caramel-colored hair was neatly tied up, her hand resting lightly on her holstered Glock. Her eyes appeared dark and tired as she conversed with someone at her side.

Irene was found in the water by the graveyard attendant,

Iael Black, beaten, and lifeless. The news sent shivers down my spine, and questions swirled in my mind.

Gates stood with a composed posture, but the distress was evident in her demeanor. It had been over a century since Hayzun witnessed such an event.

As I stood there, my fingers absently played with the fabric of my sweater, the voices around me merged into an indistinct chatter of gossip and theories, offering nothing useful. Gathering all the available information, I realized it was time for me to show up at work.

Peering over the barricade into the ravine, I had more questions. Did she fall? How long had she been there? I planned to return later, when the crowd dispersed, to sneak under the barricade for a closer look.

My stomach churned as I turned away, the sound of dried grass and fallen leaves crunched beneath my feet. Tombstones were arranged neatly to my left, among them my father's stone, somewhere distant behind me, closer to the back of the graveyard. It had been months since I last visited.

Keeping close to the side of the church, I tried to banish the image of the body bag from my thoughts. The flaxen-colored stones appeared chalky and worn from years of weathering. Heading back down the gravel drive, I reached work within minutes. The bell chimed as I entered, heading straight to the backroom. The office door was shut, angry voices seeped through the cracks. I knocked gently and pushed the door open, unsure of what I'd find.

On the other side, an angry Miles faced me, his voice strained. "There," he hissed. "She's fine." My gaze shifted to Jesse, who stood with hands buried in his pockets. "Now, if you don't mind, I have a business to run." With that, Miles stormed out of the room, leaving me to set my things down on the desk.

"I thought you were dead." I turned to the voice.

"Why would you think that?" My mind flashed back to the body on the stretcher. "You thought she was me. Why?" He shook his head, withdrawing his hands from his pockets.

"I saw her pulled from the water." His expression conveyed the rest, but he continued. "I thought maybe you..." he trailed off. My eyes widened.

"Thought I what?" Thought I would try and kill myself again. I rubbed the scars on my wrists.

Just then, he headed toward the kennels. Before I could intercept, he opened the door. Seeing his actions, I chose not to intervene.

"What did you think?" I repeated, but he kneeled before the dog he had saved, unlatching the cage. After checking the bandages, he secured the cell and stood.

The dog whined softly as he turned toward the front door without another word.

Resisting the urge to follow, I returned to the office. A small radio sat on the desk's corner, its antenna repaired multiple times, now threatening to break again as I turned it on. Static filled the air, tuning into the local station.

"Early this morning, at the northern end of Shadow Gulch, a young woman's body from Hayzun was found," the radio crackled. "Cemetery Attendant Iael Black, who discovered the woman, claims not to have heard a sound. In other news, Mayor O'Reilly will be stepping down as he recovers at Hayzun Memorial. His stand-in will be welcomed later today."

The news dissolved into a steady stream of music as I

settled behind the desk, attempting to focus on work. Yet, my mind spun, prompting me to turn and glimpse the flashing lights from here. They lingered, casting an eerie glow on the sky well into mid-afternoon.

The ambulance departed first, likely carrying her body.

Meanwhile, the police vehicles lingered, herding onlookers and meticulously combing the area. I wasn't sure what they were searching for—perhaps standard procedure.

Hours passed before I realized I hadn't accomplished a thing. Instead, I found myself idly observing the public meandering through the graveyard like curious ants. I decided to wait until it cleared out before I ventured there myself, despite my own curiosity.

As the last police cruiser exited through the gates, I rose. Only ten minutes remained on the clock. The sun was beginning its descent, and I aimed to use that fading light to my advantage. With my workbag slung over my shoulder, I watched the minutes tick by, biding my time.

The gulch concealed secrets, and the unfolding events felt unsettling in our usually quiet town. I heard the clock tower toll from the town square, signaling the hour.

Rushing through the hall and out the front door, I stepped outside before the fifth toll ended. I didn't know what I was looking for, not sure if anything remained after the area had been scoured hours earlier. But an inexplicable urge compelled me to look. Incidents like this were rare in Hayzun—first, the mayor's attempted suicide, then a missing girl found dead in the gulch following the arrival of a seemingly well-intentioned stranger. Something felt off.

I cut behind the clinic, heading toward the gulch. Tracking it along the old Western Motel, I arrived where the gulch met the iron fence bordering the graveyard.

If there were any remnants from Irene, they would likely have flowed downstream. I planned to trace this path back to where she was found. The gulch, about ten feet deep with a foot of swift-flowing water at the bottom, presented a challenging landscape.

I gripped the cool metal fence, carefully maneuvering around and into the graveyard. Pulling my workbag to the front, I unzipped it. I always kept a flashlight, especially as the evenings darkened earlier. The sun wouldn't set for another hour or so, but the sky had already begun to dim.

Clicking on the flashlight, I directed its beam into the ravine. The water appeared clear but looked chillingly cold as it churned and frothed. The spot where they found her lay about two hundred yards away.

I wasn't typically one to interfere in other people's lives, but this situation felt different, unnerving. Hayzun was known for its quietness, making this occurrence stand out.

My head snapped to the side as a large raven landed on a nearby headstone, its beady eyes tracking my movements.

Ignoring the bird, I pressed forward. The flashlight flickered momentarily, and I tightened its end, reigniting the light. I surveyed the bottom of the valley, only encountering rocks, boulders, and the occasional piece of garbage in the stream.

Soon, I reached the barricades and yellow tape marking the area. After glancing around, I slipped beneath the barricades and the tape, standing where Irene must have fallen from. Peering down, I noticed a large boulder partially submerged, likely preventing her from being swept downstream.

The edge of the gulch wasn't a sheer drop; it was manageable if I moved carefully. I perched at the edge, slowly descending by placing my feet on small ridges on the earthy side of the gulch. Gripping rocks and roots with one hand, I held the flashlight with the other.

My descent halted when I reached the water's edge, steadying myself by placing a foot on the boulder.

My stomach lurched as the flashlight revealed red stains on the far side of the large rock. Why was I even here? This wasn't my place. I shouldn't be here. I turned to climb back up when the sound of footsteps startled me. In a quick breath, I extinguished my flashlight. It was still early enough in the evening that if whoever it was approached the edge, they might spot me.

"Who's there?" It was a male voice. Iael, the graveyard attendant who found Irene. Frozen with fear, I held my breath. The footsteps paused briefly before fading away.

When I was certain he had left, I clicked my flashlight back on. There seemed to be nothing here. The police had already searched thoroughly.

Just as I was about to ascend the embankment, my flashlight caught a glint between the boulder and the base of the ravine. Kneeling, I reached into the icy water, sending shivers down my spine.

My fingers grasped an object, pulling it from the water. It felt cold and unfamiliar—a small silver angel lay in my palm. Irene must have been here visiting someone, probably not yet placing the figurine on top of the appropriate stone.

The next question lingered: did she end up in the water intentionally or was it an accident? Did she jump or fall? Or was she pushed? I knew the emotions that surged when standing among the graves, seeing the name of someone dear etched into the stone. It was enough to unsettle anyone.

Shoving the small angel into my pocket, I made my way up the embankment and slipped back under the barricades.

My gaze flickered toward my father's final resting place. I stood torn between leaving and seeking solace among the rows.

Before I knew it, I was standing before his stone. Grass now blanketed the once-bare mound, settling to match the surrounding ground. It was a stark reminder of how much time had passed.

"Hi, Dad," I murmured, my voice wavering. I knew he wasn't really there, but being this close still brought a sense of comfort. I tucked my hands into my pockets, my fingers brushing against the small angel figurine.

Retrieving it from my pocket, I twirled the figurine between my fingers before delicately placing it on the small ledge around the base of his gravestone. A lump formed in my throat, and with a heavy heart I turned away and made my way toward the iron gates.

SHADOWED SUSPICIONS

Exiting the graveyard, I followed the gravel road as it merged into the pavement. Walkways flanked the streets, and I chose one of them walking quickly.

Stars dotted the sky above as the leaves crunched under my feet. The air had considerably cooled since I left work, and I clutched my workbag tightly to my chest. Antique tree lamps flickered on, casting light along my path.

As I reached the intersection, about to turn right toward home, a burst of applause diverted my attention.

Instead of turning, I crossed the street and veered left, making my way toward the town square.

The clock tower loomed overhead as I neared. A cement pathway stretched before me, flanked by two large brick buildings. In the center, an individual stood within the shadow cast by the towering clock. His eyes locked onto mine, and a sense of recognition lingered in the air. Unease settled in, and my instincts urged me to turn away.

Hayzun's main street was lined with quaint stores and hand painted signs. Markets with fresh baked goods and homemade crafts were held here all year round.

His eyes found me at the same time I saw him. He stepped forward, giving a slight wave. His familiarity with me made me uneasy.

Turning, I headed the other way.

"Charlotte, wait." I stopped in my tracks, cringing at the use of my name. How did he know my name? How did he know who I was? Fight or flight rushed through my body. My body was ready for flight. Why were my feet not moving? Turning, I met his honey-colored eyes. He had taken a couple of steps closer.

"How do you know my name?" My eyes scanned his body, looking for any idea how he may have known me. He paused for a moment as if working out the best thing to say.

"I know, Jesse." He took another step closer.

I nodded, though that didn't comfort me any or give me many more answers. I bristled.

"You can't recognize a person based on a name." He pondered my response, eyes darting over my face.

Pale, barely noticeable lines ran up his arms, disappearing into the edge of his sleeve. He didn't have time to say another word before he was cut off. Though the words he had already said, and his familiarity with me were curious.

An uproar echoed from the town square, diverting my attention. I turned and headed down a nearby alley thankful for the distraction, with the stranger trailing behind.

Painted murals lined the bricks depicting scenes from the

town's history and the yard revealed a crowd gathered near the clock tower's base. The town had set up a makeshift stage, complete with cameras, reporters, and curious townsfolk.

Microphone feedback buzzed as I surveyed the scene, the low lights cast long shadows across the cobblestone.

A woman with golden skin held the microphone to her warm smile. "We have gathered here to introduce the new mayor of Hayzun County," she announced. The townspeople had congregated to welcome their new leader, yet an uneasy tension permeated the air.

I stood on the outskirts of the bustling town square.

"Because of Mayor O'Reilly's current state, we were forced to make some decisions until he is able to formally resign or reembrace his role. Luckily, Mr. Montgomery, or should I say, Mayor Montgomery, comes highly recommended."

My eyes found the individual she was referring to.

The new mayor, a tall, graying man, stood off to the side.

"Mayor, would you like to say a few words?"

As he took his spot in front of the microphone, the clock tower chimed from above. Six tolls. As the previous mayor lay in the hospital, his health deteriorating, the transition of power to the new mayor had been swift and unexplained. The atmosphere was a mixture of hope and uncertainty, and the tension was palpable. The town applauded as he cleared his throat.

"Before I say too much, thank you for welcoming me to your town." The mayor's voice resonated, and another round of applause echoed off the pavement, mingling with the ambient sounds of the night. I took a few steps forward, drawn by the unfolding scene. "I also want to speak on behalf of the Walker Family." The words hung in the air, and I felt a slight chill settle into my body. "A memorial will be held later this week. Donations to Hayzun Memorial will be accepted."

As the mayor continued, blathering on, I couldn't shake the feeling that something was left unsaid. They found a body in the gulch, and that was all he had to say?

"Let us remember Irene Walker, a beloved member of our community, whose tragic passing has deeply affected us all. In these difficult times, we must come together to support one another. As your new mayor, I'm committed to ensuring the safety and prosperity of Hayzun. We'll work closely with law enforcement to address any concerns and maintain the peace we all value."

I turned, pushing my way through the group of people gathered behind me. My skin crawled, having that many people so close.

Voices drawled as I walked away, the static of the microphone filling the night air.

The individual who inexplicably knew my name still stood behind me. He opened his mouth as if to speak, but I dropped my gaze, quickly heading in the other direction.

"Charlotte wait," his voice echoed behind me. "I'm sorry if I scared you."

I stopped, my breaths came out in shallow puffs and my body hummed as he stepped closer behind me.

Fingers grazed the inside of my wrist, brushing my scars and I jerked away. My body stiffened as I turned to face him.

"I have to go."

A chill clung to the atmosphere, but I brushed it aside, crossing the street to find solace in the nearest walkway.

Cracks lined the concrete path as I hurried southwest, away from the clock tower and toward the comfort of home.

After a while, I turned onto my street. The soft glow of streetlights illuminated the houses, each with welcoming lights except mine, which sat in darkness. Its empty windows resembled tired eyes, and I let out a heavy breath as I ascended the worn wooden steps of the porch. Paint peeled off the wooden awning above, revealing the wear and tear of time.

With a soft click, I pushed the door open and stepped into the dim interior. A white envelope lay face down on the floor, having fallen through the mail slot.

I hung my work bag up on a hook before bending down to pick it up. My knee cracked as I stood, the familiar sound echoing in the quiet space.

Flipping the letter over, I saw my name written in crisp red ink across the front. There was no return address, only mine, printed neatly in the center.

I broke the seal and pulled out a single piece of paper. It was addressed to me from—my mother.

6

ECHOES OF THE PAST

The paper, though only the size of a postcard, felt heavy in my hands and the room felt stifling as I clutched it. My mother's scratchy handwriting, more uneven than usual, sprawled across the surface forming a disjointed tapestry of words:

Hayzun was never my home, and it never will be.

Her signature marked the bottom, a jagged reminder of our fractured relationship. A lump formed in the recesses of my throat, the acrid burn of unshed tears stung my eyes. My mother and I never shared a close bond, and the blame she had placed on me for taking my father away remained. His passing had been a result of natural causes, but she needed a scapegoat, and I became the unwilling target.

For a moment, I stared at the letter, the weight of abandonment settled heavily in my chest. The unlit bulb in the ceiling cast a cold pallor on the room, a deliberate reminder of her indifference. She hadn't paid the bill, a calculated move to convey her apathy.

I shoved the letter back into its envelope, suppressing the urge to scream into the silent darkness. Alone. I was utterly alone.

The room held a stillness broken only by the muffled sounds of the outside world.

With a defeated sigh, I let the letter fall to the floor, a discarded relic of severed ties.

Picking up my work bag, I faced the door, the weight of isolation heavy on my shoulders. The stranger who knew my name, the peculiar markings on his arms that resembled Jesse's—questions swirled in my mind, demanding answers.

I slammed the door shut behind me, leaving the oppressive atmosphere of the empty house in my wake. It was late, but determination fueled my steps. I was done hiding, done evading.

All my life, I had kept a low profile, yet here I stood in the unraveling mystery of Hayzun. The stranger held the key to the answers I sought, and I had nothing left to lose.

The clinic was empty at this time of night. Nothing but soft barks and whimpers echoed off the walls from the back room as I let myself in.

My steps echoed through the empty space as I maneuvered to the front desk. Faint shadows flickered across the walls, playing tricks on my peripheral vision.

He would have left his information at the front desk when he showed up with the dog. I had gotten his name for the paperwork, but someone at the front would have asked for an address. Whether he gave one, or the correct one was a different question.

Bones seemed to scoff from his small bed on the counter as though I had woken him from a deep sleep. I patted his light wispy hair, a soft hiss exiting through his teeth. He never had been very friendly.

Settling into the metal chair, I faced the computer screen, fingers dancing across the keyboard in a jittery dance.

His name—Jesse Carter—typed into the search bar, the anticipation of what I might find knotted in my stomach. A moment of tense waiting ensued, each second amplified my impatience.

Finally, a ping heralded a hit on the registry. Clicking the result, I scanned the details hoping for an address, yet dreading the implications.

The cursor hovered over the screen, revealing a piece of information that tugged at my conflicted feelings.

Twenty-seven Cherry Street.

An unexpected surge of emotions washed over me. Did I truly want to find him, or was I better off not crossing paths again? The dilemma raged within me as I grappled with conflicting desires.

I closed the program and pushed the chair back.

A swift fleeting movement in my peripheral vision caught my attention—a dark shadow flitted past the door behind me. A shiver raced down my spine, prompting me to respond. Was someone else here at this hour, or was it just my imagination playing tricks?

"Hello?" No one would be here at this hour. It was in my head. A dog let out a low snarl. Maybe it wasn't in my head.

I made a run for the front door, grasping the cool metal in my hands. I cringed letting it go and turned around. I said I was going to stop running, I wasn't going to hide any longer.

What was I even going to do if I did find someone?

The hallway beckoned; each step accompanied by the apprehensive rhythm of my heartbeat.

Peering into empty exam rooms I navigated past darkened kennels, shadows disappeared when I flicked the lights on. I found no trace of another presence. Yet, the sense of being watched lingered, an inexplicable chill ran down my spine.

I shook my head and turned out the lights, and made my way back to the lobby before locking the front door behind me.

I walked, following the road as it intersected another. Cherry Street was a few blocks over from mine, south of the clock tower. I quickened my steps, forcing myself to continue so I didn't turn around, and before long, I had traveled quite a distance.

Shadows clung to the streets, a chorus of whispers accompanying my solitary journey. Redbrick buildings loomed, casting elongated shadows under the dim streetlights.

My steps quickened; driven by an urgency I couldn't comprehend. The faint echo of rustling pines carried on the night breeze as I traversed unfamiliar streets, tracing the pattern of the address in my mind.

As Cherry Street came into view, I navigated the row of houses, each one a replica of its neighbors. In front of me sat number twenty-one. My eyes trailed down the road as I walked. Twenty-seven.

At the end of the driveway, a house—another small, redbrick-sided dwelling just like the others on this street.

Loose stones crunched beneath the soles of my worn shoes as I walked the stretch of driveway.

The night seemed to echo around me as I grew closer to the door. Knots formed in my stomach and seemed to grow and tighten. I did not know what I was doing here, at his house.

Lifting my hand, I rapidly banged my fist against the door before I could change my mind.

After a moment with no answer, I turned to leave. The stranger didn't want company, or maybe he simply wasn't home. It was oddly relieving that he hadn't answered, explaining my presence would've been uncomfortable.

Turning, I cut across the front lawn toward the curb, the now-damp grass swayed against my ankles. A low-clicking noise caught my attention, and I stopped, turning as a rectangle of light appeared—the front door slid open. His eyes scanned the vicinity before stopping on me, widening slightly at my presence.

"I'm sorry, I shouldn't be here," I faltered, ready to depart, but then reconsidered. "Actually, can I come in?" His silent nod, accompanied by a step back into the house, offered an unexpected invitation.

Why I was here I had no idea, but I felt a need to tell him what had happened.

As I crossed the threshold of the house, warmth

enveloped me but inside, the house was bare.

Glancing to my left, I saw a small living room with nothing more than a couch and a lamp. To my right stood the kitchen, with a small table in the middle. The dark countertops were bare, save for a soap dispenser by the sink and a lonely pen. Even the paper towel holder under the cabinets sat empty.

The door clicked closed behind me.

"Can I get you anything?"

I shook my head, navigating into the kitchen. He followed, leaning against the countertop, arms crossed lightly over his chest.

Silent, I contemplated whether I made the right decision coming here. He spoke before I could force any words into the open air between us.

"Considering you went to all this work to find me; something must be up." He eyed me, waiting for a response.

"There's a new mayor," I began, trying to gather my scattered thoughts. Jesse's puzzled expression prompted me to continue, attempting to justify my presence. He cocked his head as if he was wondering what that had to do with him. "I met someone…Someone who knew me, knew you, and…" The words stumbled out in a jumbled mess. "He knew my name, and I've never seen him before, but he said he knew you." Jesse's eyes seemed to darken. "And weird things have been happening." I babbled on, trying to explain myself and why I showed up at his house unannounced.

"What did he look like?" It sounded more like a demand than a question.

"Tall, blond and he had these weird markings up his arms, almost like…" I gestured to his arms.

"Jace." He shook his head closing he eyes as though he had just received the most disheartening news. "Stay away from him." His tone was almost a growl, low and guttural.

"Why, who is he?" I pressed on, my voice tinged with a mix of concern and frustration. His cryptic response made my blood run cold.

"It doesn't matter." His words were forced so I let it go … for now. I looked up to see his eyes fixed on me.

"There's something else." The words tumbled out as I debated whether to ask for his help. "I don't think Irene's death was an accident." I searched his eyes for any show of emotion.

Again, I had no idea why I was here or if I should trust him, but for some reason I felt that I should. I felt as though he was the only one that would understand what I had to say.

He had turned up at the shelter after they found her body. He was concerned, and he had said something. What was it he had said? He knew something, maybe more than he let on.

The small silver angel I had pulled from the gulch rang in my memory. She was there to visit someone. Someone she didn't get the chance to visit.

"I don't think it was either."

I rubbed my hands along my arms, feeling the material of my shirt beneath my fingers.

He knew something, he must. And that shadow I saw in the clinic earlier—maybe it was nothing, but it felt like someone had been watching me. I looked around again, taking in every minor detail.

My eyes focused on a small painting on the wall. Before I could make out its image, my vision began to blur at the edges. This strange sort of feeling filled my body. It had happened once before, the day in the alley.

A surreal sensation enveloped me. Reality slipped away, replaced by a disorienting whirlwind of images.

A torrent of unsettling visions—an ominous rope soaked in crimson, a sinister grin etched into the darkness, and an unsettling glint of teeth. A surge of worry gripped me as I snapped back to the kitchen, my breaths coming in ragged gasps. Finally they rushed out in one long burst as my vision fully cleared.

Without a word, I bolted toward the door, the cold knob greeting my trembling hand. Stepping out into the night, I descended the front steps, desperate for air. Panic clawed at my chest as I tried to steady my inhalations, the frigid air offering some respite from the chaos in my mind.

A firm grip seized my wrist, halting my retreat. Jesse's stare bore into mine, searching for answers, concern etched on his face. My hasty apologies were lost in the chaos, but he released his hold, allowing me to regain composure.

"Sorry," was all I could muster. He shook his head, standing me up straight from my hunched position.

"Are you okay?" His eyes searched mine as I took in a lungful of air followed by another and another. I nodded, letting him know I was. He didn't question me on anything else, and for that, I was grateful.

"I just need some fresh air I think."

His understanding silence was a relief, a temporary anchor amid my turmoil.

"Let's go for a walk then."

Why he wanted to help and not walk away after my outburst was questionable, but I was grateful.

Walking in solitude, his silent presence trailed behind me, the distance acting as a barrier of reassurance. The weight of unspoken words hung heavy in the air, a palpable tension wrapping around us.

I could sense him trailing behind me, his hesitation tangible as if debating whether to break the silence. I wasn't certain if his voice would comfort or further unsettle me.

Maintaining a distance, I walked a few feet ahead, finding solace in the space between us. It gave me a sense of control, a small buffer against the turmoil inside.

Moving forward, my steps echoed through the quiet. The sound of leaves crunching beneath our feet, the only interruption.

This trail was familiar yet not. It was a path I had trodden only a handful of times before, yet it echoed the others in Hayzun.

The crisp air nipped at my face and hands, a sharp reminder of the present, anchoring me to that point in time.

It wasn't long before a bizarre sort of darkness spread over the ground in front of me. A darkness that was out of place even in the night. A darkness that was too dark.

It rested on the ground, swaying next to the path, the center of the shadow growing even darker. It seemed to ooze and grow with each passing second.

Gradually, I realized that the darkness pooling on the ground was a thick, viscous liquid, dripping steadily.

Tracking the path of the fluid, my eyes caught a glimpse of something pale and smooth. I gasped, turning abruptly, only to collide with a solid form.

The person holding me radiated life, in contrast to the lifeless figure hanging from the tree. I jerked against Jesse's shoulder, attempting to free myself from his grip, but his hold remained firm.

"You're okay." His hand settled lightly on the back of my neck, anchoring me to him. I wanted to keep running, but my struggle soon gave way, as I knew he wouldn't let go. His attempt to soothe me was unfaltering. How could he be so calm? It felt jarring amid the haunting scene.

My limbs felt heavy as I stood on the dewy grass, my mind on the lifeless body hanging from the tree behind us.

The weight of the situation bore down on me, the air thick with a mix of disbelief and dread. A shiver coursed through my body, a silent plea for this nightmare to end.

Jesse's voice, low and steady, broke the eerie silence. "We need to call the police." His words were measured, a decisive command that snapped me out of the horrified trance.

I nodded, my throat dry and voice barely a whisper. "Yes, we have to."

A crawling weight settled upon me, standing amid the grass nearby. The young woman, still suspended from the tree, appeared pallid and marked with bruises.

Jesse stood with a phone pressed to his ear, with the police on the other end. I wanted to run; I wanted to hide. What had our quiet town become?

As he hung up, Emergency vehicles descended upon the scene, illuminating the darkness with their vivid lights. The once tranquil town was now bustling with a frenzy of activity, the flashing red and blue amplifying the disorienting chaos.

My mind felt dizzy, and I felt light-headed. Jesse spoke off in the distance, but it didn't register.

Police cars pulled up, followed by the fire department and ambulance. Officers ushered me backward as they cordoned the scene off in yellow tape. It seemed straight out of a movie.

In moments, a crowd had gathered, awakened by the flashing lights and deafening sirens. The police fought to keep peace within the group.

The battered girl was held carefully by two firefighters while a third climbed a ladder. They cut her down before placing her on a stretcher already fitted with an open body bag.

I never thought the sound of a zipper fastening closed could be so nauseating, but the metallic whir of it caused bile to rise in my throat.

The onlookers multiplied, seemingly drawn from every corner of the small town. Amid gasps and cries of shock, a piercing shriek reverberated.

Glancing back at the young woman, I noticed an older woman forcing her way through the yellow tape, accompanied by a man. Police immediately redirected them, attempting to maintain order amid the commotion.

Word traveled fast around here.

In a moment, the police tactic changed, and the two were led over to the stretcher. The woman buckled as she peered inside the bag, slowly unzipped by the officer. The man caught her as she fell. This was the reaction that could only be that of a mother and father. I turned around once again, listening to their shrieks of pain.

Muddled between sirens, cries, and pained cries was the sound of my name being carried through the wind by a familiar voice. I stood stiff, body shaking in rigid spurts. Was that my name being called? Yes, yes, I think it was. A woman's voice. A warm hand on my shoulder. I flinched at the sudden touch.

Officer Gates stepped into my line of view.

"Would I be able to get a statement from you?" She pulled a notepad from her pocket as I wiped my face.

"Where is Jesse?"

"He's waiting to take you home." She dropped her head to look into my eyes. "I would like to question you alone if that's okay. Just to keep stories separate."

I nodded, rubbing my eyes once again.

"What happened?" Gates frowned at my question.

"That's what I want you to help me figure out."

I nodded.

"Yes, of course." I pinched the bridge of my nose, feeling the pressure build.

"Tell me what happened. Anything you can remember is relevant."

I recounted the entire incident into the cold, windy air between us. Gates took notes as I spoke, and when I finished, she pocketed her notepad and surveyed me. "Let me know if you remember anything else."

I nodded once again.

"When can we leave?"

"You're free to go."

I nodded, turning on my heels. I scanned the sea of faces until I found the one I was looking for. He stood with his arms crossed, facing me, a silent assurance urging me to go to him.

Microphone feedback filled the air as a voice boomed from a nearby police car. "As of now, Mayor Montgomery has initiated a six o'clock curfew. Please return home as quickly as possible. We'll notify the public when the curfew has been lifted."

It was well past six o'clock, and it would take me well over half an hour to make it home. When he noticed me looking, Jesse gave a slight nod before heading toward his rental. As he walked by, he gestured for me to follow.

I trailed behind him without a word, understanding that it would be much quicker to reach his house than mine. Plus, his place had lights and hot water.

The forest seemed to have grown darker along the trail, and the once open sky fogged over. The air still nipped at my exposed skin.

Soon, I stood outside the small, red-bricked house. Its dark windows stared like empty eyes into the night.

With a click, he jimmied the door from its inaccessible state into a more inviting one.

The stranger held the door for me as I made my way into the bare dwelling. It had grown colder since we left.

Silently, I made my way to the couch, taking a seat, falling into the cushions. Jesse didn't say a word. Instead, he turned and disappeared down the hall. Not very convivial, but I guess he had let me stay.

I sighed, resting back against the cushions, letting my eyes fall closed. A weight in my lap caused me to jump.

"This is all I have." In my lap was a checked blanket.

"Thank you." He nodded softly as I unfolded it and sat back, draping it over my legs.

As the weight lifted off my legs, I felt myself begin to shake. My breath became shallower by the passing second as convulsions took hold of my hands.

A warm tear slipped down my cold cheek. I fought back the urge to cry, determined not to show weakness in front of a stranger. But was he even a stranger anymore? Finding a dead body together sort of erased that barrier.

The wheezing caught his attention. I hunched deeper into the couch, attempting to suffocate my feelings, as if by doing so, I could also suffocate myself.

Shadows began to dance through my vision as my lungs felt as heavy as cement. The fears and worries of a whole lifetime culminated in one agonizing moment.

A figure knelt in front of me, and I flinched as a hand settled on my knee. I fought to brush it away.

"Hey, look at me." I reluctantly met his gaze as he took hold of my hands. "No." I attempted to pull away.

"Stop." He firmly held my hands. "Take a deep breath."

"What do you think I'm trying to do?" My words came out angrily. He shook his head, not releasing my hands as I once again tried to wriggle free.

This time, he let go and stood, watching me struggle to breathe. His gaze barely left me as he turned and settled on the small window ledge across the room.

I dropped my head back into the plush cushion of the couch, allowing it to swallow my body.

I sighed deeply, feeling the thick, cement-like blockade exiting my lungs.

A shiver ran up my spine. As if on cue, Jesse, the stranger, spoke.

"You should get some sleep." I shook my head, not wanting to relive the past couple of hours in my dreams.

"I'm not tired." He nodded softly, aware that I wasn't being truthful.

"I know you're lying." He looked me over. "I will not hurt you. You can trust me." Those words stung my ears. I had learned not to trust anyone, especially those that say *trust me.*

I backed myself up deeper into the couch, tugging on the blanket.

"I'm fine," I muttered. "You can go to bed." He stood from where he sat on the windowsill.

"Get some sleep." He looked me in the eyes before dragging them down to where I gripped the blanket tightly in my lap. My scars weren't visible, but I knew by the look that took over his features that they were the center of the thoughts that filled his mind.

"It happened a couple of years ago." His eyes snapped up to mine. "Just after my father passed." I cleared my throat, looking away. "The day of his funeral, actually." His face pinched.

"You don't have to tell me." The softness in his voice calmed the apprehension in my body. I closed my eyes, not wanting to see his reaction as I explained what had happened that day.

"It was my first time leaving Hayzun. I just wanted to get away, even if only for an hour. I haven't left since." I shifted my body. "I didn't get very far before a van pulled up beside me." I felt him sit on the armrest of the couch. "They pulled me inside." I opened my eyes, catching his gaze. "You can guess what happened next." I adjusted my grip on the blanket, trying not to let the memories creep in. He angled his body as if he was going to reach for me, but then stopped. Instead, he opened his mouth to speak.

"I'm sorry that happened to you." His words were

measured, a gentle acknowledgment of the pain. "It wasn't your fault, Charlie." There was a gravity in his voice, a sincere understanding. "But you're safe here." He leaned back, giving me space. "Get some rest. I'll be in the next room if you need anything." He rose from the armrest, offering me a reassuring nod before heading out of the room, leaving my mind to linger on the impromptu nickname.

7

FRAGMENTS OF TRUTH

The morning paper was filled with news of bloodshed and panic. Hayzun had a killer in its midst.

The paper hit the door with a hollow thud, jolting me from a light sleep.

Morning light streamed through the window, casting elongated shadows across the room. The silence of the small flat was oppressive, broken only by the faint rustling of the fleece blanket as I pushed it aside.

I lowered my feet to the floor. The only sounds I could pinpoint were my breathing and the ticking of a clock that I could not locate.

With a groggy haze lingering, I swung my legs over the edge of the couch, the cold floor sending an unexpected shiver up my spine through my socks. As I rose, the disheveled mess of my hair seemed to mirror the scattered thoughts in my mind.

Twisting the doorknob, I was surprised to find it unlocked. The door opened with an almost reluctant scrape, revealing the rolled newspaper that had landed with an unexpected force, cascading down the front step.

Though the sun shone brightly, it was very bittersweet. A family had lost their child, but the world seemed at peace.

The trees had begun to change, the dried corpses of leaves falling to the ground. Everything in this town seemed to be dying, even its residents.

Cool cement met my feet as I ventured outside, down the pathway. The tightly rolled paper was black and gray, blurred with spots of white. Birds chirped in all directions, singing a song of sorrow.

Stepping back inside, the paper unrolled in my quivering hands. Bold lettering filled the heading like a thick warning. A countywide curfew had been put into place, restricting anyone from going out past six o'clock. Something had gone seriously wrong in this sleepy town.

Voices echoed from the back of the small house, one of which I recognized. The second, thick with an accent I couldn't quite place, caused my skin to prickle. Who else was here, and why? I took a step closer, but the voices were too muffled to make out any of what was being said.

Entering the small kitchen, I placed the paper next to a set of keys and a wallet, the latter holding the promise of answers—or perhaps more mysteries.

Hesitantly peeking around the corner, I strained to discern the conversation, but the words remained frustratingly indistinct. Palpitations in my chest escalated, a knot tightened in my throat as I contemplated delving into the wallet. I was more afraid of what I might find than I was of being caught. Fear battled curiosity, but the need for answers prevailed.

Approaching the island, I grabbed the wallet with both hands and carefully opened it. Without having to pry, a plastic identification card fell out. The name matched neither of the two individuals present, but the photo did. Jeremiah Carson sat next to a picture of the stranger. If his name wasn't Jesse, then who was he?

Sliding the ID back into the wallet, I paused, uncertainty looming like a specter. My fingers trembled as I withdrew a grainy photograph nestled within the wallet's clear pocket. Jesse's eyes bore into mine from the faded image, the flipside marked with a single word—Jeremiah—and a blurry set of four numbers. It looked like a one, maybe followed by a nine, and an unfinished zero. Was that an eight at the end? It didn't make sense. The disjointed message only deepened the mystery, leaving me more perplexed than before.

Struggling to return the photo to its concealed pocket, my ears pricked up to strained, heated voices emanating from somewhere nearby.

He had been lying to me this whole time.

Stepping back, I peeked down the hall. It remained empty, but the sound of muffled voices resonated from a slightly ajar door to the left. Slowly ensuring not to make a sound, I stepped closer until the voices became clear. They sounded strained and angry. Bits and pieces melded together, but one sentence stuck in my head. It came out in a quiet grumble, but it spun me on my heels. The words playing over and over in my head.

"Jeremiah is long since dead."

The abrupt slam of the back door snapped me out of my trance, igniting a surge of adrenaline. Racing to the front door, I grasped the knob, I pulled it open hastily, then turned to shut it firmly behind me. My heart raced as I turned, only to find Jesse—no, Jeremiah—standing before me, his eyes widening at the scene in the kitchen.

A moment of realization flashed across his face, prompting a swift charge forward. I pivoted and bolted down the steps, a surge of panic propelling me into a frantic sprint.

"Charlie, wait." That nickname stung, but I didn't turn.

The fresh air was heavy as I sucked in a deep breath, replaying the encounter. Each inhale burned my lungs as I raced away from the house, the chilling words echoing in an endless loop within my mind.

Jeremiah is long since dead.

What exactly did that mean? Had he killed someone? Was he behind the deaths? I wasn't going to stick around long enough to find out. Pushing myself further away from the house, I struggled down the leaf-covered walkway.

The air smelled cool and crisp, sharp against my exposed skin, whipping around me, its bite sending shivers down my spine. Crunching leaves beneath my frantic steps echoed against the silence of the deserted street. Footsteps thundered behind me, growing closer with each passing second.

I made a desperate attempt to put distance between us, barely managing to cover a couple of houses before a pair of arms encircled my midsection, halting my escape. Panic surged anew, and I fought against his hold, my desperation lending strength to my struggle.

"No!" I pushed against him, trying to break free.

"Charlie, stop." His urgent voice cut through the air,

filled with a plea for understanding. The use of that nickname struck a nerve, conjuring memories of a past I was trying to outrun. I bristled at its repetition, reminiscent of the same nickname my father used to call me.

"Don't call me that." His arms remained fastened around me. "And let me go."

"Only if you let me explain."

"I'll scream." We weren't near the town square, but someone would still hear me if I were to scream, especially with two murders in the past week.

His arms relented slightly, granting me a slight freedom.

Seizing the moment, I moved forward, creating distance between us before turning to face him. Emotion choked my voice, making my next words tremble.

"Did you kill them?" My bottom lip quivered.

"What?" He seemed taken aback, as if that wasn't the conclusion I would come to after what I had heard and found. I secured my stance. The weight of the accusation hung heavy in the air, a long pause stretching between us. His initial confusion gradually transformed into comprehension, the gravity of the accusation slowly registering.

"Did you ... kill them?" The words seemed to finally sink in.

In a split second, he had hold of my hand, jerking me back toward his rental.

I tried to pry my fingers from his, but he turned, scowling, and jerked me forward. I planted my feet on the ground like a disobedient child, and he sighed, tightening his grip, pulling me with him. My mind drifted to the images of the two women being shipped to the hospital where they were no doubt laying in a cold freezer.

I followed, knowing he was stronger than me, but I didn't make it easy.

In the heat of the moment, my pulse thrummed against the resistance of Jesse's grip, an undercurrent of defiance driving my futile attempts to break free. Frustration simmered beneath my skin, a blend of fear and indignation fueling my struggle against his incessant pull.

As we ascended the front steps, his urgency was unmistakable, and my stomach churned with apprehension. The door clicked shut, a wave of unease washed over me, the solitary sound echoed like a prison sentence.

"You never answered my question."

I lifted my chin, trying my best to keep my composure.

He raked his fingers through his dark mop of hair, turning to face me.

He let out a deep sigh.

"Charlie, do you really think I killed them?"

I bristled once again.

"Don't call me that." I crossed my arms over my chest. "And you can't answer my question with another question."

"I know how it may seem." He took a step forward, causing me to stiffen. His sigh was heavy, laden with an inexplicable mix of weariness and urgency.

His attempt to explain was met with my rigid resistance. The way he evaded my question only fueled my suspicion. I felt a knot of anxiety tighten in my chest as he ran a hand through his disheveled hair, the sense of importance hanging thick around me.

He stopped as a knock sounded at the door. "Don't move." His words were callous, but I did as he said.

He opened the door to reveal two men dressed in blue:

cops. They looked tired. The two officers at the door seemed genuinely concerned, but their presence only amplified my sense of entrapment. Jesse's silent warning was clear, urging me to comply with the situation unfolding.

"We received a call about a disturbance at this address." The officer who spoke looked from Jesse to me. "Ma'am, are you okay?" I almost scoffed at the use of the name, but I took a step forward, opening my mouth to speak.

Jesse glanced at me, his eyes hardening. The one officer noticed the apprehension and stepped aside.

"Ma'am, can I talk to you outside for a moment?" I stepped through the open door and followed the officer down cement steps to the walkway. "Is everything all right?" I looked at Jesse and the second officer standing in the doorway, contemplating what I was going to say. This was my opportunity to get away. My attention was diverted as a raven made a loud gurgling croak as it flew overhead, disappearing on the other side of the house.

I looked at the officer, then at Jesse.

"Everything is fine."

"Are you sure?" I looked back at the officer and nodded.

"I just need some space," I said, my voice carrying the weight of uncertainty and the desperate need for answers. My eyes flickered between Jesse's inscrutable gaze and the officer's concerned expression.

"Is there anyone who can come and pick you up?"

"I'll walk." He nodded slowly. "Can I go now?"

"You're free to leave." I gave one more slow glance behind me before turning and heading down the drive.

When I reached the end of the street, instead of heading home, I turned left.

Two women were dead. One was an accident, or maybe an isolated event. Two was something more, and I needed to know what it was.

The hospital was on the opposite side of town from my house. It would take me a while to walk there from Jesse's as he was about halfway between, but I needed the fresh air.

The earthy scent belonging to autumn filled my senses as I trekked the distance.

The hospital was a large cement building with a parking lot to the right as well as one at the rear. An ambulance was parked in front of the double doors.

I shuffled around the ambulance and slipped through the automatic doors, instantly hit by the scent of overly sterilized air. Each step echoed my struggle, doubts entwined with determination guiding me through the labyrinth of thoughts, pushing me deeper into the unknown, craving resolution amid the swirling chaos.

To the right lay the entrance to the emergency room, while to the left, corridors wound away into the harsh glare of fluorescent lights. Directly ahead stood the elevators. Seeking discretion, I veered right, choosing the stairwell instead. The morgue, I knew, would be in the basement.

With every step down, the air grew heavier. Dim, pale lights flickered faintly. I moved cautiously through the corridors, my breath quickening as I approached the morgue's door.

Peering through the plexiglass window, my gaze fixed on the lone figure shuffling through documents. I swallowed hard, waiting for the right moment.

Hidden in a small alcove nearby, I held my breath, close enough to hear the door opening but distant enough to evade sight.

Seconds stretched into agonizing minutes and into wat seemed like hours, though who knows how long it actually was. The door creaked open, shattering the oppressive silence. I stayed concealed, ready to act once the way was clear.

As the door softly thudded shut, I cautiously emerged. The weight of my actions pressed down on me as I gripped the door handle, an irrational fear clenching my chest.

With trembling hands, I grasped the handle and turned, pushing the door open, feeling the air grow dense as I stepped inside.

My stomach churned as I glimpsed the small steel doors lining the far wall. A metal examining table occupied the room's center, accompanied by another next to it.

The filing cabinet was my target. Nestled beside a desk, it held what I hoped were the autopsy reports. Approaching it, I grasped the metal handle, only to find it locked. The key had to be close by.

My fingers traced the desk's drawers, desperately searching for the key. With each passing moment, fear coiled tighter within me.

A box of paperclips rested atop the desk. I'd never picked a lock before, but it was worth a shot. I pried open the box, and paperclips scattered onto the floor, their clicking noise echoing off the white tile.

I quickly tried to gather the scattered clips, clutching at them as they fell through my fingertips, dropping what I could into the box. Then I saw it, a misshapen one—the key to the filing cabinet. With trembling hands, I inserted it into the cabinet's lock, the click of success resonated through the room.

File folders filled the metal brackets, papers organized alphabetically. I sought the name of the first victim—Irene Walker. However, the name of the second victim eluded me.

Sorting through the papers, I retrieved Irene's autopsy report. My hands shook as I held the document.

Scanning through, I extracted the vital details. Blunt force trauma to the back of the head was the probable cause of death. There was also a non-fatal stab wound on her left shoulder, not deep enough to be lethal.

My gaze traveled down to the body chart. Curiously, a portion of her radius was missing. My heart raced, fingers trembling as I absorbed the grim details of her injuries.

After returning the papers to their original place, I realized I needed information on the second victim, though her autopsy hadn't been completed yet.

My eyes drifted to the small steel doors to my right. Eight compartments were visible, making my stomach churn. Palms slick with sweat, I wrung my hands nervously. Despite my hesitation, my feet propelled me toward the array of doors.

Each metallic handle I gripped sent an echo of impending dread through me. One by one, the chambers revealed emptiness, until the fourth.

I pulled the handle, feeling the cold air rush against my face as the chamber door swung open. The icy chill enveloped me, a stark reminder of the grim reality.

At first sight, I recoiled—a lifeless form lay silently

within, the air thick with antiseptic scents and the undeniable hint of death. Panic clawed at my chest, urging me to flee. Yet, an insatiable curiosity pushed me forward, my fingers trembling as I approached the shrouded figure.

A tag hung from the end of the slab: Annabelle Gibbs—victim number two. Glancing inside the solitary compartment, I returned my focus to the tag. The white blanket covering her body seemed to dip slightly on the right side where her thigh should be.

I closed my eyes for a moment before summoning the courage to pull the slab further out. The slider screeched, metal on metal. Her pale form lay under the white blanket. My fingers trembled as I reached out to expose her wound, the coldness seeping through.

The gruesome sight seared into my mind—an appalling injury, an empty void where her thigh should have been. The torn flesh spoke of a savage removal. I staggered back, a wave of nausea crashing over me, threatening to spill my insides. A part of her femur had been gruesomely taken.

Retreating, I pushed the slab back in and shut the cell door, pressing a hand against my mouth to stifle the rising vomit. I fought against the burn in my throat, struggling to contain the bile threatening to escape.

Rushing toward the morgue's door, I flung it open and stumbled into the hallway, not caring if anyone saw me. I heaved, gasping for air that seemed tainted. Bent over, I labored to fill my lungs until the bile settled back in my stomach where it belonged.

I felt unclean, an urgent need to scrub away the harrowing image from my mind, cleanse it from my skin, and expunge it from my senses.

I stood beneath the showerhead as icy water poured over my shoulders and down my back, numbing my skin. Despite its coldness, it served its purpose.

A shiver crawled deep into my bones as I lathered soap into my hair and across my arms, creating suds that trickled onto the chilly shower floor. At least the water was still running.

I remained under the brisk stream for as long as I could bear, trying to wash away the haunting images from the morgue. The torn flesh, the absence of bones—why were they missing?

Switching off the water, I wrapped a towel around my shoulders, relishing its softness against my skin that brought some warmth back to my chilled body.

Padding down the hall, I entered my room in search of some clothes.

As I opened my closet, a scant selection of worn-out clothes greeted me. Shopping choices were scarce in Hayzun, especially when money was tight. I reached for one of my favorite shirts, feeling its soft fabric between my fingers.

A sudden clearing of a throat made me freeze. Clutching my towel tighter around my chest, I turned slowly, and a shadow loomed across the floor.

"What are you doing here?" Jesse sat on the edge of my bed, his arms resting on his knees. "How did you get in?" His gaze shifted from my eyes to the towel I held, a slight smirk tugging at his lips.

"Why didn't you turn me in?" His sudden question

caught me off guard. He advanced toward me, and I instinctively stepped back, my back brushing against the clothes in the closet. "If you thought I killed them, why didn't you report me? You had the perfect opportunity." My throat tightened with a mix of uncertainty and hope. I glanced down at the shirt in my hand.

"Can I please get dressed?" After a pause, he turned and left the room; his gaze cautioning me against attempting to flee.

As the door closed, I swiftly dressed in the shirt and pants, waiting for a moment before signaling for him to return.

The door clicked softly as he entered, flicking the light switch with no response. He glanced at me, then sighed. A flush of embarrassment heated my cheeks, and a prickling sensation crept into my eyes.

"Why are you here? Why did you come to Hayzun?" My voice quivered under the weight of the unknown. I hesitated for a moment. "What happened to them?" Memories of the unfortunate woman on the metal slab flooded my thoughts. Another victim lay in that cold chamber, equally unfortunate.

The air felt charged, as if it held the tension of untold secrets, waiting for truth to emerge from the shroud of darkness enveloping us both.

VEILED CONFESSIONS

He stood in front of where I sat on the end of my bed. My questions hung in the air between us. Why had he shown up just days before the murders? Why was he here?

"Why did you come here?" The question ricocheted in the quiet, my gaze locked on his every move. I needed answers, an explanation for his sudden appearance coinciding with the tragic events that unfolded.

He raked his fingers through his dark hair before crossing his arms over his chest.

"Did you kill them?" That was the most important question, so I asked it again. A muscle popped in his jaw.

"No." His eyes locked on mine. "But I might as well have." I held my hands in my lap, picking at the skin on my fingers.

"What do you mean?" I ventured, my voice barely above

a whisper, almost afraid of the answer. I looked to the pearl-colored slashes on my wrists. They matched the white lines that marked his forearms. His eyes flickered toward the pale marks on his arms, stark reminders etched into his skin. "What are those?" I prodded gently, my eyes following his silent acknowledgment. "Reminders."

"Reminders of what?" Jesse came over and sat beside me on the bed and I stiffened slightly. "Charlie, I'm not going to hurt you. If I was going to I would have already. I've had plenty of opportunities." He leaned forward, resting his arms on his knees.

"Please don't call me that," I murmured, raw memories flashing before my eyes.

"Why not?" he inquired, his voice softer now, a symphony of understanding. I flinched, revisiting a past I sought to escape.

"My dad used to call me that before—before he died." I braced myself, expecting a rush of emotions to flood in. His presence shifted, a silent acknowledgment of my pain.

"I'm sorry," he offered gently, the weight of sympathy evident in his voice. I shook my head, grappling with the lingering ghosts of the past. "I'm trying to avoid it as long as I can."

I turned to face him, determined not to let him sidestep the crux of our conversation.

"If you don't have anything to hide, why are you stalling?"

"I never said I didn't have anything to hide," he countered calmly, a layer of mystery veiling his words. "I simply said I didn't kill them."

"You're not doing anything to stop my suspicion." My

words lingered in the charged silence, hanging in the air like an unanswered plea. He nodded slowly, his hands clasped in his lap, a gesture betraying a weighty truth he hesitated to unveil.

"I belong to a group of people that have been tracking a string of … violent crimes." I nodded slowly. "They led me here to Hayzun." I put the pieces he had given me together, however they seemed to be the outside of the puzzle and the middle was still missing.

I absorbed his words, piecing together the fragments of his narrative. I caught the drift, but the pivotal details remained shrouded, teasingly just beyond my reach.

"So … they weren't the first." The realization struck like a jolt, the puzzle pieces scattering in my mind forming a picture that still eluded completion.

The trail of violence seemed longer, weaving a darker tapestry that enveloped our quiet town. My body tensed going back to the image of the ragged skin of the ghastly incision on Annabelle Gibbs leg. Her lifeless body still sitting cold in the morgue. I felt the blood drain from my face. "And we think they have at least two more in their sights."

"Why were parts of their bodies missing?"

"What do you mean?" He eyed me strangely.

"Don't lie to me."

I wrung my hands.

"I went to the morgue. I saw the bodies."

I had only seen one, but the autopsy report stated a missing bone as well on the other.

"The missing femur and radius?"

He shook his head, so I switched to a different question.

"Who were you talking to this morning?" The voice

echoed in my mind, the foreign accent ringing in my ears. "And that picture in your wallet, your ID?" The questions poured out in a torrent. "The guy in the alley … how did he know my name?"

"Whoa," Jesse let out a soft chuckle, trying to ease the tension. "I have answers for all of your questions, but maybe one at a time, okay?" I nodded, trying to steady my racing thoughts. "I was talking to my superior this morning, Reece. He came to check on my progress." His explanation felt like a lifeline in the chaos. "My real name is Jeremiah Carson, named after my grandfather, the one in the photo." He sighed, the weight seemingly easing off his shoulders. "And about the guy in the alley, he was a former member."

"Former?" I probed, seeking clarity amid the muddled revelations.

Jesse ran a hand over his thigh, a gesture of discomfort. "He did some … distasteful things in the past."

"Why is he here then if he's no longer working with you?"

"He likes to stick his nose where it doesn't belong." My mind ran over everything he had just told me.

"Is he staying in Hayzun?"

"Unfortunately, he is for the time being."

"Where?" A muscle in his jaw popped as he looked to me.

"Ch—"

"So, I can avoid him." I blurted before he could chastise me. He rolled his eyes knowing exactly why I wanted the information.

"Somewhere on Orchard." He leaned forward. "But please, Charlie." He stopped shaking his head. "Charlotte, be careful."

He had answers for all my questions. Plausible answers too, but then why did something still feel not quite right?

Jesse's shadow crept up the far wall as he stood. It grew from the corner in a dark silhouette. I looked to Jesse, startled to see him, still seated beside me. My head jerked back to the wall.

"Are you okay?" My mouth hung open, words filtering through my mind.

"You're going to think I'm nuts." A small laugh escaped, startling us.

"You'd be surprised." His words held sincerity, urging me to share despite the uncertainty. The shadows I'd seen earlier, dismissed as ordinary occurrences, now seemed suspect.

"I've been seeing this thing … this shadow," I confessed, my voice tinged with uncertainty. "Just glimpses of it at first, out of the corner of my eye." I gestured beside me thinking back to the fleeing shadow at the clinic and the other times it had flickered in and out of existence.

"But?"

I shook my head standing.

"But nothing. I'm obviously just seeing things." Right? The weight of doubt lingered heavily, threatening to unravel my grasp on reality.

9

THE TOLLING BELL

The brisk air nipped at my skin, a tangible reminder of the impending curfew, urging me to quicken my pace. Answers eluded me, and the stranger from the alley seemed to hold a piece of the puzzle.

Jesse's cautionary words lingered, but curiosity overshadowed the warning.

I knew little about him—only Jesse's advice to stay away. If they once worked together, he couldn't be entirely malicious.

My steps echoed on the pavement as I ventured toward Orchard Street, southeast of the clock tower, aiming to unravel the mysteries veiled within Hayzun's streets.

The only question now was, how do I find him? He was staying somewhere on Orchard. Hayzun wasn't huge, but it was large enough to make finding someone you didn't know difficult. A street, however, was a start.

Reaching the corner of the road, I continued heading east. The houses got more significant and more stable the further I went. The lawns got greener and vaster.

With each step, the houses grew larger, more imposing. The aroma of decay mingled with the crispness of the air, the scent of fallen leaves heralding the autumnal rotting. Minutes blurred into each other until a worn metal sign confirmed my location: Orchard St.

The street boasted only a handful of driveways, mostly belonging to lifelong residents of Hayzun, except one. It had transitioned to new ownership after Mr. Jenkins, an elderly man well-known for his dedication to the animal shelter, had passed away.

A circular driveway signaled the one place that held potential answers. The grandeur of the home surpassed my imagination, an opulence I couldn't fathom affording, even temporarily.

The lengthy walkway snaked toward a porch constructed from interlocking stones, flanked by sizable wooden doors adorned with intricate ironwork. My trembling hand reached forward, hesitating before finally knocking. Each rap against the door seemed to reverberate, either in the surrounding woods or in the palpitations of my racing heart. Perhaps both.

Footsteps resonated from within, drawing closer until they halted abruptly. The anticipation knotted in my chest, a symphony of nervous energy and eagerness playing in my ears.

Just as the door creaked open, I instinctively ducked around the corner, senses heightening as a surge of adrenaline coursed through me. Should I have been more cautious? A shuffle followed by the door closing echoed through the air. I held my breath, counting the seconds before cautiously peeking around the edge.

A pair of mocha brown eyes met mine, forming into a growing smirk. My heart raced, and I hastily retreated, pressing myself against the cool wall. His chuckle sent a shiver down my spine.

"I know you're there." His voice, tinged with amusement, taunted me. "Charlotte?" His words hit their mark, and I shut my eyes tight. "I knew you'd come looking for me eventually." I cursed my predictability. "What's he done this time?" The implication in his words made my stomach churn. Jesse was the only connection I had with this mysterious figure. "He means well," the voice continued, a mix of insight and mockery.

Feeling the need to escape, I edged further along the house, seeking refuge amid the shrubbery lining the walls. The man's silence intensified the eerie atmosphere.

"What did he tell you about me?" His question breaking the silence went unanswered by my trembling lips. "Judging by how you're hiding, it wasn't flattering. But my brother would do anything to protect those he cares about, even lie, especially when the clock is ticking." His laughter reverberated, the implications of his words unsettling.

Brother? My mind reeled.

I pushed myself along the side of the house, inching farther away from the chuckling voice. Shrubs lined this side of the house, and I slipped myself between them and the cold wall. As I neared closer to the back of the house, I prepared to flee. The voice fell silent for a moment.

The hairs on the back of my neck stood up. What about

kill? The thought rang through my head like a buzzing bee. No, he said he didn't hurt them. Brother? It popped back into my head. Jesse had failed to mention that. What else had he failed to mention?

I ran over the rest of what he had said. The clock is ticking. I shook my head. The clock is ticking. The words grew louder and louder until they were screams. The clock is ticking.

Stumbling over a branch, I teetered backward bracing myself with my hands and unintentionally revealing myself to Jace—That was what Jesse had said his name was right? His eyes widened with recognition, and I could see a mixture of concern and familiarity in his expression. I stood, dusting my hands off on my pant legs.

The air outside was frigid, carrying a hint of wood smoke from nearby chimneys.

He saw me. I might as well finish what I came here to do.

As Jace opened the door, a rush of warmth greeted me, contrasting sharply with the night's cold embrace. His eyes fixed on me.

"Charlotte," he greeted, ushering me inside the dimly lit home. The door closed behind us with a soft thud, muffling the outside world and cocooning us in a blanket of hushed secrecy.

I couldn't help but feel like an intruder in a place of secrets. Jace gestured for me to follow him, and I complied, stepping further into the large, bare house. It felt devoid of any personal touches, just like Jesse's.

"I was expecting you to come around eventually," Jace said, his voice calm. "Jace." He extended a hand in my direction. When I ignored it he pulled his hand back, tucking it into his pocket.

I couldn't contain my curiosity any longer. "Why did Jesse have a second ID in his wallet, and why did he warn me to stay away from you?"

Jace hesitated for a moment as if choosing his words carefully. "I can't explain everything right now, but things are happening in this town that you're not aware of. Jesse, he's not entirely who you think he is."

As I listened to Jace's cryptic words, I realized that My world was shifting, and I was caught in a web of mysteries that reached far beyond my understanding.

I couldn't deny the unease that had settled in my chest. His demeanor and the cryptic way he spoke only deepened my curiosity.

I took a step closer, my voice trembled with both fear and a growing determination. "You can't just drop all of this on me and expect me to understand. I need answers."

"I wish I could give you all the answers right now, but it's not that simple. I don't even have them all yet."

I couldn't deny the urgency in his voice. I nodded, looking down.

As the gravity of the situation settled in, Jace offered to drive me back to Jesse's place, reminding me of the town's curfew. However, I declined his offer, feeling a newfound sense of independence and the need to process the information he had provided.

"I'll walk back," I said with determination. "I need some time to think."

Jace nodded in understanding, and I stepped back into the night, the weight of newfound knowledge heavy on my shoulders, and a sense of foreboding hanging in the air.

My feet moved with an almost automated determination, tracing back the steps I had taken earlier. Passing through the narrow lanes and winding paths, I found myself standing once more at the familiar sight of the large clock tower. The town's centerpiece seemed to echo my thoughts, its chimes echoing with eerie resonance. *The clock is ticking.*

The tolling of the bells resonated through the air, vibrating within my skull as if trying to unlock a hidden truth. A raven startled by the clamor took flight from its perch atop a nearby building, adding to the surreal atmosphere.

As the bells continued to toll, my mind began to grow fuzzy. The dizziness forced me to my knees. I braced my hands on the interlocking stone floor beneath me to keep myself from tumbling further. The ground was prickly and cold against my skin, and my right hand absentmindedly curled itself around a sharp stone. It cut into my flesh and pain seared up my arm.

The bell tolled once again and drew me back to the present. When I attempted to open my eyes, it was as if a veil had descended upon the world. Panic seized me until I realized the sky had darkened, the sun having disappeared beneath the horizon. The realization hit me like a jolt. How much time had passed? The tolling continued, and I counted, bewildered by the twelve rings that signified hours had vanished without my knowledge.

My attention shifted to my hand; it was covered in blood where the sharp edges of the stone had pierced my skin; I opened my shaky hand and watched as the worn stone clattered to the ground. I pushed myself to my feet, my legs feeling like Jelly.

The darkness around me grew ever so slightly brighter as my eyes adjusted. They caught the contrast of the bricks on the ground. The cement around me was all one shade however in front of me it was muddled and marked. Graffitied with thin lines. I gasped, realizing the scratches formed an image. An image I had carved into the weathered man-made floor with a small pebble. An array of flowers marred the stone.

Before I could fully comprehend this strange occurrence, a cruiser pulled up beside me. An officer emerged, casting a beam of light in my direction.

"Ma'am, curfew's been in effect. You shouldn't be out at this hour," the officer stated, concern etched into his features.

"Yes, I know," I stammered, unable to explain the lapse in time, the inexplicable marks on the ground, or the lost hours.

He noticed my injured hand. "You're hurt. Let's get that taken care of at the station."

He closed the gap between us, looking at my injury.

The officer, identified as R. Quinn, guided me into the back of the car, the faint smell of cigarette smoke lingered around him. He glanced to the markings on the ground before entering the vehicle himself, driving us to the station.

The drive was brief, and soon, I found myself seated in front of a weathered desk while Quinn worked on his computer clacking away on his keyboard.

"You won't be charged this time, but curfew violations are recorded," he informed me, his fingers tapping away at the keyboard.

I nodded, my mind a swirl of confusion and anxiety. "Can I make a phone call?"

His expression was a mix of concern and duty. My mind was still clouded with confusion, struggling to piece together the lost hours.

"You're not being arrested, Miss," Quinn reassured me; a faint hint of empathy filling his voice. I nodded once more, a pang of relief flickering through the perplexity gripping me. "I will drive you home once I gather all of your information."

"Thank you." A female officer approached, deftly tending to the cut on my palm before leaving. I managed a grateful smile before she disappeared.

I thought back to the drawing; An array of wilted flowers that had been snipped off at their stem. The same flowers I saw on my walk to the clinic. I thought of the man who planted them. He had arrived just before the murders.

"Officer Quinn?" He nodded, bringing his gaze to mine for a moment. I took that as a go-ahead. "I saw someone on my way to work the other day."

"The town is filled with someones Miss. Lowrey what's your point?"

"Behind the high school. A new janitor maybe. How much do they know about him?" Quinn let out a low sigh.

"I imagine they did their due diligence." I nodded dropping the subject.

A few minutes later I had answered all of R. Quinn's questions and was taking my seat in the back of the cop car once again.

Instead of giving him my address, I gave him Jesse's. I'd rather be with someone I barely knew than by myself.

The drive was silent, punctuated only by my soft *thank you* as I stepped out of the car. Quinn lingered, a silent sentinel as I approached the house.

I knocked, a sense of urgency pulsating within me. The curfew was in effect; he had to be here. But as seconds stretched into minutes, uncertainty crept in. Had he left despite the curfew? Or was I simply being ignored?

A faint creak broke the silence, a sliver of light appearing as the door inched open, revealing a slice of the dimly lit interior.

His tired eyes found me with a slight look of surprise, but he stepped aside, allowing me entrance to the small house. Jesse glanced outside, a small smile catching his lips when he spotted the cruiser.

Once the door was closed, I allowed myself to let out a shallow sigh. Was I comfortable? No! But at least I was inside and warm.

My body stiffened, and his eyes searched me. The taunting smile disappeared from his full lips as he realized something was wrong.

"I went to the town square," I blurted out, the words tumbling incoherently from my mouth, again trusting him without cause. Maybe the loneliness since my father passed had really taken its toll.

I struggled to recount the lost time, the inexplicable drawing, and the disconcerting gaps in my memory. When I finished, Jesse guided me to the couch, his demeanor unexpectedly serious.

"Wait here." With these words, he was on his way out of the door. Before I could protest, he was gone. I squeezed my hands in my lap to try and contain the mix of emotions that brewed inside of me. I sunk deeper into the couch and pinched my eyes closed.

The creak of the door reopening startled me, making me

realize how much time had passed since Jesse left. He re-entered, and I sensed he had gone to inspect the cryptic drawing I described. The click of the lock as he closed the door sent shivers down my spine.

His eyes found me in the same spot he had left me. It was more the loss of time that had me startled.

"Until whoever this is, is caught…" his voice was grave, "I'm not letting you out of my sight."

He looked me up and down before gesturing down the hall with a jerk of his head; I sat unsure of what he wanted. When I didn't move, he clarified.

"Follow me."

I swallowed hard, trying to clear the lump that had formed in my throat. He sensed the unease, and his expressions softened.

"Just so I can keep an eye on you," He shifted his weight. "Make sure you stay safe."

Why was he so worried? Did he think I was in danger?

"The Victims," he stated, snapping my attention back to him. "They all look the same."

I nodded in agreement, thinking of the girls who had been killed. They looked strikingly similar.

"They look like you!" His words cut me to the core. Suddenly, I felt empty and utterly alone. The person I was closest to was the stranger standing in front of me. Even my own mother had left.

I looked down at my hands, which were clasped tightly in my lap. They pulled restlessly at one another, the bandage wrinkling.

I shifted my weight, looking at him for confirmation. He gave me a slight nod, and I stood watching as he turned and headed down the hall. I followed along the small hallway. Two doors sat closed to the left and an open bathroom door to the right. At the end of the hall sat another closed door. He pushed it open and stood to the side, letting me walk in.

Against the back wall sat a neatly made bed with end tables on either side. A window was above, clad in black curtains. He stepped inside and pushed the door closed while I looked around.

Unsure of what to do, I stood, rooted to the ground, watching as he dragged the sheets down on one side of the bed. He then stood back and took a seat in a chair I had not noticed before.

"You can have the bed," his words were calm and matter of fact. I looked from him to the bed one more time before slowly making my way over to it.

I sat on the edge of the bed, feeling the soft black sheets beneath my palms. He eyed me from where he sat a couple feet away as I pulled my legs up and slowly slid them beneath the covers. My clothes from that day were not the most comfortable to sleep in, but I pushed that out of my mind and laid down in the unfamiliar bed, pulling the covers up around me.

As I let myself sink into the mattress, the fresh scent of the washed sheets filling my senses, exhaustion hit me. My eyes found Jesse once again as he reached over and flipped the light out, plummeting us into darkness.

The tightness of fear filled my chest until a small lamp on the bedside table turned on. He sat back down, eyes flicking back over to me.

A small smile formed on his lips, quickly vanishing once he caught me looking. I adjusted myself, pulling the blankets higher, closing my eyes.

I focused on what I could hear instead. The buzz of silence filled my ears, diluted slightly by the sound of Jesse's breaths and my own.

For the first time in a long time, I felt content. I felt safe with him here. He shifted his weight in the chair, and I could smell him from where he sat across the room—a warm earthy scent.

I nestled myself deeper, cocooning myself in blankets as I tried to push all thoughts from my whirling mind.

I let the exhaustion take over as sleep pulled me into its massive embrace. But fear, it's relentless, it sneaks in, and wraps itself around you, suffocating your thoughts. My nightmares became a canvas of the night, an unwelcome visitor in the silent darkness.

Fear isn't conscious. It lives everywhere, whether or not you know it. It manifests when we are awake and even when we are asleep. Everyone experiences it differently, and everyone handles it in their own way. Me, I lived with fear. It had become one of my closest friends. Fear is loud, and it doesn't care who or what it hurts. Like a siren in the night's quietness. A siren warning of danger.

It grew louder and louder until I could no longer bear it. My eardrums felt as though they were ready to burst.

I covered my ears with my shaking hands, a scream startling me. Something wrapped tight around my body, and I struggled to get free. Another scream pulled me back to reality, and I realized it was mine. Hands grasped me gently, and my eyes shot open. I gasped at the figure in front of me. His eyes were filled with worry, a nightmare. I shook my head, trying to catch my breath. My eyes locked with his.

"I'm sorry," was all I could say. His eyes softened as he looked me over. I let the warmth of a tear gently slide down my cheek. Before I could wipe it away, Jesse gently dried it with the side of his hand. His presence was oddly calming.

I could feel my body shaking, and he looked me over once again. This time It wasn't fear, a chill had set into my bones.

"Cold?"

I nodded slightly, and he stood making his way over to the dresser where he pulled out another blanket. He laid it over me before reclaiming his spot on the chair. I settled back down, feeling the cold snake its way through my body.

"What were you dreaming about?" I thought back to a few moments ago.

"It was deafening," I stammered, recoiling from the memory. Jesse nodded, in understanding, his silence allowed me to collect my thoughts. I pinched my eyes shut.

Movement on the opposite side of the bed caused me to jump. He lifted the sheets gently before sitting down beside me, warmth radiating off him.

His eyes found mine as he stretched his long body out beside me. I looked at him warily.

"Come here," he said, lifting his arm closest to me. I looked at him for a long moment. "I'm not going to hurt you," his words were tender, reassuring.

I swallowed hard and slid myself over to him. He guided me to his chest before fixing the blankets up around us. My body was tense, and he noticed, running a hand gently up and down my arm. I relaxed into his embrace, letting the warmth of his body dispel the cold creeping inside me.

"Get some sleep," he whispered softly, and I allowed

myself to succumb to the comfort of his presence, drifting into a restful slumber. I closed my eyes and once again cleared my head of any bouncing thoughts. His body stole the cold from me as I drifted off.

I woke to a cold and empty bed in a dark room. The door was pulled closed, and the rental was eerily silent. I had a feeling I was alone.

The sheets cascaded softly off my arms as I sat up, my feet landing on the chilly floor. A shiver ran through me, even through my socks.

I edged toward the door, its creak protesting the movement in the quiet room. Pushing it open, a faint glimmer of light illuminated the hallway.

The sound of a ticking clock grew louder as I neared the end of the corridor. All the curtains were still pulled, keeping this little house closed off from the outside world.

Nearing the end of the hall a rattling caught my attention. The doorknob twisted before the door clicked open. Jesse stood on the other side with a grim expression on his face, though it softened a little when his eyes found me.

His somber expression softened briefly upon seeing me but quickly reverted to its previous gravity. Without a word, he strode to the counter, dropping a handful of papers beside the fridge. One stray envelope, bearing the name Jeremiah Carson, drifted to the floor. As I bent to retrieve it, Jesse snatched it from my grasp with a heavy sigh. Gathering the rest of the letters, he disappeared down the hallway, leaving me in the silence only to return a moment later.

"Gardening shears," he stated quietly, his gaze locking with mine.

My stomach churned at the thought of those tools matching the victims' wounds, capable of inflicting the gruesome injuries I saw in the morgue. The image of tearing flesh apart as easily as snipping a flower from its stem was too vivid.

"There's still a missing girl; Piper Adams." He swallowed hard, "But he won't tell the police what he did with her." The muscle in his jaw ticked "They've lifted the county curfew."

I nodded slowly to him.

"Does this mean it's over?" My heart clenched.

"No." His eyes darkened. "He didn't do this."

10

ECHOES OF THE PAST

"What are you not telling me?" My words came out angry. "Does it have to do with your brother?" I bit the words out. Just now remembering the little tidbit of information I had been told. His eyes widened, but he ignored my words.

"Your drawing," he started.

"What about my drawings?"

"Drawings … as in many?" his tone was probing, insistent.

I nodded; drawing had always been my solace.

"What have you drawn in the past week?" His urgency sent a chill down my spine.

"I … I drew gates …"

"Gates to the graveyard?"

The confirmation felt like a punch to the gut. I simply nodded, unable to voice the confirmation.

"Where they found the first body." He pushed his fingers through his hair. "What else?"

I struggled to find words.

"Nothing, but I had—"

"Had what Charlie?" his voice came out harsh.

"You're going to think—"

"Had what?" It was a growl now.

"A vision … I had a vision," I said as he crossed his arms over his chest. "Just before we found the second girl."

"That's why you ran."

It was a sharp observation, a cutting truth. "The graveyard, the woods, the flowers. They match the incidents. It wasn't a coincidence you found that body."

My mind spiraled in disbelief. This couldn't be real, but the pieces aligned too perfectly.

My mind whirled. This was some sort of sick joke, but he was right, wasn't he? My sketches, my thoughts. They matched. The realization knocked my breathing off-kilter and my body too.

"You think I had something to do with it?"

I went to straighten, but my legs quivered, making me sit on one of the kitchen chairs.

"You do, don't you? How else would I know these things?"

"No, no, no," his voice softened as he took a step forward. I pulled back at his movement, and he knelt beside me, shrinking his stature.

I looked to Jesse where he was kneeling on the ground.

He reached beside us, opening a small drawer where he pulled out a pen and a pad of paper, sitting them both on the table in front of me.

It was as if he expected my drawings to unveil the truth behind the chaos.

"It doesn't work like that." My voice quivered, my fingers fidgeted with the edge of the paper. This was beyond my control; these visions were elusive and unpredictable.

I looked at the paper that sat in front of me. I knew what he wanted. He wanted me to draw. To predict the terror. "It doesn't work like that," I repeated as I pulled at my hands. Though the dots were just connecting, I knew it wasn't something I could control. I was a sort of slave to these ideals.

"It's okay, take your time."

I nodded slowly. The air seemed thick and stale, though I knew it was just the knot of panic forming in my core. My drawings were a part of me; they were my imagination. They had no ties to the real world. Though I suppose if you looked hard enough, you could read too much into anything. However, the faster I produced an image, the faster I could put this to rest. Or maybe prove him right. I shook that last thought loose.

Each breath felt more labored than the last. My drawings were merely creations of my imagination, detached from reality. Yet, here they were, being scrutinized for clues to a grim truth. I pushed away the irrational thought that they could somehow predict horrors.

Picking up the worn pen, I touched the tip to the paper. The nib gobbed with ink transferring messy color to the wrinkled stark canvas, blank and begging to be used.

I didn't know what triggered the ideas to form in my mind. I imagined it to be the same way a writer creates a story, or a musician picks their notes. It becomes a sort of thing that just happens. Like the way we don't have to think about breathing. The ideas formed in my mind, uninvited and haunting. It was like an involuntary reflex, a creative surge that I couldn't stop.

The labored breaths beside me were like bees buzzing in my ears, and a soft ticking evenly spaced marked the passing time. A clock. Where, I was still not sure? Its rhythmic clicking stole my thoughts. I tried to recall how artists describe their process, how inspiration strikes them. Was this akin to that? A cascade of images flooded my mind, unfiltered and unsettling. The struggle to translate these visions to paper was like wrestling with a restless spirit.

Minutes trickled by; the weight of the situation hanging heavy in the air. I stared at the paper, but no images formed, no visions came forth. Just emptiness.

Jesse's hand found its way to my leg, offering comfort. A warmth spread under my skin, momentarily distracting me until a knock at the door pulled us from the moment. Jesse stood, his movements deliberate, and made his way to the door. With a slow turn of the handle, the door creaked open.

At his feet sat a small, wrapped box resting on the front stoop. I brought my eyes back up to his, and he gave a slight shrug. I stood making my way to his side and knelt. The box was carefully wrapped in a light-colored paper. A bow sat neatly on the top. I picked up the card and my eyes crinkled as I found my name printed on the envelope.

"What does it say?" The voice snapped me back, and I looked up at him.

"It's for me." He furrowed his brow. "Does it say who it's from?"

I shook my head, flipping the envelope over in my hand, and pulled the card from inside. Words sat scratched on the paper.

Your time is running out.

Jesse took the card from my trembling hands, studying it intently. While he focused on the message, I cautiously turned my attention to the box, fingers gingerly unwrapping the thin paper.

Once the top of the box was revealed, I hesitated for a moment, a sense of foreboding tugging at my gut. Slowly, I lifted the lid, a knot forming in my throat. As the darkness inside the box emerged, my fingers grazed something soft, sending shivers down my spine. Pulling it from the box, a chill swept over me.

I held it for a moment, unaware of what it was until I felt its texture against my skin. Horror curled in my stomach as I watched it unfurl in my trembling grip. Without warning, a sharp, guttural scream tore from my throat, and I dropped it to the ground; my body recoiled in sheer terror.

It took a moment for my mind to process the sight—the dark lock of hair still attached to the scalp. A rush of bile rose in my throat, and I stumbled backward, trying to distance myself from the grotesque object.

A rasp of air escaped my throat as I tried to stay upright. Jesse knelt to inspect what I had thrown from my hands. Once he realized what it was, he shook his head and put it back into the box. He sat it back down on the front stoop before standing and stepping toward me. I felt a warm tear trickle down my flushed cheek. Jesse was oddly calm as his eyes searched my trembling body.

I shook my head, pushing back my dark hair from my

face. Red caught my attention, and I wheezed, looking down at the sickly red blood staining my hands.

Jesse approached me gently, his touch comforting yet urgent. He led me to the sink, turning on the faucet he guided my hands under the running water. I watched in a daze as the crimson hue washed away, swirling down the drain, leaving my hands clean but my mind in turmoil.

His fingertips brushed over the scars on my wrists, a silent acknowledgment of what I went through. After a moment, he turned off the tap and fetched a towel from a nearby drawer. With tenderness in his gaze, he dried my hands, his touch surprisingly soothing amid the mess.

"We should take that to the police," I managed to say, my voice trembled as another tear rolled down my cheek. Jesse hesitated for a moment, a flicker of concern passing over his face before he gently dried my cheeks.

"The police can't help us," he murmured, his voice tinged with a sense of resignation. After tossing the damp towel onto the countertop, he dried his own hands on his jeans, his eyes locking onto mine, a silent promise of protection and resolve.

"I wasn't completely honest with you before," he began, his words causing my body to tense involuntarily, taking a step back.

"What do you mean?" I asked, my voice betraying me and showing my anxiety. He leaned against the countertop, running his fingers through his hair, his expression troubled.

"The person committing these murders is part of a worship," he stated, his tone measured.

"A cult?" I raised my hands in disbelief. "And you're just thinking of telling me this now? Why not tell the police?" My frustration seeped into my voice, but he didn't answer, continuing as if I hadn't spoken.

"They call themselves The First Chosen. They worship Disias, the God of Shadows."

"I have never heard of—"

He cut me off with a shake of his head.

"Most people haven't," he admitted. "It's a long and complicated story, but they believe that Disias was imprisoned to maintain the balance between good and evil. They believe that an individual with a void soul must be sacrificed to release him."

"A void soul?" I furrowed my brow, trying to grasp the concept.

Jesse nodded.

"Someone born both good and bad." My forehead wrinkled. "Someone born from both the Sol and Ember bloodlines, the two major bloodlines they … believe in." His words broke off as he looked me up and down. "Someone like you."

"Me?" the words sputtered out of my mouth. "These zealots think I'm who their looking for?" I asked. Jesse nodded. "Why?"

He stood silent, the seconds ticking by. The longer I stood the more enraged I became.

"Better yet, when?"

He quirked an eyebrow. "This so-called sacrifice, when?"

His gaze dropped to the floor.

"When the clock strikes midnight on the eve of your birthday," he finally answered, his voice laced with dread. "This year, it just so happens to align with the lunar eclipse— the blood moon needed to complete the ritual, The Eclipse of Shadows."

"That means I have less than eleven days?" A lump rose in my throat.

"No, I will not let them hurt you."

I laughed turning, feeling a warm tear streak down my cheek.

"They've already killed two and taken a third in Hayzun alone," I stated, wiping my cheeks. "They know where I am," I added, gesturing to the box containing the lock of hair and bloodied scalp. Darkness loomed at the end of the hallway, causing me to inhale sharply. The shadow. I watched it move toward the wall, disappearing into the darkness.

Hands grasped my hips, gently turning me toward him.

"I won't let them hurt you, Charlie," he said again, softly, tilting my chin. "I made that decision the moment I saw you." Despite his attempt to comfort me, there was an undercurrent of something else in his words, something ominous that chilled me to the bone. My bottom lip trembled involuntarily.

"You didn't come here to save me, did you?" I asked. He paused, his hand still lingering on my cheek. His silence spoke volumes, confirming my suspicions. "Did you?" The words tumbled out of my mouth, each syllable weighted with a mix of hurt and anger.

"No."

As I took a step back, his hands dropped to his sides, and his expression remained unyielding. My anger began to seethe beneath the surface.

"Why were you sent?" I asked, my voice barely above a whisper, but I knew he had heard me. He stood silently, his stoic facade unwavering. "Why?"

"I came to remove the problem," he answered bluntly, his eyes devoid of emotion. "The First Chosen won't stop until they get what they want."

His words were like a dagger through my heart, and I took another step back, a surge of fear and anger welled within me.

"And I am what they want?" I demanded, my voice quivered with a mixture of emotions.

"Yes."

The starkness in his response sent shivers down my spine, solidifying the gravity of the danger that loomed over me.

11

FEAR AND RESILIENCE

"Why didn't you kill me?" I shouted the words. "Now they are dead, and it should have been me."

His eyes softened as he took a step forward. "Don't." I held up my hand. "What's your plan now then?"

"Can you please just calm down."

"No."

His eyes closed momentarily, a hand combing through his hair, frustration evident.

"I was meant to wait," he began cautiously. "The ritual would draw them out, and that's when I was supposed to intervene ... to end it all. Them. And you." His words lingered, bearing a weight I struggled to carry.

I ran over his words in my head. His expression became more and more pinched as the seconds ticked by.

"And now I'm bait. You were going to ask my

permission, weren't you?" I turned away, my arms wrapped tightly around me, a feeble shield against the situation unraveling. "I didn't think so."

"Charlie." I tensed at that name. "Thousands more will die if we don't stop them." I felt him take a step closer. "And those who have died will have died for nothing." He grabbed my arm, gently turning me around to face him, eyes solemn, the blue churning like the waves of the ocean. I met his gaze and held it.

"I will do it, but I'm doing this for the people that died." His fingers tensed on my arm, turning the inside of my wrist toward him.

"Why are you so indifferent to your own life?" He pressed a thumb into the puckered scars, his touch gentle yet insistent.

"The world can be cruel," I murmured, trying to pull my arm away, but he held it firmly.

"You've only seen such a small fragment of it. There's so much more." His features softened as my eyes prickled.

"I haven't been fortunate enough to witness that," I confessed, the weight of past experiences heavy in my voice. The room fell silent, except for the relentless ticking of the clock.

"You will, I'll make sure of it."

I grabbed his hand that remained on my wrist, holding his fingers in mine.

"Promise me something."

He nodded, shifting his weight.

"If it comes to that … if I have to die."

His eyes squeezed shut, bracing for the weight of my words.

"You'll let me. If it's a choice between me and the lives of thousands." Before he could respond, I held his gaze, my grip firm, then released his hand, letting it fall to his side.

"I hope it doesn't come to that." A frown formed on his lips, and I turned. Why his emotions affected me the way it did after he had lied and hid things from me, I had no idea, but they did. This stranger though maybe morally confused had become important to me. Though I guess when you are deprived of human connection you grasp onto whatever you can.

"But if it does?" I left the question hanging.

"If it does, then yes."

I nodded, lowering my head.

12

SHIFTING SHADOWS

Once again, the familiar path to the clinic guided my steps. The sky, shrouded in a heavy cloak of clouds, mirrored the ground strewn with the dry carcasses of leaves. Every step I took crunched these remnants beneath my heels, releasing an earthy fragrance that mingled with the crisp air.

Voices trickled in around me, coming from different directions. Their words too far away to decipher.

As I neared the Western Apartments, a cool wind pulled on the hair at the nape of my neck, the icy fingers of death. I shivered releasing their hold on me, but a few steps later they grasped me once again. It was as if a wall of ice had hit me, before slowly melting away. It froze every inch of me, causing my muscles to tense. I hurried forward, hoping to get to the warmth of the clinic as quickly as possible.

Each step felt like a conscious effort, pushing through

the numbing cold, knowing that warmth was an elusive sanctuary ahead.

As I quickened my pace, I felt a pull, a pull on my mind. Before I could stop myself, or even know why or how I had gotten there, I stood on the edge of Rainbow Bridge. Its colorfully painted boards spanned the distance over Shadow Gulch. I had only crossed it once before, and it was an act I regretted. I thought of the puckered scars that marked the events of that day.

The aged boards creaked underfoot as I tentatively stepped onto the bridge, each movement causing an unsettling wobble. Why was I here? A question that resonated with every uncertain step I took. Yet, despite my inner protests, I found myself halfway across the span. With one more step, clarity pierced through my mind, urging me to turn back toward Hayzun. But an inexplicable force pulled me in the opposite direction, compelling me to stay.

I braced my hands on the railing, letting my shaking body relax. Black blurred the edges of my vision, pinning me to the spot. I stood, unable to move, arms shaking. A dizzying sensation filled my head.

To my right, the dark silhouette transformed into a large-winged raven perched on the rail, its low croaks reverberating, disorienting me further. I winced, pulling my eyelids shut and clenching my jaw, trying to block out the ominous sound.

Initially soft murmurs, they grew louder, a name repeated with increasing urgency—*Charlie*. I remained still, but the bird's eerie croaks intensified. Suddenly, the individual to whom the voice belonged charged onto the bridge, causing the old structure to groan and sway under the abrupt weight.

Again, this time louder. And again. *Charlie?* The voice

was panicked and getting closer.

"Charlie?" Jesse's hands encircled mine, gently prying my fingers from the splintering wood. His panicked eyes met mine, his hands cupping my face, radiating warmth that eased the tearing cold inside me. "You're freezing."

His words felt distant against the icy grip tightening around me.

"What's wrong?" His panicked eyes filled my vision as he turned to me, cupping my face in his hands.

"The …" My jaw clenched tighter, refusing to form the words.

"What, Charlie?" His panic did nothing to subdue mine.

"The Shadow."

Realization flooded his eyes as another shiver racked through my body. He swiftly removed his jacket, draping it over my shoulders before kneeling, an arm folded behind my knees as he lifted me against his chest.

With each step he took over the bridge, a new sensation crept through me, a myriad of tiny icicles formed beneath my skin, pricking with each movement. The further he walked, the sharper they became.

"I'm taking you home." His breath warmed my cheek as I tried to focus on anything but the icy pain. I let myself go limp in his arms, tracking the passing seconds with the beating of my heart.

It felt like an eternity until warmth enveloped my body, yet it failed to thaw the spears of ice beneath my skin.

Jesse settled me onto his bed, gently tucking a blanket around me before stepping away down the hall. He returned swiftly, sliding in beside me.

My heart thudded so loud it was all I could hear.

"I'm not going to hurt you," he whispered. I nodded.

"I Trust you."

He held a cup out to me.

"Drink it."

"What is it?" I took the cup and looked at the contents. A red liquid stained the sides of the glass.

"Just drink it."

With a hesitant breath, I tipped the cup back, the viscous liquid pooling on my tongue, trailing down my throat. Its warm metallic taste clawed at my senses, but I forced it down, a testament to my trust in Jesse's intentions.

I knew Jesse had a reason behind this. I downed the cup and handed it back to him, dragging the back of my hand over my mouth. As he took it, his sleeve slid up his arm, exposing a deep slash across his wrist like mine.

"Jess, what's that from?" He pulled his sleeve down as he stood, yes hard. "What was in the cup?"

"It doesn't matter."

"Yes, it does."

I lunged for him, but my legs felt like rubber, and I fell hard to the floor, vision blurring, and body now erupting with heat. Arms closed around me and lifted me off the ground. I could feel sweat rolling down my back and off my arms. The air around me felt thick and stale, I couldn't get in a full breath no matter how hard I tried. The arms around me laid me down onto the bed and Jesse's face flicked into view.

"Jess." I choked on my own words. "Jess," I gasped only being able to draw in short raspy breaths. I grasped blindly at the air trying to reach him, but my fingers only caught air.

The bed shifted suddenly, and I felt like my body was going to tumble over the edge and onto the floor, but it was only Jesse sitting down. I tried one more time and this time I was able to grab onto his wrist.

"What's going on?" Sweat rolled from every pore in my body without any sign of stopping.

"Shhh." Jesse ran his hand over my hair. "It's going to be okay."

"I don't feel okay." My body convulsed.

"I know." A tear slid from my eye as a shot of pain gripped at my stomach. I grabbed at his wrist so hard it hurt my hand.

I heard a scream resonate and soon realized it was mine. My body felt like it was on fire. "I can't breathe." I rolled onto my stomach, but it only made it worse. My throat was closing, and I gagged feeling my heart flutter in my chest. Swinging myself over onto my back, another scream filled my ears. I gasped not being able to get enough air into my lungs.

I clawed at my chest, nails digging into my flesh even through the fabric of my shirt.

"Charlie, stop." I ignored his warnings, I needed air. "Charlie." His voice came out hoarse. My heart felt ready to burst and my lungs burned as if I was underwater. "Stop fighting it."

I coughed.

"Charlie," he warned. "You're making it worse."

I couldn't breathe. Was I dying? My hands clawed roughly at my body. Jesse swore. Soon he was on top of me, straddling my hips. I hit at him, trying to get him off, but he wouldn't budge.

He grabbed me by the wrists and pinned them to the mattress above my head. I kicked my legs, but he adjusted his body over mine, immobilizing me.

"Jess, get, off." My chest heaved.

"I'm sorry Charlie." He held me pinned to the bed, knees digging into my hips.

"Jess!" I pleaded. "Please."

"Shhh." He closed his eyes. I wriggled my body, but he held me securely.

"Shhh." Jesse's eyes shut tightly as he held me firmly in place.

"Jess." Tears streamed down my cheeks; each drop a searing testament to my anguish. Breathing remained a struggle; it felt as though a snake coiled around my lungs, constricting, depriving me of air and consciousness.

Pain filled my body as my stomach twisted and my skin burned. I was covered in sweat; it rolled off my skin. "What is, happening?" I wheezed. I wanted Jesse to get off me. His fingers dug into my wrists, cutting off the circulation.

His eyes opened slowly, pain flickering across them. I screamed with more pain, vision blurring; fists clenched tight. "Jess." I sobbed. "I can't, it hurts." A ringing began in my ears getting louder and louder until it was all I could hear. I could feel myself losing consciousness by the second. I knew I wouldn't last long.

"Charlie?" Jesse's voice took over the ringing in my ears, but I didn't have the strength to answer him. swearing under his breath he said my name again. I couldn't muster an answer no matter how hard I tried. My body went limp, and he released my arms knowing I could no longer fight.

"Charlie!" His hands cupped my face, soft and smooth against my damp skin. "This should be over by now." I heard the fear in his voice. "No, no, no."

I was dying.

"Charlie."

My head rolled to the side as white clouded my vision before fading to black. Jesse's voice began to get quieter until everything was gone including me.

RESTLESS NIGHTS

I gasped opening my eyes. Light trickled into my vision as I sat choking, trying to regain my breath. Air trickled into my lungs, slowly at first, but then I was able to get a full breath followed by another and another.

"Charlie?" I whipped my head to the side. Jesse stood by the window, eyes tired. "Charlie!"

"What happened?" I struggled to clear the fog from my mind as he approached, taking a seat on the edge of the bed. "Jesse?" The mattress shifted as he leaned in, his weariness evident. He hung his head, palms pressed against his eyes.

"You're alive," he whispered.

"Yes, I'm alive. Why wouldn't I be?" I pulled his hands from his face and looked up to his eyes. They looked red and tired. Had he been crying?

"I thought you were dea—" He cut himself off, a momentary panic flashing in his eyes as he stumbled over his words, leaving a lingering silence.

"Dead?" I voiced the question that lingered unspoken.

"You don't remember?"

I shook my head waiting for him to continue. When he didn't, I urged him on.

"Tell me."

He sat still for a long moment.

"I found you on the bridge." He stopped again. "It was as if you couldn't move." I pushed, pushed my mind to try and remember. Pinching my mind closed I thought. Black blurring the edges of my vision. Black that flourished, turning into dark wings.

"A bird." I looked up to him. "I remember a bird." I shook my head looking away.

"A Valing." My eyes snapped back to his.

"What?"

"Valing." He repeated as he wrung his hands in his lap. "Like a raven, but they're used as messengers." I thought for a moment.

"Messengers for who?" I pressed. His eyes dropped.

"The First Chosen." I nodded, picking the skin around my fingers. The bird I saw following me as I walked, the one that hit the window at the clinic.

"I carried you back here, but the further we got the colder you became." I remembered the warmth of his arms cutting through the icy chill.

"The shadow." He nodded.

"I had to get it out of you."

I remembered the red viscous liquid I had choked down

before the fiery pain took over.

"I had no choice …" words kept spilling from his mouth, but they didn't register as I thought back to the cup he had handed me.

"What was it?" I demanded, my tone sharp and urgent. His voice faltered momentarily, a vacant expression replacing his usual composure. "Don't lie to me." Leaning forward, I pressed myself closer to him, a surge of anger supplanting the panic that gripped me moments before. "Jesse."

"Blood," he confessed, the word slipping out. "Mine."

Nausea churned in my stomach, causing me to stand abruptly, distancing myself from the bed.

"Charlie—" he began, but I raised my hand, halting him.

"I'm not sure I want you to explain," I interrupted, my fingers tightening around the doorknob. As I attempted to leave, his hand seized mine, preventing my escape. Panic swelled within me, and I struggled to break free, but his grip remained firm. I retreated until the door pressed against my back.

"Please," he implored, his palm flat against the door, blocking my exit. Feeling cornered between him and the closed door, I attempted to pull away once more, and this time, he released me. He leaned against the wood preventing me from opening it. "I want to show you something."

Glancing up at the arm pinning the door, I noticed his wrist emerge from the sleeve of his shirt. The cut, which I had assumed was the source of the mysterious liquid, was nothing more than a faint line.

I took a step back, followed by another, until my legs brushed the side of the bed. He dropped his arm, knowing I would no longer try to run. He took a small step forward.

"You drank my blood. It was supposed to react with the shadow and force it out. It didn't want to let you go, but I guess it didn't have a choice when your heart stopped."

Dizziness crept in at his words. I still didn't know the connection between his blood and the shadow I had been seeing.

His eyes searched my face, knowing the question that was turning in my mind.

He pinched his eyes closed.

"I'm sorry," his voice was soft, remorseful. "I didn't anticipate that outcome. If I'd known, I wouldn't have taken that step." He remained standing, eyes still shut tight.

I wanted to assure him that he did what he believed was necessary, that he had rescued me. But the uncertainty about what he actually did lingered in my thoughts.

Studying him intently, my gaze wandered, trailing down to his neck where a small silver pendant hung. No, it wasn't the pendant that glinted, but the skin surrounding it. A faint halo-like shimmer emanated from its hollow, stretching out in a delicate ring around his throat.

I took a step back, stumbling when the bed came harder up against my legs again.

His eyes opened, glowing an eerie blue before taking on their normal shade. My breath hitched, pulling his eyes up to mine.

"Charlie?" He inched closer, his eyes softening. The confined space felt suffocating.

"I said no more secrets," I protested, my tone edged with frustration.

"Charlie, this isn't something I am supposed to tell you."
My stomach squeezed.

"What are you?" I demanded, my hands involuntarily tensing at my sides.

"Charlie—" He tried to placate me, stepping forward.

"What are you?" The words surged out, louder and more intense than I intended.

"I'll explain it to you, but you need to calm down." He took a step forward.

Feeling defeated, I exhaled heavily and sat on the bed's edge. He recognized my surrender and moved closer, kneeling before me, gently clasping my hands, allowing me to observe the faintly glowing circle on his skin. His relief shone through a soft, almost grateful smile.

"It's not something-" He paused, carefully choosing his words. "It's hard to find words …" He shook his head looking down at our hands.

"Please," I urged, meeting his eyes. The glow diminished, his skin nearly back to normal. He nodded in response, softly agreeing to disclose the mysterious truth.

I knew whatever he was about to confess wasn't something I would normally think was in the realm of possibility. However, the words that came out of his mouth were even further from what I expected.

"Everything I've told you has been true," he affirmed, and I nodded slowly, trying to absorb the unexpected turn. "Except for who I work for." An unfamiliar sense of unease tingled in the back of my mind. "What humans refer to as angels."

"Angels?" The glowing halo I had just witnessed came back to the forefront of my mind. Before I knew what I was doing, or before I could stop myself my fingers grazed the skin on his neck. He sucked in a short breath. Just then everything else started to make sense. The lack of food in his kitchen. The way his rental didn't look lived in.

"That picture?" He looked to me, knowing what I was asking. The picture I had found in his wallet, the one he had said was of his ancestor.

"It was me." His confession settled heavily between us, and I looked away, absorbing the weight of his admission. "Charlie?" His voice held concern, and I nodded, confirming my understanding.

This revelation shook the very foundation of what I thought I knew about him, weaving an intricate web of questions and uncertainties in my mind. Yet, amid the complexity, a sense of connection remained, grounding us in this unexpected moment of shared truth.

"I think … I believe you." I kept my gaze fixed on the far wall, absorbing the weight of his confession. His revelation felt like connecting dots that had been scattered across my mind. "The First Chosen …" I shifted my gaze back to meet his, seeking some semblance of clarity. "If they succeed …"

"It won't be good."

A tight knot formed in my chest.

"Is it okay if I have a shower?" I needed time to think. Time to let the water clean away all I had just gone through.

"Of course." He let go of my hand and stood, leaving the room. He returned a moment later with a clean towel. "If you leave your clothes outside the door, I'll wash them for you."

His considerate gesture brought a small but genuine smile to my lips. I nodded in gratitude before rising from the bed and making my way into the hallway, taking a left turn into the bathroom.

Setting the towel on the counter, I twisted the shower knob, the rush of hot water instantly filling the small space with soothing steam.

Dropping my clothes in a haphazard pile outside the bathroom door, I stepped into the torrent, the water searing but comforting against my skin. Each droplet felt like it was washing away not only the grime but also the worries, fears, and newfound truths that had surfaced. It was a temporary solace amid the storm raging both outside and within.

I shook my head vigorously, sending water droplets careening in all directions, creating a symphony of splashes against the shower walls. A gentle knock on the door interrupted the tranquility of the cascading water.

"Charlie?"

"I'm almost done I just …" I just needed a few more minutes.

"No, take your time." I heard him cough lightly. "Your clothes won't be ready for a while so I picked out something you can wear until they are." I braced my hand against the acrylic wall.

"Thank you." There was a pause.

"Is everything okay?" His concern was unmistakable, but I wasn't ready to articulate the chaos swirling within.

"Yes." The word hung in the air, marking the silence that stretched for several more minutes. I turned off the water, enveloping myself in the towel before opening the door quietly. The clothes he'd left for me—a long-sleeved thermal and a pair of oversized sweatpants—felt fresh and comforting against my skin as I pulled them on.

As I stood, I studied myself in the small mirror. All of it was me, but I wasn't quite sure who that was anymore.

Staring at my reflection, I saw myself, yet the image felt distant, fragmented by the recent revelations. A flicker of movement caught my eye—a dark shadow slinking into the corner—a familiar ominous presence.

Flinging the door open I ran into the hallway, colliding with Jesse.

"Are you okay?" he asked, as I grabbed onto his arms. "Charlie?"

"It's here." My words came out strained.

"What?" He took me by the shoulders and looked down at me.

"The shadow."

Jesse muttered a curse under his breath, his grip tightening around me protectively.

"It's okay; it shouldn't be able to do anything with my blood still in your system." His attempt to reassure me brought little comfort as tears streamed down my cheeks. Jesse gently lifted my face, his touch tender as he wiped away my tears with his palms. His eyes held a tenderness that pierced through the fear and sadness.

"I don't want to die." The words escaped me in a sob, an admission I hadn't allowed myself to voice until now. Fear of mortality seized me, and for the first time, I truly felt the weight of it.

"Charlie, you're not going to die. I'm not going to let it hurt you." My body shook.

"I'm scared." I glanced up at him, my eyes reflecting a vulnerability I hadn't intended to reveal. Jesse seemed momentarily taken aback by the admission, a rare moment of openness between us.

"It will be okay." His reassurance fell short, but his

attempt to console me was evident in his tone.

"How do you know?" The silence that followed showed that he didn't.

This stranger who I met not too long ago had now become so important. Important in keeping me sane.

I looked up to him and put my arms around his neck. His body was so sturdy, so strong. I felt as though if I was with him nothing could go wrong, though I knew that was not the case.

"We'll figure it out."

I sat on the edge of Jesse's bed, the sleeves of his thermal extending far past my wrists, covering all signs of my past.

Jesse stood in the doorway as I nervously wrung my hands in my lap. His eyes stayed focused on the wall behind me. I could almost see the thoughts rampaging through his mind.

The silence that filled the room was almost deafening, so much so that I finally had to break it.

"What are you thinking?"

His eyes snapped to mine, an unearthly shade of blue. The silence continued for another moment.

"I don't know what the shadow has to do with the rite." He shook his head. "But the only way to ensure that it can't harm you is to keep my blood in your system."

Bile rose in my throat at the thought, but it was only a few days until the eclipse.

"Why can't we just leave Hayzun?"

His eyes softened as he took a step forward.

"We could."

Hope filled my senses before it dropped away.

"But they'd still find you. The First Chosen, they have people everywhere." His body tensed. "And this is our chance to take out their leader."

Fear filled my throat, restricting my breathing.

"This is the closest we have been able to get."

A sense of emptiness filled my stomach, causing my head to feel light.

Jesse settled into a chair beside me, his eyes reflecting a mixture of concern and determination. He attempted a reassuring smile but worry clouded his expression.

"Why don't you try to get some sleep?"

I nodded, laying down at the head of the bed, pulling the covers up and over my body.

I turned to face him. Worry floated around his irises, but still he forced a smile.

I closed my eyes, settling beneath the covers as the room landed in darkness.

I'm not sure how much time passed before the piercing ice of fear filled my bones. I shot to a sitting position, air wheezing from my lungs.

The light blinked on a moment later, Jesse's face coming into view.

"What's wrong?"

I grasped at my chest; the air was too thin, too void of oxygen to properly fill my lungs.

"Charlie?" His hands found my shoulders as my dream

resurfaced. Damp darkness filled my senses, along with the soft cries of someone in pain, of someone being held against their will.

A hot wet tear fell, rolling against my flushed skin. His grip tightened.

"She's still alive." I blinked heavily, sucking in another breath.

"Who?" Jesse's eyes searched mine, trying to make sense of my cryptic statement.

"Piper, the one they haven't found yet." Recognition flickered in Jesse's eyes, understanding settling between us. The third victim disappeared without a trace. My mind raced, but I couldn't pinpoint her whereabouts.

"Do you know where?" His urgency was evident, but I could only shake my head. Suddenly, a vivid image flashed before my eyes—reflections glinted off a blade as it pierced flesh, filleting it from her skull. The bloody patch of missing scalp caused my stomach to turn as a shallow cry escaped my lips and a chill filled my body.

His hands moved from my shoulders, cupping my face gently.

"Just breathe."

I nodded, grasping Jesse's hand, seeking comfort in the warmth that flowed through my fingers. I concentrated on each breath, focusing until the dizziness faded, leaving only the lingering chill.

"You're cold," Jesse observed, eyeing the dresser. "Let me get you more blankets."

I held onto his hand tighter, urging his attention back to me.

"Charlie?"

"Yes?"

His gaze dropped, withdrawing his hands from my face before he stood, making his way to the dresser. He retrieved a blanket from the top drawer.

"This should keep you warm." A small, sad smile spread over his lips as he unfolded the blanket and sat back down beside me on the bed. He draped the blanket around my shoulders, pulling it together at the front.

Pausing, he stared at his hands on the blanket.

"Jess?" I inquired softly, watching him. "Is everything okay?" His nod was almost imperceptible. "Please, don't lie to me." I caught his arm, feeling a slight tremor beneath my touch. "Please."

His attempt to respond faltered.

In a swift motion, he shifted, balancing on one knee while using his other leg for support. Our eyes met briefly before he leaned in, his lips touching mine.

Shock spread through my body.

His one hand moved from the blanket, reaching up to touch the side of my face.

When I didn't pull away, he rose higher, moving closer. A small sigh escaped him.

My mind flickered from the here and now, to the first and only time I left Hayzun. To the men I encountered. The sensation of his touch triggered a surge of memories, intertwining with fear in my mind.

I recoiled; the fear that seized me apparent in Jesse's widening eyes.

"Hey," he rushed to assure me. "I'm not going to hurt you." His hand hovered in the air, hesitant. I could almost feel the warmth radiating from his palm, a stark contrast to the cold sweat that gathered on my skin. I squeezed my eyes shut, battling to shake off the echoes of the past.

"I know," my voice wavered slightly as I fought to steady my trembling hands, anchoring myself in the present. "I'm sorry." I felt his gentle touch on my arm.

"Don't apologize." His thumb gently grazed my wrist, and I knew he knew the origin of my fear. "I can't even imagine what you went through." I gave a halfhearted laugh.

"I don't even want to think about it." I met his gaze, finding him fixed on me as if I might vanish if he blinked. The room felt small, suffocating almost, as if holding its breath along with us. My heart thudded in my chest, reverberating through my entire being.

"I think I just need some sleep."

"Of course." He stood, making his way to the chair, but I grabbed his arm, stopping him. He turned back to face me. I slid over in the bed, giving him room to lie beside me.

When he realized what I wanted, a smile filled his eyes as he turned back to me. The mattress dipped as he settled into the vacated spot, the warmth from his presence spreading comfort.

"Thank you."

"Anything for you, Charlie."

14

CAUTIOUS ALLIANCES

Someone cleared their throat behind me as my fingers reached for the cool doorknob leading out of the front door. The subtle sound sent a jolt through my body, freezing me in place. Slowly, I turned, finding Jesse leaning against the wall near the hallway, his expression marked with concern.

"Where are you going?"

I raised an eyebrow at his question.

"Work."

"Are you sure that's safe?" His eyes focused on the ground by my feet. I ignored his question.

"And I need to get some food, considering you don't have anything here." I tried to lighten the mood, but his eyes met mine, filled with a mixture of guilt and regret.

"I'm sorry, I didn't think." His apology felt sincere, yet

the weight of our situation lingered.

"It's fine." I shook my head reaching for the doorknob once again. He took a couple of long strides forward.

"Wait."

"I'm going to be late."

"Just please, wait." A small amount of panic in his tone caused me to stop. Or maybe it was fear or anxiety, I couldn't quite place it.

With a hesitant motion, he retrieved something from his back pocket, holding it tightly in his closed hand. He extended his palm toward me. I eyed it cautiously, unsure of what lay concealed within his grasp.

"What is it?" I questioned, but instead of a verbal response, he reached for my hand with his free one. Turning my palm upward, he released the object, allowing it to rest against my skin. A small dark vial with a black cap lay balanced in my hand. I scrutinized it, feeling the weight and smoothness against my fingers.

The vial held a darkness that was more than just the absence of light; it was the red, thick liquid sealed within that struck me. I rotated it between my thumb and forefinger, the contents swishing gently inside.

"No, absolutely not." The words fell from my mouth as I held the vial back out to him.

"Charlie—"

"No—" My protest was cut short as Jesse closed the gap between us in swift strides. He seized my wrist, his grip insistent, forcing my fingers to close back around the vial with his other hand. The firmness of his hold conveyed a hint of irritation, his eyes hardening with an intensity I hadn't seen before.

"If this is what will keep you safe," his words were clipped, laced with an underlying anger that resonated through his tone. I could sense his frustration, though I knew it wasn't directed at me but at the circumstances. "Then so be it." A swirl of intensity danced within his blue eyes.

He stepped back abruptly, releasing my hand. His expression softened when he noticed the fear etched on my face. His frustration seemed to falter, replaced by a sense of regret and remorse.

Eyes softening, he ran a hand through his hair, cursing under his breath.

"I'm sorry." He shook his head cursing again. I stood silently not wanting to tell him it was okay because it really wasn't. "I just—" His words trailed off as my fingers instinctively twisted the cap from the vial.

Before he could finish his sentence, I lifted the vial to my lips, pouring the liquid into my mouth. I tried to block the taste, contorting my tongue in an attempt to prevent the metallic tang from overwhelming my senses. Yet, the flavor persisted, making me gag as I struggled to suppress the thought of what I was ingesting.

Jesse's eyes lingered on the empty vial in my hand, his expression a mix of resignation and gratitude. He exhaled a heavy sigh, his shoulders slumping slightly.

"Thank you." Despite the gratitude in his tone, a flicker of irritation arose within me. I nodded curtly, sealing the vial before striding over to the table and dropping it down with a definitive clink. I wiped the back of my hand over my mouth, trying to rid myself of the lingering taste.

"I have to get to work," I announced, breaking the tense silence.

"At least let me drive you," he offered, his voice carrying a trace of concern. I eyed him warily.

"I didn't know you had a car." He offered a soft, reassuring smile. It momentarily eased the tension, prompting a small nod from me.

"It's parked across the road." Jesse moved past me, opening the door to let the cool fall air into the room. I inhaled deeply, the musky scent of autumn wrapping around me, offering a brief reprieve.

I followed Jesse out of the rental, waiting as he locked the door behind us. He unlocked a sleek black car, courteously pulling open the passenger door for me. Once in, he closed the door before rounding the car and claiming the driver's seat.

I watched as he put the car into drive and pulled away from the curb, expertly maneuvering around the corners.

His eyes moved from the road to me.

"Is everything okay?"

I nodded softly, watching as his hands turned the wheel.

"I haven't been able to get my license," I confessed, meeting his gaze. "Can't afford a car either, so it never felt necessary." I shrugged, turning my attention to the passing scenery outside the window.

The remainder of the short drive passed in silence, the only sound being the faint hum of the car engine. Jesse maneuvered the vehicle expertly, pulling up in front of the clinic and shifting into park.

"Thank you," I murmured, reaching for the door handle and giving it a tug until it clicked open.

"Charlie?" His voice stopped me as I moved to step out. I turned to face him. "Please be careful and call me if you need anything. My number should be on the paperwork." I offered him a small smile, acknowledging his concern, before finally exiting the car and shutting the door.

The gentle chiming of the bell greeted me as I stepped into the clinic, immediately accompanied by the sterile scent of antiseptic that filled the air.

The small office lay vacant, and I settled into the chair behind the desk, focusing on the tasks at hand.

Time seemed to blur as I delved into the paperwork. The quiet was finally disrupted by the creak of the office door, signaling Miles' entrance.

"Will you go with Mason please and take kennels B, C, and F to the shelter? We have some clients coming in and need to have some empty spaces."

I nodded, standing from my seat.

It wasn't uncommon for owners to abandon their pets here, unable to cover the bills, or for cases like the dog Jesse found, housed in kennel B. Eventually, the unfortunate choice was made to transfer them to the shelter across town, hoping for a chance at adoption.

Mason had already loaded the dogs from kennels C and F into the van, securing them snugly in the built-in crates. All that remained was kennel B, housing a dog with dark fur that stood slightly on end as I approached.

"It's okay," I murmured, aiming for a soothing tone as I unlatched the kennel door. The dog observed me with intense eyes as I secured a collar and leash around his neck.

Extending my hand, I offered it to him. His nose twitched, sniffing the fabric of my shirt. Recognition dawned in his brown eyes, instantly softening his fear. It wasn't me he was sensing; it was Jesse, his scent lingering on my clothes.

Mason entered from the side door where the van was parked outside.

"Want me to lift him?"

"Yes, please." I smiled as Mason rolled up his sleeves, revealing elaborate tattoos adorning both his forearms. He gently lifted the large dog, setting him down on the ground.

The dog shook himself off before obediently following me to the van, where I secured him in one of the built-in kennels and closed the trunk with a soft click.

"Ready to go?" Mason questioned, stepping out of the clinic through the side door and closing it behind him.

"I think so." I nodded, making my way around the van and sliding into the passenger's seat. Mason settled into the driver's seat, waiting until I was securely buckled in before putting the van into gear and departing from the clinic.

"So, what's new?" Mason glanced over at me, a friendly grin lighting up his face. He tapped his fingers lightly on the steering wheel, awaiting my response.

"Not much," I started, trying to stifle a smile.

"Not much?" He wrinkled his nose in mock disappointment. "That's all I get, not much?" His expression made me chuckle, and I shook my head at his playful inquiry.

"I don't know what to tell you." I shrugged, glancing out of the window at passing buildings. "I can make something up."

He snorted, flipping the radio on low.

His tall, lean body looked somewhat silly driving a minivan. Dark, raven-colored hair swept in different directions, shorter at the sides but tousled atop his head. A hint of stubble outlined his jaw, adding to his rugged charm. Although not as broad as Jesse, his features were undeniably attractive.

Mason had always been kind to me in his months at the clinic.

My stomach let out a low growl, hunger suddenly taking over. I had forgotten to stop for food, as Jesse had driven me to work. Mason's eyebrows pitched upward as he looked over at me, my cheeks flushed pink.

"Sorry." He chuckled softly, turning the van around another corner. The shelter was all the way on the east side of town.

"How about I buy you lunch after we drop the dogs off?"

I looked over at him.

"It's okay, I can buy my own lunch." In truth, I was financially strained, and he knew it. Mason had overheard one of my phone conversations with a debt collector at work, prompting me to explain my and my family situation.

"It was my idea. I'll buy." His insistence was gentle, and I nodded gratefully.

"Thank you." He nodded, giving a smile.

Minutes later, the van pulled into the shelter's parking lot and settled near the back door. Mason expertly aligned the van, ensuring the back faced the shelter entrance, a precaution after a previous runaway dog incident.

Undoing our seatbelts, we stepped out, and I released the van's trunk, revealing the dogs in their kennels. Soon after, a young blonde employee answered our knock on the door, her cheeks flushed as Mason explained our purpose.

"We called earlier about bringing three dogs from the clinic," he stated, the girl's reaction prompting a stifled chuckle from me.

"Right this way." The shelter employee led Mason and

me inside, each with a dog, her hurried steps echoing through the hallway. Mason engaged in a conversation with her, leaving me to return to the van alone. I unlocked the kennel, allowing the dog inside to step out. His hesitant gaze sought reassurance from me.

My heart sank for the dog. The shelter was no place for any animal, especially one as gentle-looking as him. How long would he wait for someone to adopt him?

"It's okay, come on." I offered a comforting pat on his head, guiding him toward the entrance. He whimpered softly before following me, his steps hesitant and unsure. As I rejoined Mason, the hallway filled with other voices. I glanced at him, raising an eyebrow in question.

"The mayor is here speaking to Piper's mother.," Mason explained, a hint of concern in his voice. "She works here."

"I didn't know that," I admitted, my curiosity piqued.

"Neither did I, until now," Mason confirmed.

"He's strange," the blonde employee remarked, catching my attention.

"How so?" My curiosity got the better of me. She leaned against one of the kennels, tapping her acrylic nails while chewing gum noisily.

"He's always got this intense look," she began, her voice lowered. "And he's too fixated on finding the missing girl. Sometimes it feels like he's trying to control the situation rather than help." Her expression reflected a mix of uncertainty and wariness.

I glanced toward the office where the conversation seemed to be taking place, a feeling of unease settling within me.

Her overdrawn lips pursed. Dismissing her claim because

most men over thirty probably gave her 'weird vibes' I turned back to the dog.

I refocused on the dog, unlatching the kennel door and allowing him to walk inside. Kneeling down, I gave him a comforting pat.

"Be good, okay?" His cold nose nudged against my hand, and for some inexplicable reason, a pang of attachment hit me. I wished I could keep him, but the thought faded as I latched the door and turned to Mason.

I tried to shake off the wistful feeling, reminding myself of the reality of my situation. I couldn't afford to care for another living being.

As the mayor concluded his conversation, he turned and swiftly walked toward us, his expression a mix of formality and something harder to decipher.

"Good day," he greeted us with a controlled smile before reaching out his hand. His handshake was firm, almost too firm, as if trying to assert dominance.

"I'm Charlotte," I introduced myself, gesturing to Mason. "And this is Mason. We work nearby at the clinic. We've just brought some dogs over."

The mayor's eyes lingered a moment longer on us, an air of suspicion subtly clouding his otherwise composed demeanor. "Indeed. Your help is appreciated," he remarked, his tone polite but guarded.

"We're always willing to support the community," I replied cautiously, sharing a glance with Mason, who seemed equally perplexed by the mayor's unexpected appearance.

Mayor Montgomery nodded, acknowledging our words, but his attention seemed divided, as if there was something he was eager to tend to. His gaze flitted to the distressed mother, and a flicker of concern briefly crossed his face before he regained his composure.

"Please, excuse me," he said briskly, as if reluctant to linger. "I must attend to some urgent matters." With a nod, he pivoted, striding purposefully, leaving us standing there. Mason and I exchanged glances laden with unspoken questions.

The shelter buzzed with quiet activity as staff went about their tasks, the mayor's presence having caused a ripple of curiosity among the employees. I turned to Mason, noting the furrow in his brow, a reflection of my own confusion.

"Did that seem odd to you?" I murmured, keeping my voice low.

Mason nodded slowly, his eyes darting back to where the mayor conversed with the mother, his demeanor guarded, as if sensing something was amiss.

"Yeah, it did." Mason replied, his tone reflecting his uncertainty.

The mayor bid everyone a swift farewell, turning away to exit the shelter. His departure left us with an unsettling feeling, a sense of unease lingering in the air.

Mason and I exchanged looks.

"I'll meet you in the van," Mason replied. I nodded and exited the shelter, relishing the cool breeze on my face.

Once back at the van, I closed the trunk and settled into the passenger seat, waiting for Mason. The quiet hum of the engine filled the air until he joined me a few moments later.

"Still hungry?" His question was met with a grateful nod from me. Hayzun's limited dining options didn't leave much room for preference. A simple burger and fries later, we returned to the clinic, where I resumed my place behind the desk while Mason took care of the now empty kennels, cleaning them meticulously.

The air was cool against my face as I walked, the temperature dropped rapidly with the fading light. The evening was eerily quiet, the usual bustle of the neighborhood replaced by an unsettling stillness. My steps echoed in the silence, the sound unnaturally loud in the dimming twilight.

Halfway to Jesse's rental, a shiver ran down my spine, making the hairs on the back of my neck stand on end. A low, ominous rumble of slowing tires grated on my ears, triggering an instinctive dread in my chest. It was a sound etched into my memory; one I couldn't forget.

The large van coasted to a stop beside me, the window rolling down with a mechanical whir. My heart pounded in my ears, drowning out any other sound.

"Get in." The voice was gruff, commanding, and it sent a surge of fear coursing through me. I was paralyzed, unable to move.

When I didn't comply, the driver's side door creaked open, and a figure emerged, circling around the front of the van. Panic seized me, and I squeezed my eyes shut, hoping against hope that it was all a terrible dream. Strong hands suddenly gripped my shoulders, pulling me back to a blurred reality. "Charlie, look at me."

Struggling to steady my breathing, I summoned the courage to open my eyes, finding myself face-to-face with Jesse. An array of emotions flooded me, relief mingled with a rush of overwhelming fear, causing my legs to wobble beneath me. His arms enveloped me, providing a much-needed anchor in the midst of my turmoil.

"What's wrong?" His voice was laced with concern, his grip firm yet gentle as he steadied me.

"I saw…" I looked to the van, shocked to see it wasn't there. Instead, I saw a small black car. "That sound." I pinched my eyes shut again.

"What sound?"

He cupped my face in his hands, using his thumbs to gently wipe the tears from my cheeks.

"The slowing tires." I shuddered, the memory searing through me like a bolt of lightning. It triggered something deep, a wound still raw. My lower lip quivered.

"Charlie, I'm sorry." Jesse's voice held a mix of concern and frustration, his jaw clenched in empathy.

"I just hate how it makes me feel…" I opened my eyes to find Jesse's expression tight with empathy. "Powerless and weak."

"No." Jesse's response was firm, a muscle flickering along his jaw. "You're far from weak."

"I'm crying on the sidewalk in the middle of town." A soft chuckle escaped me, mingling with tears that Jesse tenderly wiped away once more.

"What you went through." He moved closer. "No one should have to go through that."

I nodded, feeling silly.

"Let's go home."

Another pulse of fear filled me.

"Your home?"

He smiled, giving a nod, erasing the latest wave of panic. "Thank you."

He looked at me.

"For what?"

"For not making me feel like it was my fault."

Jesse's gentle touch as he tucked a stray hair behind my ear made me feel strangely vulnerable and comforted all at once.

"Why would it be your fault?" Jesse's eyebrows furrowed in genuine confusion.

"My mom always told me it was my fault." As Jesse's fingers lingered behind my ear, I couldn't help but feel a rush of warmth amid the whirlwind of emotions.

"It's not your fault." His voice turned sharp, not directed at me but at the injustice of the situation. I nodded, turning toward the car. Jesse caught my hand, halting my movement. "Do you understand?" His grip was gentle yet firm, a plea for me to believe his words. I nodded again, feeling the weight of his sincerity.

He enveloped me in a hug, his sturdy arms offering a shield against the guilt that had become all too familiar. His warmth wrapped around me, dispelling the shame I carried within.

After a brief moment, he released me, ensuring I was settled in the car before closing the door. He quickly moved to the driver's seat, and we soon arrived in front of his rental. Stepping out into the crisp autumn air, I followed Jesse up the steps and into the house as he swung the door open.

Watching as he dropped his car keys on the table, I eyed two large paper bags on the counter. Out of place in the normally bare house, I couldn't help myself but ask.

"What is that?"

A smile kicked up the corners of his mouth.

"What?"

He reached into the paper bag closest to him, pulling out an array of food. His grin broadened as he sat it on the kitchen table and went back for another handful.

"I figured if you're going to be staying here, we should have food in the kitchen."

"That's usually where people keep their food."

He snorted, rolling his eyes.

"You know what I mean." He sat a carton of eggs and a pack of bacon on the table. "I thought we could make dinner and then go to your place and get some of your clothes."

I nodded, my heart pinched with the feeling of how thoughtful he was being.

"Do you have a pan?" I gestured to the eggs to which he replied by reaching into the second paper bag pulling out a small stainless-steel pan.

"I do now." A wry grin took over. "Take a seat."

I pulled a chair from the table and sat, watching as he set to work.

I watched, confusion taking over as he expertly cooked the bacon before cracking eggs into the pan.

"If you don't eat, how do you know how to cook so well?" He turned, flipper in hand, still smiling.

"I can eat, I just don't have to." He pulled paper plates from one of the bags. "I do love some bacon."

"I thought angels would be vegan if anything."

He snorted a laugh.

"Why?"

"I don't know, something about not eating gods' creations."

He rolled his eyes, turning back to the pan, offloading

the eggs.

"Just eat." He placed a paper plate in front of me, a smile still dancing on his lips. He placed a second plate in front of himself.

"Do you have—" He reached into the bag yet again and pulled out a bottle of ketchup. I grinned widely.

"Thanks." He picked up a piece of bacon, popping it into his mouth.

Stale air hit my senses as I opened the front door and stepped into the dark foyer of what should have felt like home, but it didn't. I had lived here my whole life, yet I felt more at home in Jesse's small rental than I did here.

Instinctively I reached up and flicked the light switch, shaking my head with a sigh when nothing happened.

Jesse pushed the door closed with a click behind us.

"I'll wait in the kitchen for you."

I nodded, making my way in and to the left where I hurried up the stairs and into my room.

I hastily grabbed a bag from the closet and hurriedly stuffed in what I thought would suffice for about a week. The urgency to leave this place grew with each item I shoved into the bag.

Back at the top of the stairs, I glanced toward the kitchen, only a partial view visible from my vantage point. The uneasy feeling I'd been trying to ignore crawled beneath my skin, the hairs on the back of my neck standing on end.

Starting down the stairs, I felt a cool chill prick the hairs on the back of my neck.

Shaking it off, I took a couple more steps, the chill intensifying.

"Jess?" My nerves caused a pit to form in my stomach. I heard his footsteps getting closer, but before he came into view, the ground slipped out from under me, pitching me forward.

I let go of my bag, putting my hands out in front of me to soften the blow. The palms of my hands skidded against the wooden steps before giving way, letting my shoulder hit the nosing of the bottom step.

I came to a stop when I hit the ground and had nowhere else to fall, my bag of clothes landing with a thud beside my head.

"Charlie?" The warmth of Jesse's hands enveloped my shoulders. "Are you okay? What happened?"

Struggling, I pushed my palm against the floor, attempting to sit up.

"I think I was pushed." As I rose, a sharp ache throbbed in my wrist, making me wince.

"By what?" Jesse's expression twisted with confusion as he knelt beside me.

"What do you think would push me?" I spat bitterly, running my hand over the shoulder that collided with the step.

"The shadow." Jesse closed his eyes, his voice heavy with unease.

"Bingo." My fingers traced over the blossoming pain.

"Can you stand?"

"I think so."

Jesse stood, extending a hand in my direction. I took it, pulling myself to my feet, pain blooming in many spots around my joints and muscles.

He picked up my bag, slinging it over his shoulder. I took hesitant steps, favoring my left leg, which had borne the brunt of the fall more than the right.

"Can you make it to the car?" Jesse asked, I nodded, limping toward the front door. He trailed closely behind, ensuring everything was securely locked before joining me in the car.

I slumped against the seat, feeling a mixture of pain and confusion while Jesse stowed my bag in the backseat. The engine hummed to life as he reversed out of the driveway, the events in the house leaving me unsettled.

INVISIBLE THREADS

As I stared at the angry welts marring my skin, a mixture of frustration and apprehension knotted in my chest. The knock on the door startled me, prompting me to hastily tug the fabric of my shirt over the forming bruises along my shoulder blade.

The door clicked open, exposing Jesse with a solemn look imprinted on his handsome face. His eyes flitted to my attempt at hiding the marks, and a subtle tension crept into the room.

"Let me see," he urged gently, his tone carrying an unmistakable edge of worry. I shook my head in reflexive denial, my hand instinctively falling back to my side.

"I'm fine," I insisted, trying to mask the discomfort that rippled through me.

"Charlie," Jesse's voice was firm, his jaw tightening as he stepped closer, his presence commanding the room. He reached into a drawer, extracting a white tub with a scent that carried hints of mint. "Let me see."

Knowing he would not let up, I turned my back to him, feeling his hands grasp the fabric. He lifted it, pulling it up to expose my back.

A curse rang through my ears as I watched as his eyes inspected my skin. He stood silent for a moment.

"Can you take this off?" His request was tentative, his fingers lightly tugging at my shirt. "I'd like to put some of this on it." He gestured toward the tub of cream, his intent clear. But a surge of fear welled up within me, a resurfacing of memories I wished to bury.

"Do I have to?" I pleaded with a quiver in my voice, feeling the weight of panic clawing at me. His touch was gentle as he turned me to face him, his eyes seeking to reassure me.

"You can trust me." His words held a warmth that softened his expression, momentarily easing my apprehension.

"You came here to kill me, remember?" The words slipped out before I could hold them back, the sting of fear causing my mind to blur with mistrust. His face fell, and my heart sank with the weight of my own words. "I'm sorry."

"No, you're right." He pulled on the hem of his shirt, the muscles in his arm tightening. Pushing every worry I had back inside, I turned and pulled my shirt up and over my head, keeping my chest covered.

A sharp twinge coursed down my left arm, prompting a stifled sound from Jesse. I glanced over to see that the bruises had deepened, the vibrant purple now etched darker against my skin. Bruises typically took days to develop, but the purple masses had taken in over in less than a couple of hours.

"I'll be as careful as I can."

I nodded as he reached into the tub and began to gently rub the minty cream onto my skin. Pain surged under his fingertips.

"I have never seen bruises get this bad this fast," he murmured softly, his voice laced with concern. I stood silently, uncertain of what to say, allowing him to work the cream into my battered skin. After a few minutes, he finished and rinsed his hands under the tap, sealing the tub shut. "I wonder if it's my blood reacting with your system?" I turned to look at him. "Your Ember blood probably doesn't appreciate it much." He shook his head, stepping away. We both knew it was his blood keeping me safe, but was it also destroying me from the inside out?

"Thank you." He nodded, exiting the room, giving me space to gently pull my shirt back over my head.

Grabbing the cool metal of the doorknob, I paused as voices filled the small rental. One of them was Jesse's, but the other I couldn't identify. Wait. I pulled the door from its resting place and listened. I knew that voice.

They echoed from somewhere near the front of the house, either the kitchen or the living room. The voice, it was the same one I had heard the day I found the picture in Jesse's wallet.

Torn between revealing my presence and retreating to the solitude of the bedroom, I hesitated, my hands clenched and unclenched at my sides. Against my better judgment, curiosity spurred me on, drawing me silently down the hallway.

I soon pinpointed the voices to the living room on my right. The voices stopped as I exited the hall. Jesse sat on the small couch, elbows resting on his knees. The stranger that belonged to the voice stood in front of the large picture window; eyes trained on me. Jesse's jaw tightened.

"Charlie, this is Reece." Reece eyed me for a second.

"Jeremiah this is not what we agreed upon." Anger flared in his features, and I instantly wished I had gone to the bedroom instead. Jesse shook his head, hanging it between his shoulders.

"She is not the problem." Jesse's eyes flashed toward me, a mix of emotions swirling within them, leaving me wondering what exactly was transpiring between the two men.

"Maybe not the whole problem, but she is definitely a part of it," Reece asserted, his voice thick with an accent that hinted at an English origin. With broad shoulders, clocking in at well over six feet, black cropped hair and the same fine tattoo-like lines along his forearms, his stature was just as threatening as his voice.

"I have it under control." As tension escalated, Jesse moved protectively between Reece and me, his stance a barrier against the palpable hostility. I felt both vulnerable and utterly bewildered, unsure of my place in this confrontation.

"I know you have a big heart, but I've never known it to get in the way of an assignment." I stood in silence. An assignment, that's all I was. "Has he told you everything?" Reece's eyes focused on me.

"Yes." The voice that came out of me sounded too small,

too weak to be mine.

"Reece don't." It was Jesse speaking now, I looked to Jesse.

"What?" He shook his head in my direction, "what?" I asked again.

"Should I tell her, or do you want to?"

"Reece," Jesse's tone was laced with a ferocity that was unexpected, drawing my gaze to him for some explanation.

"Someone please just tell me." I felt my bottom lip tremble as Jesse turned to me taking a deep breath.

"You're adopted, Charlie," he finally revealed. The revelation hit me like a physical blow, my breath catching in my throat as the ground seemed to slip from beneath my feet.

After figuring out my involvement with everything, I had assumed my parents had hidden their past from me, but not my own. I guess that did explain my mother's hatred for me.

"And your birth father is behind all of this." The words exited Reece's mouth filling the air around me. I looked to Jesse as a muscle jumped along his jaw. The weight of the revelations pressed down on me, the shock and confusion mixing with a newfound sense of danger. It was as if a door to a hidden world had been flung open, revealing a reality that I never knew existed.

"Is that true?" I turned to Jesse, seeking confirmation or perhaps some form of denial, but his silence was telling. His jaw clenched, an undeniable acknowledgment of the truth in Reece's words. I directed my gaze back to Reece, my voice shaky with disbelief. "Who is he? My real dad, who is he?"

I cleared my throat to try and push down the tightness I felt.

"We don't know for sure, except that he is a part of The

First Chosen," Jesse's voice dropped.

"He's helping with the upheaval," Reece spoke with disgust.

"Why?"

"Why else?" Reece asked, "To gain power." I guess in the end it did always come down to power. "Disias promised his followers chaos and to show the Sol bloodline that they are not to be dismissed. But before he could make good on his promise Nykarus had him imprisoned. He needed to remain alive to keep the balance, but he was too dangerous to roam free," he explained. "And you're the key to setting him free," Reece added, his tone turning grave. The weight of his statement hung in the air like a foreboding storm cloud. "As long as you are alive, someone will try to use you."

The realization sent a chill down my spine, the hairs on my arms stood on end as fear tightened its grip. The mere thought of being a pawn in a game of such magnitude was paralyzing.

Fear perked the hairs along my arms.

"I have a plan." Jesse's words came out forced, but Reece didn't seem convinced.

"Who is my mother?" I needed to grasp at something tangible amid the unfathomable chaos. Jesse's gaze turned contemplative, attempting to unravel the fragmented knowledge.

"All we know as of now is she was of the Sol bloodline." His words barely scratched the surface of my yearning for identity and understanding. I couldn't help but feel a pang of emptiness, realizing how little I knew about my own origins.

"In order for you to be useful," Jesse paused, his expression clouded with the weight of a secret he hesitated to voice. "You had to be born of both bloodlines, something that is forbidden."

The prohibition, the forbidden union between the Sol and Ember bloodlines, whispered of a profound and ancient pact. I felt the weight of their history upon me, like an invisible shroud of inevitability.

"A void soul is very powerful, capable of many things." Jesse's eyes held an intensity that mirrored the gravity of his words. "Thousands of years ago, Nykarus and the other gods signed a treaty prohibiting procreation between the two bloodlines. Sol: good and Ember: evil, as a void soul could become powerful enough to overthrow even the first God."

The revelation was overwhelming, a tapestry of myths and laws interwoven with my very being. My breath hitched as I tried to absorb the sheer magnitude of what I was hearing.

"When Nykarus entrapped Disias, he made it so only the blood of such an individual could release him." The implications echoed in the hollows of my mind. "The blood of something that shouldn't exist."

The phrase lingered in the room, resonating within me, its weight unbearable. A sensation of being an anomaly, a contradiction to the laws of existence, gnawed at my sense of self.

I had always felt displaced, but now it was as if my entire existence was an affront to ancient laws, a discordant note in the symphony of life. The revelation that I was the embodiment of a forbidden existence crushed against the fragile walls of my understanding, leaving behind a hollow sense of disquiet.

Reece's eyes darkened with a stern resolve, his demeanor unyielding. "We can't keep her hidden forever. It's too risky.

We need to move forward."

Jesse's jaw clenched in a tense silence, a conflict evident in his eyes. "Reece, there has to be another way. We can't just throw her into this."

"It's not a choice, Jesse," Reece's tone remained resolute. "She's the key, and we can't afford to let the wrong hands find her."

I had had enough of this conversation.

Turning on my heels, I headed back down the hallway, ignoring Jesse's voice calling after me.

Closing myself in the bedroom, I tried my best to ignore the now muffled angry voices as my mind flitted through the brief conversation I had just had. With each breath, I tried to shake off the labels thrown upon me like chains, the weight of their expectations pressing heavy upon my chest. An assignment. A pawn in a game I never signed up to play. But the more I dwelled on their words, the more they seemed to seep into my consciousness.

An assignment, something that shouldn't exist, a burden; that is what I was …no, that is what they wanted me to think, my mother, Reece, the men in the truck. And they had all put in a good effort, believe me, but I was done being scared.

Tears streaked down my cheeks, carrying with them a cocktail of frustration, fear, and an underlying sense of defiance. I pulled down the silky sheets and climbed in, tucking myself between a blanket of obliviousness and silence. I wasn't just going to be a bystander in my own life. With each wipe, I reclaimed a fragment of my determination, a refusal to be caged by the expectations of others.

The muffled voices outside slowly morphed into an indistinct murmur, a distant hum that gradually faded into silence. I curled tighter under the covers, embracing the solace of the bed's sanctuary, seeking refuge in the quiet recesses of my own mind.

I'm not sure how long I laid in silence, the blankets strangling the iciness of reality. It was an hour maybe two, before I heard the soft click of the bedroom door being pushed open. A few seconds passed before the far side of the bed dipped down under the weight of a body. He let out a sigh before leaning against the headboard. The room still sat in darkness, but I could feel the tension that was no doubt etched across his face.

"Charlie?"

I laid still hoping he would think I was asleep so we wouldn't have to relive our earlier conversation.

"I know you're awake."

How he knew I had no idea, but I let out a sigh, feeling him adjust his weight behind me.

"Can we talk, please?"

Resigned to the inevitable, I flicked on the bedside lamp and sat up, avoiding meeting his gaze. I couldn't bear the thought of seeing sympathy reflected in his eyes. Pity was the last thing I needed.

"I'm not an assignment," I declared, my voice carrying the weight of my frustration. Anger simmered within me, a mixture of hurt and indignation. "Is that all I am to you?"

The pause that followed felt interminable. The silence hung heavy between us, charged with unspoken emotions, carving a deepening chasm. I didn't expect to mean much more, but to have it said to my face was a different kind of hurt.

"Charlie, no." His voice was soft, an attempt at reassurance. But the flames of resentment still burned within my chest, and his words didn't douse them.

"Then what am I?" My voice trembled slightly as I faced Jesse, but he averted his gaze, refusing to meet my eyes.

A heavy sigh escaped me, and I stood, my steps deliberate as I moved toward the door. "I need some air." I didn't wait for a response, pulling the door open, ready to escape the tension coiling in the room.

"Don't go too far." His words halted me, the implication of his concern irritating me after all the hidden truths.

"The curfew," he added, and a shadow flickered across his jawline. My gaze homed in on the darkness, and as I attempted to scrutinize, he turned away, hiding whatever mark lay beneath.

"What happened?" I demanded, my concern bleeding through my frustration.

Silence lingered between us, and my worry deepened when I noticed the deep purple bruise gracing the side of his jaw. "What happened?"

"It doesn't matter," Jesse's voice remained flat, his legs dropped to the floor as he stayed seated on the bed.

"Doesn't matter? Like hell it doesn't matter." I strode to stand in front of him, my anger directed not only at his injury but at his dismissive tone. "Did he do this?" I inquired, referring to the stranger who had visited earlier.

"No."

"Who?" When he didn't answer I made my way to the bathroom and rummaged through the drawers until I found the same cream he had used on my bruises. I made my way back into the bedroom and unscrewed the lid, sitting the jar on the nightstand. The cream was cool on my fingers as I brought my hand to the side of his face.

As I neared his jaw, he reached, grabbing my wrist. My eyes met his.

"You're not an assignment, Charlie." His words were gentle, and I nodded in acknowledgment as he released my wrist.

"I was. That's why you're here." Jesse closed his eyes briefly as my fingers touched his jaw.

"That changed when I saw you." His admission twisted something inside me as I worked the cream into his skin. I paused, noticing the muscle tensing along his jawline.

"Who did this to you?"

Jesse reached up, grabbing my hand in his before standing. He used his grip on my hands and pulled me closer, guiding my arms around his waist. His grip tightened around me, and I sunk deeper into his body.

A long moment passed before he reached up, tilting my head back, fingers grazing my chin. When I didn't move away, he leaned down closer, warmth radiating from his skin.

The palm of his hand slid to my cheek, fingers winding into my hair as a shot of tension ran through my body. Jesse noticed, gently rubbing his thumb under my eye, bringing his forehead to rest on mine. I pinched my eyes shut.

"What is it like?" He hummed softly in response. "Death, I mean." His thumb stilled for a brief second.

"What do you think it's like?" His words warmed my skin.

"I don't know." I thought for a moment. "Everyone has

a different idea…"

"But what do you think it's like?" His interruption was gentle, and I opened my eyes to find his softly closed.

"I'd like to think I'd see my father again." I paused, swallowing the lump forming in my throat. "Even if he's not my biological father."

"Blood doesn't make family, Charlie." His voice held conviction. "You'll see him again." I nodded, comforted by his words. "Heaven is whatever you make it."

"What do you mean?" I questioned, trying to comprehend his words.

"A person's beliefs in life…" Jesse paused, choosing his words carefully. "Shape their afterlife. That's why there are so many beliefs." His explanation lingered in my mind, a puzzle I couldn't quite solve.

"I don't understand," I admitted, feeling lost in the complexities of it all.

"If you believe in nothing, then there is nothing." He paused, collecting his thoughts. "Similarly, if you believe in reincarnation, then that becomes your path. If you wish to see your father again, then you will."

A flicker of warmth spread through me, a glimmer of relief amid the uncertainty.

His eyes snapped open, a small smile tugging the corner of his lips. A flutter worked its way from my stomach before turning to knot of panic in my throat once again. The knot worked its way higher, causing tears to prickle before dropping into my lungs, forcing out the air. The feeling of hardening cement filled my lungs. Jesse took a step back grabbing my hands in his.

"Charlie…" Worry etched his face. I wheezed feeling the

panic spread.

"It's just…"

"A panic attack."

I nodded bending forward, resting my hands on my knees.

"Just breathe." Jess grabbed my hands leading me to the side of the bed. Dizziness swirled in my mind. "Count with me." He paused. "One."

I repeated after him focusing on the way the words formed. "Two-three-"

Slowly I felt the panic subside, my breath working its way back into my lungs.

"Thank you."

He nodded sitting beside me on the bed.

"I'm sorry."

Surprised I looked over to him.

"For what?" I asked. He sighed and I shook my head. "That was not your fault."

"I brought up your past." His eyes found mine. "What those men did to you." Anger crept into his voice, and I looked down.

"I still get these flashes of panic." I stopped for a minute. "Even the smallest of things can set it off. Sometimes I don't even know why it happens, like now."

He nodded folding his hands in his lap, hanging his head between his shoulders.

Summoning a deep breath, I pushed down the overwhelming fear, burying it deep inside. With a delicate touch, I traced my hand along his jawline, guiding his gaze to meet mine. The fading bruise marred his skin, and a sudden surge of protectiveness swept over me. He sat deathly still as

I leaned into him, stopping just before touching his lips. His breath hitched.

"I'd never hurt you," he murmured. I closed the gap, the briefest brush of my lips against his. Pulling away, I dropped my hand, but he caught it, pressing it against his chest. A heartbeat thumped beneath my palm, echoing my own.

We sat in silence before he finally spoke.

"You should get some rest," his voice, filled with care, nudged me gently. I nodded, releasing my hand from his hold and shifting to the far side of the bed. Jesse reclined, leaning against the headboard, and I turned to face him, our eyes lingering a fraction longer than before.

"You never told me what happened to your face." I prodded gently, sensing reluctance in Jesse's expression.

"There's a sect of The First Chosen a couple of towns over. I went to see if I could get any information."

"Did you?" I leaned in, pressing for details, feeling a knot of worry twist in my stomach. "Jesse?"

"Nothing yet." He sighed, his eyes clouded with a mixture of frustration and concern.

"Yet?" My voice hitched, and he hesitated, weighing his words carefully.

"I found one of the lower-level members." His gaze met mine, carrying the weight of an unspoken story. "He was alone." A pause lingered. "When I approached him, he started to cause a scene."

"The bruises." My voice faltered, connecting the dots before he confirmed it.

"I secured him for later questioning." His words left me feeling very uneasy.

"Secured him?" I questioned, the uncertainty in my voice

mirroring the confusion in my mind.

"There's a safehouse—"

"You kidnapped him?" My shock was unmistakable, the reality of Jesse's actions sinking in.

The silence stretched, thick and heavy. "I want to be there when you question him." The words tumbled out of my mouth before I could stop them, a surprising assertion that startled us both.

"Charlie, I don't think that's—"

"I'm not asking." The newfound strength in my voice surprised even me, fueled by a mix of concern and determination.

His eyes widened for a moment, then softened, a faint smile playing at the corners of his mouth.

"Okay." He paused, standing. "I have some work to do."

16

FLICKERING FLAMES

I stepped into the warm glow of the kitchen, the scent of beeswax and aged parchment instantly enveloped me. Jesse had transformed our usual meal space into an impromptu library, with an assortment of faded papers sprawled across the table. Candlelight cast dancing shadows across the intricate inscriptions and faded illustrations that adorned the aged pages.

"Hey," I greeted softly, observing Jesse absorbed in the collection of ancient tomes.

He glanced up, a faint smile lighting up his features as he acknowledged my presence. "Can't sleep?"

I shook my head, folding my arms across my chest.

"Hey, come take a look at this," he invited, gesturing for me to join him.

"What's with the candles?"

Jesse snorted softly.

"The fluorescent lights emit ultraviolet rays." His eyes followed me. "They can damage the inks and paper." His fingers tapped gently on the table. "Probably not at this level." He gestured to the lights. "But I didn't want to take the chance."

I eased myself into the chair opposite him, drawn in by the centuries-old secrets and forgotten wisdom laid out before us.

My eyes traced the intricate patterns etched onto the pages, each symbol seeming to hold a story of its own. Dust motes danced in the air as I skimmed over the faded ink and weathered illustrations, feeling a sense of reverence for the ancient knowledge preserved in those pages.

"This is incredible," I murmured in a hushed tone, as if my words may damage the papers. The weight of history felt tangible, thickening the air around us. "Where did you get all of this?"

"This is everything I could gather about the ritual and The First Chosen," he explained, gesturing toward the meticulously arranged assortment of parchment scrolls and weathered papers strewn across the table. "I've been collecting it since I came to Hayzun." His body tensed. "But deciphering this language is beyond me." A fleeting touch of frustration swept across his face. The pages, worn and delicate, bore faded illustrations, cryptic symbols, and hints of verses, each teasing a fragment of the enigmatic puzzle we were attempting to unravel.

No doubt the ancient lore spoke of destinies intertwined and dangers lurking in the shadows, presenting a daunting challenge that we were determined to confront.

The pages before us were adorned with intricate depictions of celestial alignments, obscure runes, and symbolic representations of figures in ceremonial attire. Although the meaning eluded us due to the unfamiliar language, the vivid visuals spoke volumes.

"These patterns," I pointed to a series of circular glyphs interwoven. "This could be the eclipse," I pointed to a sequence of circles slowly disappearing behind one another. "It looks like the moon disappearing into the shadows."

Jesse leaned in, his eyes narrowing as he observed another illustration. "Look here," he indicated a mosaic of interlocking triangles surrounded by a series of smaller circles. "It's a symbol of unity and convergence, maybe signifying the joining of forces or the gathering of energies."

We pieced together hints from the visual tapestry, deciphering the symbolism based on our limited understanding.

Each illustration unveiled a layer of ancient lore, hinting at a convergence of powers and an intricate ritual whose complexity surpassed our current comprehension.

Jesse's brow furrowed as he studied an intricate series of lines and dots. "These symbols might signify an alignment of the stars."

The parchment scrolls seemed to hold secrets steeped in secretiveness and shrouded in obscurity. Each drawing and symbol hinted at a larger narrative, one that wove together elements of mysticism, celestial alignments, and cryptic messages from an age long past.

As we examined the pages, the patterns and puzzling symbols created an air of wonder, yet the meaning remained elusive, veiled within the layers of time and the intricacies of an ancient script.

JOURNEY INTO DARKNESS

I woke with a scream, a primal sound that tore through the silence of the room. My chest tightened, suffocating me as the remnants of the nightmare clung to my mind. It was as if the past had slipped its shackles, clawing its way back into my present.

The dream resurfaced in my mind and a tear slipped down my cheek. I wiped it away, pushing the dream into a box, shoving it into the corner of my brain. This corner was filled with dusty boxes, cobwebs, and remnants of old nightmares. I rarely went into that corner of my brain. I used it as a place to shove unwanted memories, thoughts, and fears, but occasionally one would sneak out and make its way back to the surface. I could still feel their rough hands on my skin.

The room lay shrouded in darkness, the empty space

amplified the echoes of my terror. I felt the slickness on my skin, the sensation of sweat mingled with a chilling fear that snaked around me. I reached out, flicking the lamp on the bedside table, its soft glow revealing the scene before me.

My gaze fell to my wrists, the sight sending a jolt of shock and confusion through me. Blood welled up from the slashes, trailing down my arms and staining the sheets.

"What the hell were you thinking?" Jesse's voice sliced through the air, full of concern and urgency. He had heard my scream, witnessed my distress.

He approached, dropping beside me, his hands carefully examining the cuts. "Why?" His eyes pleaded for an explanation, and I struggled to find the words.

"I didn't do this. I mean, I did, but these are old." My voice wavered, barely audible above the storm of emotions raging within me.

He rose abruptly, retreating before returning with a towel in hand. Taking my hand again, he gently wiped away the blood, revealing the faded scar tissue. I saw his face contort in a mixture of anguish and concern. The crimson-stained towel fell to the floor, a silent testament to a past that had never truly faded away.

Jesse remained silent, his eyes still fixed on the towel. His hands trembled as he clenched and unclenched them in his lap, a tumultuous storm brewing within him. When he finally looked up, his gaze softened with concern and empathy.

"Charlie, I'm sorry." His voice was raw with emotion.

"I didn't mean for you to see that," I murmured, feeling the weight of the past pressing down on me.

"I shouldn't have reacted like that," he replied, the anguish evident in his eyes. "I just … I care about you."

Silence enveloped us, heavy with unspoken words and emotions swirling in the air.

"It's okay, Jesse," I whispered, trying to reassure him. "I've … I've been dealing with this for a while. But it's not your burden."

He nodded slowly, absorbing my words. "You don't have to carry it alone."

We sat in the quiet of the room, the air thick with unspoken understanding. Jesse's presence felt reassuring, a lifeline in the darkness threatening to engulf me.

"I want to understand," he finally said, his voice gentle yet filled with determination. "But only if you're ready to share."

I hesitated, unsure if I could lay bare the darkest corners of my mind. But the sincerity in his eyes urged me to try.

"I'll tell you," I whispered, a tremor in my voice. "Not now, but soon." I thought for a moment, confused as to where the blood had even come from. The old wounds didn't reopen and there weren't any fresh ones.

A small smile touched his lips, a glimmer of hope and solidarity. He reached out and squeezed my hand, a silent promise of support.

The weight on my chest felt a bit lighter, as if the darkness within had started to recede in the face of his compassion. It was a small step, but in that moment, it felt like a leap toward healing.

He stood, leaning down to press a kiss to my forehead.

"Get dressed, we should get going soon." With that he turned, tossing the bloody cloth into the room to his right on his way out.

In the bathroom, the tap ran, the water streaming hot as

I tried to scrub away the crimson reminders etched into my skin. Each rub of the cloth was an attempt to erase the pain and fear that lingered beneath the surface. Tears blurred my vision, their heat mixing with the warmth of the water.

A fleeting shadow crossed the doorway, and my breath caught in my throat. Blinking away the tears, I found Jesse standing before me, a crimson vial in his hand. His presence felt like a sudden intrusion, yet a soothing balm all at once.

"We should get going," he started, but the tenderness in his voice faltered, recognizing my distress. The vial landed gently on the counter as he approached cautiously.

I forced a smile onto my lips, quickly wiping my face with the palms of my hands. I tried to push past him, but he grabbed my arm, pinning me next to him, lowering his head.

"I don't like to see you cry."

I forced my smile wider, feeling my bottom lip quiver. "But—" He let go of my arm. "I hate seeing you pretend you're okay even more." His hand slid up to cup my cheek, his eyes the color of freshly polished blue sapphire.

"I'm not pretending."

A gruff sigh rolled from his throat as he turned me to fully face him.

"Don't lie to me, Charlie," he implored, his voice a breath against my skin. "You don't have to hide from me."

I closed my eyes, a silent admission of the truth I couldn't voice.

"I'm going to die, aren't I?" I asked. His fingers tightened on my jaw.

"No."

I opened my eyes to see his still open wide.

"I thought we weren't supposed to lie."

His other arm encircled my waist, pulling me flush against him, bringing his forehead to mine.

"Charlie, I'll do anything to keep you safe." His words were a whisper against my lips, tinged with fervor. I felt his sincerity in every word, his determination reverberated through his touch. It was a promise he seemed willing to stake everything on.

"We should go," I managed to murmur, the urgency of our situation gnawing at my thoughts. But neither of us moved, held captive by the electric tension that crackled in the charged atmosphere.

"Jess?" The sound of my voice was a hesitant plea. He remained silent, a pillar of strength and vulnerability all at once.

The sound of rain pelting the roof filled my ears, drowning out the sounds of our breathing. A loud crack of thunder sent a pulse of shock through my body causing me to jump. Jesse's smile was an unexpected comfort, and he straightened, a determination glinting in his eyes.

He reached past me, placing the vial he had retrieved into my palm. Its crimson contents caught the dim light, refracting the intensity of our emotions. Jesse disappeared down the hall, leaving me standing there, contemplating the significance of that small glass bottle.

A few minutes later I made my way down the hall and out the front door. Jesse stood under the eave, sheltered from the relentless rain. As I approached, he pulled the door closed behind me, the lock clicking with finality.

My clothes clung to my skin, the cold seeped through, sending a shiver down my spine. I hastily tucked the vial into my front pocket and climbed into the passenger seat without a second thought.

The engine roared to life, and the car began its journey, navigating the winding roads toward the town's outskirts. The closer we got to the limits, the tighter the knot in my stomach twisted, constricting my breath.

Memories of the last time I left Hayzun flooded my mind, vivid and unwelcome. I shut my eyes tight, trying to block them out. "Take a deep breath," a calming voice urged me, but the images persisted, refusing to fade. I gripped the seat, my knuckles white with tension.

Amid the chaos of my thoughts, warmth encased my left hand. Jesse's touch gently pried my fingers from the fabric of the seat. "Look at me," his voice urged, steady and reassuring.

"Charlie," Jesse's voice reached me through the storm within. "Look at me."

I struggled to obey, the fear welling up inside. His firm yet gentle touch guided my other hand away from its vice-like grip, and it was then I realized the car had halted.

"Open your eyes."

I shook my head, trying to focus on his hands, letting them pull me back to the present. I focused on their warmth, their strength, but also their gentleness. The exact opposite of what I remembered from that day.

With a determined inhale, I pushed my eyelids apart, allowing my vision to slowly adjust. The scene outside came into focus, the raindrops painting the car windows with trails of water, and Jesse's gaze, a beacon of stability amid the chaos.

He sat in front of me, holding my hands in his. He didn't ask me if I was okay. He didn't need to ask because we both knew I wasn't. He also didn't ask if I wanted to turn around because he knew this was something I needed to do for myself.

I looked out the windshield seeing the rain patter on the glass. The sign that signaled Hayzun's barriers sat, blurred in the streaming water.

Taking my hands back, I sat straight.

"I'm ready," I announced, pulling my hands away and straightening my posture. Jesse didn't protest; he simply returned his hands to the wheel and guided the car forward.

As the distance between us and the town limits grew closer the more my body tensed. Bile rose in my throat, causing it to burn. Taking a deep breath, I held it. Held it until we had surpassed the brightly colored sign that marked the invisible boundaries of the town. Held it until my lungs burned and I had a choice between passing out or letting go of the air I had barricaded in my chest. I chose the latter, letting out a shaking breath followed by another and another. I had finally crossed the border, and this time nothing bad had happened.

Time became elusive as we drove on, lost in the blur of landscapes and thoughts. The car slowed and veered into a narrow gravel driveway, halting with a soft crunch.

"You can wait here," Jesse suggested softly. I shook my head, unfastening my seatbelt. His hand reached out to mine. "Charlie…" he started again. "It might not be the most pleasant thing to witness."

I looked over at him.

"You're just going to question him, aren't you?"

Jesse's jaw hardened.

"Yes, but…" He shifted in his seat. "He might need a little bit of…persuading."

"Persuading?" It was a question, but I instantly knew the answer. "I understand."

He nodded, but his body stayed tense as he undid his seatbelt and opened the driver-side door exiting the car. Rain spilled in from the outside as I forced open the door and took steps onto soil that didn't belong to Hayzun.

18

DARKNESS DESCENDS

Rust-colored stains smeared the ashy tiles, dripping from metal that tore into flesh. Wrists bound by cuffs that tightened with any attempt to get free.

The man sat on the floor; head hung; arms connected to a metal bar that had been screwed into the floor. Shoulder-length hair the color of darkness fell forward over a tired face hearing us approach, the body leaned against the wall twitched before raising its head. His hair cascaded backward, unveiling a pair of obsidian eyes framed by scars etched deeply beneath his right eye. My gut clenched, a sour taste rising in my throat. Seconds later his top lip pulled back exposing crooked teeth.

"A wilted flower with tender skin, tear-stained cheeks," his voice emerged, dark and guttural. "You're but a scarred body, soulless," he muttered, his words hanging in the air, haunting and eerie. "May the king of shadows come upon us with a sordid war." The sinister verses resounded, echoing in my mind like a ghastly refrain. His words stung my ears, playing over and over. Turning quickly I rushed back the way we came, finding the front door of the safehouse.

"Charlie?" I pulled the door from the deadbolt strike in time to hear a soft chuckle fill the room. Cold damp air filled my lungs as I stepped out under the eve, rain pattering heavily. Jesse rushed out behind me as I buckled at the waist, retching. His face flashed once again.

"Charlie?"

I raised my hand, feeling my whole-body tremble." Charlie?" His voice was filled with anger. Not at me at the fact he didn't know what was going on.

"I just need a minute." My head spun, and the only thing that stopped me from falling was a strong arm wrapped around my midsection. Hot wet tears collected on my cheeks as I gripped his arm, digging my fingers into his skin. I stood still bent at the waist. He swore lightly under his breath as my nails marked his skin. After a moment he spun me to face him, lifting my head in his hands.

He muttered a soft curse, enduring the imprint of my nails on his skin before gently turning me to face him, cradling my face in his hands. A flicker of recognition passed across his eyes.

"You know him." His voice held a note of realization. I nodded weakly, attempting to steady my voice, to explain the horror that lingered in my memory.

"He hurt you," Jesse's tone darkened, a trace of anger threading through his words. My lips quivered, making it difficult to speak.

"He was one of them." The words caught in my throat, painful memories clawing their way back into my consciousness. "He…" I hesitated, the words stuck in the chasm of my horror. "He held me down … while the other…" My voice broke, the words too raw to fully articulate. "They knew who I was. They were watching me."

"Wait in the car." His demand was stern, edged with protectiveness. My head shook in refusal, stubbornness rising against the swell of emotions.

"Charlie…" Jesse's voice carried a deep-seated anger, his concern and protectiveness evident. "I'm not asking, wait in the car."

"I want to know what he has to say just as much as you do, Jess." My voice, matching his anger, was a resolve fueled by defiance, a defiance against the lingering fear and haunting memories. Jesse's jaw clenched, his eyes burning with a mixture of concern and anger. He reluctantly released his grip on me, his hands falling to his sides.

"Fine," he growled, "but stay close. I don't want you anywhere near that man."

I nodded, wiping away the tears that still clung to my cheeks, and followed Jesse back into the dimly lit room. The man, still shackled to the floor, grinned maliciously as we re-entered.

"What do you want?" Jesse demanded, his voice sharp and unyielding.

The man's laughter echoed in the room. "What does anyone want, Jesse? Power, control, a taste of the forbidden."

Jesse's nostrils flared with restrained anger. "Cut the cryptic crap. Who are you, and what does The First Chosen want with Charlotte?"

The man's eyes flicked to me, a wicked glint dancing in their depths. "Ah, the wilting flower," he mused. "Charlotte, born of Sol and Ember, the key to our salvation."

My stomach churned at his words, and I steadied myself against the wall. Jesse shot me a concerned glance before refocusing on the man.

"What's the ritual they're planning?" Jesse pressed.

The man chuckled, the sound sending shivers down my spine. "Rituals, sacrifices, and a dance with the shadows. The First Chosen believes that releasing Disias will bring about a new era, a world cloaked in darkness."

"Why Charlotte?" Jesse's voice was sharp.

"Ah, my dear, she's the void soul. Born of forbidden bloodlines, a perfect vessel for the God of Shadows."

My mind raced, trying to absorb the information. "Why do they need Disias? What's their endgame?"

The man leaned back against the wall, a sinister smile playing on his lips. "Power, my dear. Unimaginable power. The world is a puppet, and Disias will cut its strings, leaving chaos in his wake."

Jesse's fists clenched at his sides. "How do we stop them?"

The man's laughter echoed once more. "You can't. The First Chosen's plans are already set in motion. The ritual, the sacrifices—it's all underway. You're too late."

Jesse lunged forward, grabbing the man by the collar. "Tell us everything, or I swear—"

The man's laughter cut through Jesse's threat. "You can't stop the inevitable, Jeremiah. The shadows will rise, and your precious Charlotte will play her part in the grand design."

The room seemed to close in around us as the man's

ominous words hung in the air. We were left with more questions than answers, and the weight of impending darkness settled over us like a suffocating shroud.

Enraged and frustrated, Jesse released his grip on the man, who slumped back against the wall, a triumphant glint in his eyes. I could feel the tension in the room, a sense of impending doom.

"We need to find out more," Jesse muttered, his jaw clenched. "There has to be a way to stop this ritual."

I nodded, determined to uncover any information that could help us thwart The First Chosen's plans.

"But first I need you to go wait in the car." He wrung his hands. "I don't want you to see this."

The relentless rain drummed on the roof, and distant thunder punctuated the heavy air, the flashes of light sliced through the gloom. The car door slammed shut, the sound a sharp contrast to the relentless downpour outside. Jesse took his place behind the wheel, his knuckles white as he gripped it tightly.

My fingers grazed the sleeves of his shirt, pushed up to reveal a new, angry white scar on his forearm, marking the finality of the man we left behind. Each of those scars told a story, one that was too vivid for me to ignore. A mix of emotions churned within me—remorse, anger, a sense of freedom tainted with fear.

"How many?" The words were a whisper, hesitant, but I needed to know.

"Too many," he responded, his voice distant, lost in the

storm outside. The weight of his admission suffocated the silence that followed.

"What … what happens now?" My voice was barely audible, the question lingered in the tense atmosphere.

"Reece is going to deal with it." The amount of disconnect in his voice was alarming. "I'm sorry you had to see him again."

A shiver ran across my skin.

"You didn't know."

"No, but I should have."

I shook my head. How could he have known? I tried my hardest to block the man's face from my memory, the way his harsh hands felt on my skin, brutal and unforgiving. It was something I would never wish upon anyone. Even though he hadn't been the one to inflict the worst harm, he had played his part. He deserved what he got. Or at least that's what I would tell myself. It then occurred to me that I had not only just witnessed a kidnapping, but also a murder. The murder of a sick, sadistic individual, but a murder, nonetheless. I shut my eyes, sinking as far into the seat as I possibly could. Maybe if I sunk in far enough it would be enough to disappear.

The car eased down the driveway as Jesse reversed, then shifted into drive, leaving the gruesome incident in our wake.

We were about forty minutes from home, in an unfamiliar town that I had never set foot in. Outside Hayzun, my world had been confined, but the stark reality of that encounter urged me to break free. "I don't want to go home yet." My voice was small but determined.

"Are you sure?" Jesse glanced over from the driver's seat.

"I just faced one of the reasons why I stayed locked in Hayzun for so long. It feels like my fate is sealed, so maybe it's time to see beyond this town, even if it's just a few towns over."

His nod was understanding as he turned the car in a different direction, steering us toward an unknown horizon.

Puddles stretched across the streets, streaming toward the storm drains in shimmering rivulets. The car plowed through the water, spraying droplets against the sides. The unfamiliar buildings and landscapes whizzed by; a peculiar sense of achievement creeping over me.

"You'll see." Jesse's smile was cryptic, fleeting, as he glanced over before focusing back on the road. Thunder rolled in the distance, lightning danced across the darkened sky.

The rain intensified, tearing the last remnants of leaves from their branches, casting them to the ground in a flurry. I gazed out through rain-streaked windows, the world outside cloaked in a watery haze.

Then, as if the earth had parted, the landscape changed abruptly, revealing a valley submerged in water. I had never witnessed the coast, never expected to, and without a conscious thought, I unfastened my seatbelt and leaped out of the car as it came to a stop.

"Charlie?" His voice echoed from the car, but a moment later his door opened as he followed me into the rain. I didn't stop until I met where the water lapped the rocks. "You're going to get sick." I turned to look at him, rain slicking his hair to his face.

"We both know that's not how you get sick," I retorted, a smirk played on my lips.

"Maybe not," he spoke loudly. Raindrops blurred my vision as I faced the churning water, an untamed force that seemed to mirror the turmoil within me. The rain fell incessantly, a symphony of nature's chaos.

A gentle grip on my wrist pulled me away from the open waters. Raindrops danced before my eyes, making everything blurry.

"We should get out of the rain." His words were rational, but leaving felt like abandoning something crucial, something unresolved.

"I will. I'll take you wherever you want to go, explore every shore and every sea." His tone carried a promise, a glimmer of hope amid the tempest.

"There's one more place we have to go before we go home," Jesse revealed, his expression somber. "If you're up for it?"

I nodded, steeling myself for what lay ahead, knowing that Jesse's determination meant there was more to unravel in this already complex journey. I knew the man must have given him information in his last moments. What it was I was about to find out.

"Stay here," Jesse instructed, unclipping his seatbelt, and stepping out of the car. I watched as he made his way toward a small, derelict building.

The man in front of the building was a striking figure, a cigarette hanging between his weathered lips, glowing with a tiny ember against the encroaching darkness. His fingers, no doubt stained yellow from years of smoking, plucked the cigarette from his mouth.

Jesse approached him asking something I couldn't hear.

The man abruptly gestured toward the building's door, an old, weathered structure that had seen better days. A large sign blinked in the window, its neon letters spelling out the word "bar" alongside a faded "open" sign. The place seemed to be a relic from another time, tucked away in the shadowy corners of the world.

I watched as Jesse and the man disappeared inside the dimly lit establishment, the door creaking as it swung shut behind them. The neon sign flickered intermittently, casting eerie glows that seemed to dance along the edges of the tattered curtains. I sat in the car, feeling a growing sense of unease.

Time seemed to slow as I waited, wondering what secrets lay concealed within those walls. Jesse had gone in there for answers, but I couldn't help feeling that this was a place teeming with danger.

Time ticked on for what seemed like hours, but it may have only been minutes. Finally, I reached for the door handle, intent on following Jesse.

Exiting the car out into the rain a hand gently rested on my shoulder, stopping me in my tracks.

I turned to see a stranger, a man whose features I couldn't quite place. His presence was unexpected, and I felt a rush of anxiety.

"Can I help you?" he asked, his tone polite but with a hint of warning.

Not sure what to say, I hesitated, the words caught in my throat. It was as if he could see my uncertainty and unease. My instincts screamed at me to be cautious, and I couldn't help but wonder if this man was connected to The First Chosen.

"No." I took a step back. "I'm fine thank you."

The stranger nodded, his expression unreadable. "As you wish," he replied, his voice calm but carrying an air of knowing. With one last inscrutable look, he slowly withdrew his hand from my shoulder.

As I approached the entrance, I couldn't help but wonder whether the stranger had intended to guide me away from danger or deeper into its clutches. My instincts told me that I was on the right path, but only time would reveal the true nature of the secrets hidden within the bar's dimly lit confines.

I cautiously pushed open the heavy wooden door, causing it to creak softly on its hinges as I entered. The interior was shrouded in shadows, broken only by the sporadic, flickering glow of neon lights. The atmosphere was thick with tension, and the air was heavy with the scent of aged wood and lingering cigarette smoke.

Jesse and the stranger were nowhere to be seen. I felt a chill run down my spine, realizing that I had entered this unfamiliar and potentially dangerous place alone. My heart raced, but I couldn't turn back now.

The bar was sparsely populated, with a few patrons scattered at the worn-out wooden tables. A bartender, a grizzled man with a ragged beard, wiped down the counter and regarded me with a curious, yet unfriendly, look.

Taking a deep breath, I decided to approach the bartender. I had to find Jesse, and I couldn't do it by simply standing there.

"Excuse me," I began, my voice trembling slightly. "I'm looking for someone. A man came in here a little while ago, and I need to find him. Tall, dark hair, he was with another man."

The bartender's gaze remained cold, but he grudgingly nodded and gestured to the far corner of the bar.

"They're over there," he muttered, his attention quickly returning to his cleaning.

I followed his gaze and spotted Jesse sitting at a corner booth, engaged in an intense conversation with the stranger from earlier. The stranger's face was partially obscured by the dim lighting, but it was clear that their discussion was far from casual.

I hesitated, my curiosity warring with my unease. The scene before me was tense, and I couldn't shake the feeling that I might be stepping into something beyond my understanding. Jesse and the stranger seemed deeply engrossed in their discussion, and I didn't want to intrude without cause.

Instead, I pulled back slightly, choosing to remain at the bar. I tried to blend in with the few patrons scattered around, sipping a drink that I didn't particularly want. I kept a close eye on Jesse and the stranger, straining to catch any snippets of their conversation.

As I observed from a distance, I couldn't help but feel a growing sense of unease. The stranger's gestures were animated, and Jesse appeared to be listening intently. Whatever they were discussing seemed significant, and I was left in the dark, wondering if it had to do with The First Chosen, our quest to uncover their secrets, or the impending danger that loomed over us.

Feeling like an intruder, I chose to observe from afar, eavesdropping on their discussion. Words eluded me, but the gravity of their conversation was definitely noticeable. The stranger's animated gestures and Jesse's focused attention only deepened the intrigue.

With each passing moment, my determination to unravel

the mysteries and confront The First Chosen only grew. I couldn't afford to remain in the dark, and the urgency of our mission pressed upon me.

As I sat at the bar, my anxiety continued to build. Jesse and the stranger were still engrossed in their conversation, and my growing impatience gnawed at me. I needed to know what they were discussing, especially given the dangers we had encountered in our quest to uncover The First Chosen's secrets.

With a determined resolve, I discreetly excused myself from the bar and began to make my way toward Jesse and the stranger. I tried to remain inconspicuous, moving carefully through the dimly lit bar.

As I approached Jesse and the stranger, I could see their exchange becoming increasingly heated. Their voices rose, and Jesse's expression darkened. I couldn't catch the words, but the intensity of their discussion sent shivers down my spine.

Just as I reached their table, the stranger abruptly stood up, his chair scraped loudly against the floor. He cast a final, lingering glance at Jesse before turning and heading toward the exit.

Jesse remained seated, his jaw clenched, his eyes following the stranger's departure. The tension in the room didn't dissipate, but I had a feeling that the stranger's departure signaled a new and unsettling development.

I finally reached Jesse's side, my heart pounding with a mix of anxiety and curiosity.

"What was that about?" I asked, my voice trembling with unease.

"I told you to wait in the car." He stood grabbing my

hand, pulling me in the direction of the door.

Jesse's gaze met mine as we secured ourselves in the car, and he looked both frustrated and determined. "It's not good, Charlie."

Jesse sighed, the rain tapping a dissonant melody on the car's roof. "They're fixated on Disias, but there's more to it than just unleashing an ancient being."

I leaned forward, anticipation prickling the edges of my nerves. "What else did you find out?"

"They believe Disias holds the key to reshape the world," Jesse explained, his voice carrying a mix of frustration and concern. "But they're not fully certain about the consequences. The ritual they're planning … it's a gamble, and they're willing to risk it all."

My mind raced, trying to comprehend the magnitude of their intentions. "What do they hope to achieve?"

"It's about power, control," Jesse continued, his tone grim. "They're seeking dominion, believing they can harness Disias's abilities for their own gain."

"But at what cost?" The words tumbled from my lips, a sense of impending dread settling in my chest.

"That's the question," Jesse replied, his gaze fixed on the road ahead. "The stranger hinted that Disias's release might bring catastrophic consequences, chaos that could consume everything."

I swallowed hard, the weight of the situation sinking in. "Is there a way to stop them?"

Jesse glanced at me, his expression grim. "Stopping them won't be easy. He didn't reveal much about how to halt their plans."

A heavy silence settled between us as the car cruised

through the rain-soaked streets. A dark cloud of urgency hung around us.

"Surely there's something we can do," I murmured, grappling with the rising sense of helplessness.

"We have to dig deeper, find every piece of information we can," Jesse replied, his jaw clenched. "The First Chosen are skilled in secrecy. We need to uncover their motives, their vulnerabilities."

"Where do we even start?" Frustration tinged my voice. The enormity of the situation felt suffocating.

Jesse's gaze flickered to mine, determination shining in his eyes. "We'll turn every stone, explore every avenue. If there's a way to thwart their plans, we'll find it."

DANCING WITH DEMONS

The rain had almost stopped as we crossed the town line back into Hayzun. I felt a sense of weightlessness, but also a sense of dread. A chill jarred my shoulders catching Jesse's attention.

"Are you okay?" Jesse asked, and I nodded slowly.

"Just cold."

Jesse adjusted the temperature controls, warm air gusting out from the vents, wrapping around me like a comforting blanket. "Thanks," I whispered, trying to suppress the shivers that persisted beneath my skin.

As the car made its turns and pulled up in front of Jesse's rental, the engine's quiet hum ceased, leaving an unsettling void. A sudden wave of nausea twisted my stomach, signaling a familiar discomfort.

"I think I'm going to be sick." Before the words had fully left my mouth, the passenger side door was yanked open, and my seatbelt unclipped. Stumbling out of the car I heaved feeling the contents of my stomach which wasn't much, empty onto the grass. The shivers grew until my body felt like waves of electricity coursing through my bones. I heaved again, but there was nothing left to come out.

"Can you stand?" I nodded pushing myself to my feet, feeling my legs waver beneath me. Jesse grabbed my arm, steading me as I made my way to the front door.

"Your skin is freezing." I pulled my focus from my jittering extremities to the raised bumps along my skin. The door opened as I stumbled in, finding my way to the couch. I heard the door close, and water start to run a minute later.

Dizziness spun behind my eyes, pushing me deeper into the cushions, an icy chill dancing across my shoulder blades.

"Charlie."

Warm hands took mine.

"You need to come with me."

My teeth jarred against one another.

With gentle determination, Jesse scooped me up, cradling me against his chest. Each step he took echoed in my ears, the rush of water grew louder with every passing moment. The door creaked open, and he maneuvered us into the steam-filled bathroom, closing the door behind us with a decisive thud.

The enveloping warmth suffused my senses, the heavy steam causing my chest to tighten. I coughed; my lungs startled by the sudden heat. Droplets of water sprayed across my chilled skin as Jesse settled me onto the shower floor.

The scalding water lashed against my frigid body, a searing sensation that elicited a deep hiss of pain.

"Get me out!" I pleaded, clawing at the shower wall in desperation. My hand inadvertently knocked over shampoo bottles, their clatter adding to the chaotic symphony.

"Charlie, just sit still," Jesse urged, attempting to calm the panic that surged within me. His hands reached out, but my movements caused me to slip, sending me crashing back to the floor with a jarring thud.

"Please!" I whimpered, teeth chattering uncontrollably despite the onslaught of boiling water. My body protested vehemently against the unexpected heat.

"The water's barely warm, Charlie," Jesse reassured, trying to anchor me to the present. Ignoring my protests, he swiftly repositioned himself, drenched clothes sticking to his skin as he settled behind me, his arms.

"Jess?" my voice wavered, the battle between cold and hot waging both inside and out. His humming, a soothing melody, resonated in my ears as he pressed a tender kiss to my temple. "It's burning," I gasped, feeling overwhelmed by the scorching downpour.

"We just need to regulate your body temperature," Jesse murmured, his voice laced with concern.

I nodded weakly, seeking solace in his embrace as the pounding in my head intensified. His slight flinch didn't escape me, yet he kept his focus on calming me despite the commotion outside.

The door crashed open, water droplets cascaded into my eyes, jolting me from the moment. The intrusion shattered the fragile cocoon of warmth, sending a chill down my spine. Water dripped into my eyes.

"What did you do to her?" the voice sliced through the steam, laced with anger and possessiveness.

"I didn't do anything," Jesse retorted, his tone heated and defensive.

"Something must've happened." Footsteps echoed closer, and Jesse swiftly pulled me backward. Pain shot through my leg, eliciting a sharp cry of agony from me. "She's bleeding." A second pair of hands reached out and grabbed my leg, running up to my pocket. I flinched.

"Get back," Jesse growled out the words, low and guttural. The second pair of hands didn't leave, instead grasped my pocket.

"Why is there glass in her pocket?" The words came out harsh and insistent.

"Glass?" Jesse's voice betrayed a hint of alarm. The hands didn't relent, still investigating my pocket.

"Did I stutter?" The voice was commanding and unyielding.

"Jace—" Jesse's voice dropped to a threatening growl. His hand skimmed down my side, halting where the glass shards had pierced my skin. A heavy sigh escaped him. "It's not her blood, not all of it." He cradled my face with his other hand, his touch comforting amid the chaos. "She's going through withdrawal."

"Withdrawal? From what?" I blinked heavily, trying to clear the rushing water from my eyes. Through the haze, I made out the sight of blond hair approaching, Jace kneeled beside the shower stall. He shared the same features as Jesse, but his eyes were a deep almond brown.

"Kitchen drawer, top left. There's a vial, bring it to me," Jesse instructed, his voice urgent. Jace promptly left us alone, disappearing to retrieve whatever was needed.

"Why didn't you take it?" I shivered against Jesse's warmth, the tremors ran deeper than the physical chill. "It was to keep you safe."

"And what am I supposed to do?" I trembled, my voice quivering. "Take it forever?" I shook my head, the feeling of despair sinking in.

"No." Jesse's hand ran soothingly through my hair, a gesture of both reassurance and urgency. Jace entered the bathroom, his presence adding an extra layer of tension. He handed a blood-red vial to Jesse, who twisted it open and held it to my lips.

"No." I turned my head away, refusing the vial.

"Charlie, you have to," Jesse insisted, pressing the vial toward me once more.

"She said no."

"Jace, you are not a part of this," Jesse's voice grew stern and authoritative behind me, tension radiated from his body.

"Jess, please," I pleaded, a single tear mixing with the water from the shower. I hadn't felt like myself since I was coerced into taking it the first time, as if it was slowly devouring me from within.

"Charlie, you won't feel better unless you take it. Your body is going through withdrawal," Jesse reasoned, his voice laden with concern. I shook my head, the relentless hot water beating against my skin.

"At least take half of it, it'll stop the chills, and we can wean you off over the next couple of days," Jesse implored, his words a blend of care and urgency. My body ached, and I let my head fall back against his chest, seeking solace.

He brought the vial to my mouth, but Jace's low snarl

reverberated through the room, his hands gripping the edge of the shower with intensity, his knuckles whitening. I wasn't sure why he was here, but his presence only added to the escalating tension.

Raising my hand, I silently gestured for him to stop, a plea for peace amid the chaos. Surprisingly, he quieted, though I couldn't comprehend why or how it worked.

I brought my lips to the rim of the vial, allowing Jesse to tip it back, forcing down the thick, metallic-tasting liquid. It was a struggle, and I gagged, trying to swallow it down. Jesse, as promised, made me take only half before he screwed the lid back on and handed the vial to Jace. I sat still for a moment, feeling the intense battle between the contrasting sensations of heat and cold. Gradually, the chills began to subside, and the water, which had been an onslaught before, now felt more bearable, almost lukewarm. I let out a sigh, feeling some of the discomfort gradually ebb away through my skin.

Jesse leaned back, turning off the tap, halting the steady flow of water. His hand came up to my thigh, and I felt a sudden tenderness in his touch.

"I think the glass might have cut you," he said, concern etched in his voice. I nodded weakly, each movement causing the embedded shards to sting deeper into my skin. "I need to see your leg," he continued gently. I felt exhaustion wash over me, draining what little strength I had left. Jesse carefully stood up, water droplets cascading from his soaked clothes. He glanced at Jace.

"You can leave," Jesse's tone was sharp, a clear dismissal.

"I'll wait," Jace replied coolly.

"I need to undress her, and I'm sure she doesn't want

spectators," Jesse retorted, a note of tension in his voice. Jace nodded, conceding.

"I'll be in the kitchen," he said before exiting, closing the door behind him. In an instant, Jesse was back in front of me, kneeling with a reassuring presence.

"Can you stand?" His voice held a tenderness that wrapped around me like a blanket. I nodded, reaching for his reassuring presence. He took my hands, guiding me up with a careful touch that melted away some of the unease. A sharp sting shot through my thigh, and Jesse knelt before me, his eyes fixed on the blood seeping through the fabric.

"Can you take these off?" He motioned to my pants; his gaze soft yet determined. I looked down at him, finding reassurance in his eyes. "I need to be able to get the glass out." I nodded in agreement.

"Can you turn around?" Jesse dropped his head, turning his back toward me. The soaked fabric clung uncomfortably to my skin as I carefully pulled my pants down, the glass from my pocket clattering to the ground.

I wrapped a towel around my waist, leaving the front of my right leg exposed for Jesse's examination.

"Okay." He turned slowly.

"Sit up here." He patted the countertop with his hand. When he turned to rummage through a drawer, I pulled myself up onto the counter, letting the towel rest against my skin. In a moment he had a small array of bandages and antiseptics.

Pulling the towel just off of the wound, he leaned closer, his focus on my injury. "Looks like it cut you, but there's no glass left in." His words brought a wave of relief, a small reprieve in the midst of everything. He reached for a bottle, and I expected a stinging pain under his touch. But the familiar sting of alcohol never hit. He carefully dabbed it dry before applying a small bandage, smoothing it out with a gentle touch that offered a sense of comfort.

He left the bathroom briefly, returning with a handful of dry clothes. "I'll wait for you out there," he said softly, gesturing to the door. As he closed the door behind him, I slid off the counter, exchanging my wet clothes for the dry ones he had brought, the fabric a welcomed warmth against my chilled skin.

Voices echoed down the hall; a jumble of similar tones reached my ears. The voices of brothers. I followed them to the living room, where they both cut out the minute I rounded the corner.

Jesse stood from the couch, having changed from his wet clothing as well. He looked me over, tension ticking along his jaw.

Movement caught my attention as Jace shifted his weight from one leg to another, leaning against the window frame. I looked from him to Jesse.

"Are you feeling better?" Jesse's voice was soft, his concern evident as he turned to face me. I nodded weakly, offering a small smile to reassure him.

"Yeah, thanks to you," my voice came out quieter than I intended, the lingering effects of the chills still making me feel shaky.

Jesse moved forward, his eyes never leaving mine. "You need to rest." It wasn't a suggestion but a gentle command, the kind of assertion that showed how much he cared.

"Okay." I glanced toward Jace, feeling a surge of curiosity about his presence here. His eyes held a guarded intensity that made me uneasy.

"What's going on?" I asked.

"They're holding a search for Piper after the candle lighting ceremony." It was Jace who spoke. I looked to Jesse still confused as to why he felt the need to come here and tell us this.

The candle lighting ceremony was a Hayzun tradition that occurred in the town square halfway through October. It involved the lighting of the *Candle of Protection*, a specially crafted candle believed to ward off malevolent spirits until Halloween. I always thought it was a silly superstition, but now it seemed to hold something different. Townsfolk gathered to witness its lighting and the safeguarding of Hayzun from supernatural forces. The candle must remain lit without interruption until midnight on Halloween to keep the town under its protection. I had completely forgotten about it until now.

"That's why you came here?" Jace looked to Jesse, his jaw hardening as he thought for a moment before nodding. I knew he wasn't telling the whole truth, but I shook it off.

"We should go help then," I suggested, eager to contribute, to ease the growing unease in the atmosphere. But Jesse's apprehension lingered like an unspoken warning.

"Charlie, I don't think that's a good idea," Jesse intervened, reaching out to hold my arm, his touch a mixture of concern and restraint. "Besides, I don't think they're going to find anything anyway."

"But wouldn't it be suspicious if we didn't help?" I insisted, catching a glimpse of Jace's smirk.

"You know, I think she's right," Jace agreed, his amusement evident. Jesse muttered under his breath, showing signs of reluctance. "Can we have a minute?" He looked to Jace who nodded.

"I'll be outside." He smiled at me before letting himself outside, closing the door behind himself.

Jesse turned to me taking both my hands. I opened my mouth to argue, but he shook his head, closing his eyes.

"You will stay within my line of sight or within Jace's." his eyes opened. We'll be back before the curfew, preferably before it gets dark."

I nodded knowing that if I argued his offer would be revoked. But I couldn't help but clarify one thing.

"I didn't think you trusted him." My gaze flickered toward the closed door where Jace had exited moments ago.

"I trust him less than some but more than others," Jesse's response was cryptic, leaving me wondering about the intricacies of their relationship. His concern for my well-being seemed genuine, and I appreciated it.

"How are you feeling?" His eyes probed mine, searching for any signs of discomfort or hidden pain. I met his gaze, assuring him that I was indeed feeling better. His embrace enveloped me, a tender gesture that momentarily eased my worries, his lips pressed against the crown of my head.

"I'll grab you a jacket. I don't want you to get cold," Jesse's words were caring as he slowly released me and made his way down the hallway. I felt bad making Jace wait outside by himself, so I headed to the door and pulled it open. The air still smelled damp as I stepped out. Jace stood on the small cement stairs leading to the front, his smile brightening as he caught sight of me. Despite the uncertain circumstances, his demeanor remained amiable, leaving me perplexed about his true intentions.

"What's the verdict angel?" I pinched my eyebrows at the use of a pet name. I arched an eyebrow, slightly bewildered by the term.

Shaking my head lightly, I responded, "Looks like you're going to help babysit me on this venture." His grin widened, a glint of mischief in his eyes.

"I can handle that." As Jace took a step closer, the door creaked open, revealing Jesse, holding a jacket. His eyes flitted between us before his attention shifted to me, offering the jacket for me to slide my arms into. He carefully pulled it onto my shoulders and zipped it up.

Once the front door was locked, he encircled an arm around my shoulders, drawing me closer to him and away from Jace.

A second car sat across the road, white and slightly larger, a stark contrast to Jesse's black car, it had to be Jace's.

"We'll meet you at the town square," Jess said coolly.

CANDLES QUEST

"I don't like the way he looks at you," Jesse stated, his tone tight with a mix of anger and something deeper, something almost buried—jealousy.

I turned to Jesse, surprised by the intensity in his voice. "What did he do to make you dislike him so much?"

His grip on the wheel tightened, his fingers extending and then clamping back down on the leather. In the side mirror, I noticed Jace's white car trailing closely behind us.

"It's not what he did," Jesse's jaw tightened. "It's what he didn't do." I furrowed my brow, even more puzzled now. "He didn't fight," Jesse's voice was gruff. "When things got rough, he simply walked away."

The confusion deepened, and I nervously fidgeted with the skin around my fingers. "What do you mean?" I looked at Jesse, his eyes flashed a deep blue.

"It's not my story to tell," Jesse's response was firm, indicating that it was something for Jace to explain. I nodded, making a mental note to speak to Jace about it when I had the chance.

Jesse pulled the car into a parking spot a short distance from the town square, and Jace parked beside us. As we stepped out of the vehicle, a heavy silence hung between us, unbroken as we walked toward the town square.

The anticipation in Hayzun was profound as the sun dipped below the horizon on the eve of the Candle of Protection lighting ceremony.

The town square was aglow with torchlight, casting long shadows that danced in the brisk October breeze. Halloween was fast approaching, and the Candle's unbroken, five-day vigil was about to commence.

As the gathered crowd buzzed with excitement, I couldn't help but feel a sense of wonder mixed with trepidation. The tradition had always held a special place in the hearts of the townsfolk, and the responsibilities of this ceremony were handed down through generations.

Montgomery, our town's mayor, stood beside the grand pedestal where the Candle of Protection would soon find its place. He was clad in his finest attire, a symbol of his role as the protector of Hayzun. I watched as he took a deep breath, his voice carrying the weight of tradition as he addressed the crowd.

"Good people of Hayzun," Montgomery's voice rang out, "we gather here today to light the Candle of Protection, as our ancestors have done for centuries. With each passing year, we honor their wisdom and the bonds that connect us to this town's past."

I joined the hushed reverence of the crowd, my eyes focused on the mayor as he continued. "As the sun sets and darkness encroaches, we kindle this flame, a beacon against the shadows. It's a symbol of our unity, our commitment to protect this place we call home, and our connection to the forces that shape our world."

Montgomery gestured to the elaborate pedestal, where the Candle of Protection stood, tall and unlit. "May this candle burn brightly for the five days leading up to Halloween, as it has for centuries. May it shield us from malevolent spirits, preserve our balance, and guard the town we hold so dear."

With these words, the mayor took a long taper, its flame flickering with promise, and approached the unlit Candle of Protection. I watched with bated breath as the taper's flame met the wick, and the candle slowly came to life, its radiant glow cast an enchanting aura over the gathered crowd.

As the ceremony continued, I felt a sense of unity with my fellow townspeople, bound by tradition and the knowledge that we were protecting Hayzun from the unknown. The Candle's warm, flickering light held the promise of safety, but as the moments passed, I couldn't shake the feeling that trouble loomed on the horizon, its dark presence inching ever closer to our quiet coastal town.

It only broke when we approached the information vender inside the base of the clocktower. A small line of volunteers was quickly shuffled through until we were at the head of the line.

A woman, unknown to me, stood at the forefront, her demeanor projecting a mix of urgency and hope. She ushered our group forward, and her gaze lingered on each volunteer, silent gratitude etched in her eyes.

"Thank you for coming," she began, her voice carrying a blend of determination and concern. She motioned for the others to draw closer—a middle-aged woman, a young couple, and a teenage boy. Something flickered within me, a spark of recognition when I looked at the middle-aged woman, but I pushed it aside, focusing on the task at hand.

"You seven will be paired with…"

"I'll go with them." An officer stepped forward and I recognized her immediately, Gates.

"We'll be covering the area near the old drive-in. When our grid is complete, we will be assigned a new one." Everyone nodded in understanding. "We'll provide a shuttle for those who need it otherwise we will convene in fifteen minutes in the field." Gates rubbed her hands together. "Look for any signs. clothing, hair, markings, Anything, I'll split you into smaller groups when we get their so we can cover as much area as possible" She handed us each a piece of paper. "This is security footage of what she was last seen wearing."

Studying the photo in my hand, I saw a young woman in her twenties, shrouded by her long black hair, concealing her features. Jesse's hand found the small of my back, a silent reassurance amid the building tension.

"We don't have to do this," his voice was a soft whisper in my ear, concern laced within his words.

"Yes, we do," I replied, my determination mingled with a tightening knot in my throat. If I could help find this girl, this individual who had been put in danger just because I existed at this specific point in time with two opposing blood lines coursing through my veins, then I would do whatever I could. I would do whatever was within my power. Jesse nodded, tucking the photo into his pocket.

"Then let's go," he said.

The group made their way outside the clocktower. The chilly breeze carried the scent of saltwater from the nearby coast, adding a touch of unease to the task ahead.

Fifteen minutes later Jesse and I joined Officer Gates, and the other volunteers, forming a tight-knit group as we headed toward the designated area. The atmosphere was tense, yet there was an unspoken unity among us, a shared determination to aid in the search for Piper.

The old drive-in, now a relic of the past, loomed ahead, its weathered sign barely visible in the fading daylight. The broken carcass of the screen stood abandoned in the distance. Jagged and broken pieces of plywood were the only thing left of the once pristine screen where the movies would have been projected. We scattered, combing through the overgrown remnants of the once-thriving entertainment hub. The tall grass whispered as we walked, the occasional creak of rusted metal adding an eerie backdrop to our search.

The evening air was heavy with the scent of damp earth as we made our way through the outskirts of town. My pulse quickened, not just from the chilly October breeze but also from the tension hovering between Jesse and Jace. I hesitated, casting a sideways glance at Jesse, whose expression had turned guarded as he trailed behind, his every movement restrained.

Sensing the weight of his gaze, I turned my attention to Jace, who seemed more at ease despite the unspoken tension. His small smile, though welcoming, held a flicker of something deeper, something he wasn't willing to let surface.

With a gentle motion, he gestured for me to follow, leading us to a quieter stretch where the rustle of leaves and the distant sounds of the searchers faded into the background.

The question lingered on my tongue, a knot formed in my stomach. I took a deep breath, my voice low but steady. "What happened between you two?"

Jace's gaze flicked momentarily toward Jesse, a knowing glint in his eyes. "Did he tell you to ask me?"

"Not in so many words." I wrung my hands. "But yes."

He nodded softly, pocketing his hands.

Jace let out a low, humorless laugh. "It's complicated." His eyes scanned the surrounding area, almost as if ensuring our privacy.

"Complicated seems to be a common theme," I murmured, feeling a surge of frustration at the mysteries that encircled us.

He glanced at me, his features softened. "Our families have a history of conflict, and Jesse and I ... we've been in the middle of it all for a long time. There have been choices, alliances, sacrifices ... some made willingly, others not so much."

The depth of his words lingered between us, a heavy silence settling as we continued walking. I glanced back once more, catching Jesse's eyes briefly before he turned away, his expression unreadable.

The forest grew eerily quiet as I stepped cautiously forward, Jace following close behind. My gaze darted across the ground, searching for any sign of the missing woman, Piper. Leaves crunched underfoot, and the distant rustle of branches hinted at movement, setting my nerves on edge.

"Did you see that?" I asked as I peered ahead.

Jace's response was calm, almost indifferent. "See what?"

A flicker of movement drew my attention, and a knot formed in my stomach. The silhouette of a woman emerged from the trees, a familiar face from our earlier group. The sense of recognition briefly flitted through my mind, but the urgency of the search pushed the thought aside.

As we continued forward, I noticed a glint catching the fading sunlight. My eyes focused on the object in the woman's hand—a blade. Instantly, my pulse quickened, and a shiver crawled down my spine. Her presence felt unsettling, an uneasiness that grew with each step closer.

"You," her voice trembled, filled with accusation, as she pointed the knife in my direction.

Confusion clouded my mind as her accusation hit me.

"Killed my daughter." Her words hit me hard, landing with a weight that settled in my chest. I shook my head, my thoughts a whirlwind of disbelief and alarm.

A hand pressed gently against my back, offering a sense of warmth and reassurance, but it wasn't Jesse. I turned slightly, finding Jace beside me, his touch both protective and guiding.

Instinctively, he positioned himself between the woman and me, shielding me from the sharp tip of the blade.

The woman's anguished eyes bore into mine, accusing me of a crime I hadn't committed. Memories surged within me, piecing together fragmented images—a lifeless figure hanging from a tree, the second victim, and the woman's heart-wrenching grief.

Recognition dawned upon me. She was the mother of the second victim, and I had encountered her after discovering the body. Her accusation was driven by unbearable pain and unfathomable loss, directed at me with trembling hands and tear-filled eyes.

The forest seemed to hold its breath, tension filling the silence Images played in my mind like a montage stopping on one image in particular. I could still see her vividly in my mind like a picture, hanging lifeless from a tree in the forest.

The rustling of leaves indicated the arrival of others in our group, their footsteps halting abruptly in the tense air.

"No," my voice was barely audible, muffled by the overwhelming emotions that surged within me. "I found her that night." I attempted to lean around Jace, eager to offer solace to the distraught woman, but his protective grip held me in place. "I'm so sorry." My cheeks flushed, the tragedy too heavy to bear.

"Lower your weapon," Gates's commanding voice sliced through the tense silence, her gun drawn with the safety clicked off. "Put it down." The woman surged forward, and a sharp shot echoed in my ear as the blade was raised.

The scene unfolded in a blur—a swift, tragic motion. The blade cleaved through her flesh, crimson spilling across her clothes, while the gunshot tore through her shoulder. Horror froze me in place as Jace swiftly turned, enfolding me in his arms and guiding us away. Before I could avert my gaze, I saw the lifeless body slump to the ground, a slit gaping in her throat and a growing pool of blood marking her violent end.

I guess grief can make a person do extreme things.

Overwhelmed by shock and horror, I pressed into Jace's chest, my ears ringing from the cacophony of the tragic events. Another set of arms gently took hold of me, their familiarity offering a semblance of comfort, yet my mind struggled to process what was happening.

I felt myself being moved around, absently answering questions. It was as if my body was present, but I was not.

Warm hands gently turned my face, coaxing me back to awareness. I found myself facing the sight of a gurney carrying the lifeless body away, the scarlet pool of blood left behind seeping into the earth.

"Hey." Jesse's touch was gentle as he smoothed his thumb over my cheek. "Let's go." His eyes scanned my face, trying to reassure me. "This isn't your fault." I nodded, though the weight of guilt hung heavy on my shoulders. His hand rested reassuringly at the small of my back, guiding me toward the car.

I could feel eyes on me stopping me in my tracks.

"Just a minute." I turned scanning the growing crowd behind us, finding the face I was looking for. Jesse grabbed my hand, giving it a squeeze.

"I'll wait here for you." His eyes were sad, but he forced a smile, leaning down to press his lips to my temple. "Then will you let me take you home?"

I nodded turning in his grasp.

I made my way through the crowd toward the figure I'd spotted. He smiled when he saw me but faltered briefly when his eyes glanced past me to where Jesse stood observing us. His smile returned as he refocused on me, yet I noticed the blood staining the right sleeve of his shirt, creeping up to his chest. My gaze trailed from the blood to meet his eyes. He shook his head softly, stepping closer.

"Don't worry about me, Angel," his voice was gentle, trying to reassure me. I moved closer, wrapping my arms around his shoulders.

"Thank you," I whispered against his shoulder. His arms

enveloped me, holding me tight against his chest.

"Anytime." I could feel him glance back to where I knew Jesse stood, as he gave me another squeeze, holding me longer than a normal hug would last.

"I should go." His arms slowly released as I took a step back. His smile fell as I turned to walk back to Jesse.

As we made our way in the direction of the car, I glanced back to see Jace standing under the spotlight of the cast iron streetlamp, hands in his pockets. Within minutes we were back in the car.

Jesse cleared his throat as he pulled out of the parking spot and turned in the direction of his rental. The drive home was silent, save for the clicking of the blinker as we turned.

Entering the rental, Jesse turned to face me after closing the door behind us. "Are you okay?" His concern was evident as I removed my jacket, hanging it on the back of a kitchen chair. He called my name again when he noticed a stray tear rolling down my cheek. Before I could respond, more tears cascaded down my face, and he acted swiftly.

"Hey, hey, hey." Jesse was by my side in an instant, tenderly wiping away the tears with his thumbs. But the floodgates had opened, and I couldn't stop.

He pulled me close, wrapping his arms around me and lifting me off the ground. Seating us on the couch, he cradled me against his chest, allowing the realization of what had just transpired to hit me.

"I feel like all I ever do is cry." I shook my head "She killed herself." My body began to shake against his. "She was so angry, and sad." I looked to him. "She recognized me." The tremors moved to my arms.

"You found her daughter's body," Jesse murmured

softly, wiping my eyes once more. "Of course, she would recognize you." His understanding was comforting, but beneath it all, I felt something deeper, something unspoken that I couldn't quite articulate. I didn't say that to him, but I felt it deep inside.

He eased me down, letting my head rest on his shoulder. His cheek brushed against my hair as he ran a comforting hand up and down my arm, pushing a chill deep inside my bones. I shivered against him.

"Cold?" Jesse's voice was soft as he wrapped a blanket around me, cocooning me in its warmth. "Are you hungry?" I nestled closer, seeking comfort in his presence. "What can I make you?" I nestled closer.

"Nothing," I murmured, not quite ready to let go just yet, not after everything that had transpired.

"Charlie, you need to eat." His concern was evident, his touch gentle against my arm.

"But I don't want you to let go just yet." I recalled the fleeting expression on his face when I hugged Jace, the hint of fear I caught before I left. "You don't have to worry." He hummed softly against me in question. "I saw the look on your face." His hand stilled on my arm. "I know the look of fear."

He stayed still and quiet.

"He helped me tonight. That's all."

He cleared his throat.

"What do you want to eat?" he asked, trying to shift the focus.

"A grilled cheese?" I suggested, craving something simple and comforting. "And for you to tell me about you and your past." Jesse's breath caught, a weighty pause hanging between us.

"Why don't you go have a hot shower? I'll make you your grilled cheese, and then I will answer any questions you have." He tipped his head to the side. "But only if you do the same for me."

"What could you even want to know?" I asked, my curiosity piqued.

"Go shower," he gently urged, his hand resuming its comforting motions on my arm. "You need to warm up."

EMBRACE OF FEATHERS

I sat at the kitchen table, with the plate of food in front of me, feeling a knot of apprehension tighten in my stomach. Jesse took the seat opposite mine, his posture relaxed yet attentive.

"What do you want to know?" His hands clasped together on the table, a mix of emotions flickered across his face.

I hesitated, nervously picking at the grilled cheese on my plate before the words spilled out, unfiltered. "Are those for all the people you have killed?" I asked as I glanced at the faint scars on his forearms, a silent testament to his past.

"Right off the bat?" He shook his head slightly, his gaze steady. "Yes," he confirmed. His voice was soft, laden with the weight of his admission. Hearing the confirmation sent a shiver down my spine, a stark realization settling heavily in my chest. I pushed the plate away, feeling a wave of nausea rising within me.

"You need to eat," Jesse insisted, gently nudging the plate back in front of me. I reluctantly picked up the grilled cheese, forcing down a bite, struggling against the turmoil churning inside.

"What does that necklace mean?" I gestured toward the pendant nestled against his chest, hoping to shift the focus away from the discomfort.

"Not so fast, it's my turn." Jesse's tone held a quiet resolve. I took another bite, my apprehension growing with each passing second. "What is your earliest memory?"

I glanced at Jesse, feeling the weight of his question as I delved into the labyrinth of my memories, each one a tangled thread waiting to be unraveled. A knot formed in my throat as I attempted to navigate through the haze of the past, trying to pinpoint the earliest recollection.

A touch, warm and reassuring, slid over my hand, drawing my attention back to Jesse. He leaned forward in his chair, his eyes reflecting a mixture of concern and understanding, and gently rested his hand over mine.

"Forget I asked," he murmured, his voice laced with empathy.

"No." I met his gaze, my expression a mix of uncertainty and determination. "It's just that … my earliest memory seems too late." Jesse's brows furrowed; confusion written all over his face.

"The first thing I remember is my dad taking me to work with him at the clinic for the first time." As I spoke, realization dawned on Jesse's face. "That was when I was at least seven." I added as I glanced down at my hands, feeling the disappointment. "Memories usually form much earlier than that though, don't they?" I asked. Though I knew the answer already—they did.

Jesse's concern deepened, and he shifted in his chair, a clear sign of his contemplation. He reached out, pulling his chair closer and encircling both of my hands in his.

"It could be nothing," he offered, his voice soft, attempting to provide solace. I looked up at him, my eyes reflecting a mixture of resignation and confusion.

"When is it ever nothing?" The question slipped from my lips before I could stop it. Jesse started to respond but then hesitated, his thoughts clearly wrestling with his words.

In a quiet gesture, he stood, gently coaxing me up from the table to stand by his side.

He guided me down the hallway, his steps deliberate yet gentle, leading us toward his bedroom. An uneasy knot twisted in my stomach, luring bile to the edge of my throat. Jesse halted outside his bedroom door, turning to face me. His eyes studied my expression, he must have noticed the flash of fear that danced across my face, but he remained silent.

"Wait here," he said softly, a reassurance without making me feel inferior.

I waited while he disappeared only to return a moment later with a blanket in his hands.

"Come with me." His voice was calm and warm as he beckoned me. We crossed the hall, and he pushed open the door to his right, ushering us onto a small wooden porch. A rush of cool night air enveloped us as he closed the door behind, plunging us into darkness. Jesse's hand found mine, leading me further into the night until he seated me beside him, draping the blanket over my shoulders.

I winced as my leg brushed against his, an involuntary reaction that didn't go unnoticed by him.

"How's your leg?" His voice was gentle, barely audible in the quiet night around us.

"It's okay," I breathed out softly, feeling his arm slide around my shoulders, pulling me closer to his warmth.

"Look up." His hand tilted my head back gently. I strained my eyes against the darkness, allowing them to adjust to the night sky above.

The storm had passed, leaving behind a canvas of twinkling stars. They glimmered like scattered diamonds against the vast expanse of the sky, painting a breathtaking masterpiece above us.

His breaths slowed, a quiet rhythm in the night as he leaned back, bringing me along gently.

"Thank you," I murmured, feeling a sense of calmness enveloping us.

"For what?" his voice was soft, carrying a hint of curiosity. I gestured toward the sky above us, its expanse littered with stars.

"For showing me that beauty still exists, even when your world is falling apart. Even if they are just the tiniest embers of light," I explained, my gaze fixated on the twinkling stars. The stars seemed to hold a silent conversation above us, each one a small glimmering beacon amid the vast darkness, their brilliance cutting through the night like whispers of hope.

I felt my body shift, as I was lifted into the air. Cool air ripped at my exposed skin, being replaced by warmth as my body was enveloped in softness.

Calm washed over me, quieting my mind, and I nestled deeper into the comforting warmth. It held me close, a haven I knew I could trust, an assurance that it would never bring harm.

The warmth shifted, drawing me closer still, a reminder that I wasn't alone. I leaned into it, finding solace in the hands that held me close. I wrapped my arms around, seeking comfort in their presence.

"Charlie?" his voice, a gentle murmur, accompanied the warm embrace as he rested his chin atop my head, gently rubbing a warm hand along my back. His fingers brushed against my skin, and though he recoiled, fearing to unearth unwanted memories, I found a rare sense of peace in that moment.

"It's okay," I murmured softly, reassuring him. He hesitated, keeping a respectful distance. "I trust you."

When he didn't move, I lifted my head, meeting his gaze. His eyes, faintly glowing, searched my face. "I'm tired of always being afraid," I confessed, feeling an unexpected sense of vulnerability. His gaze didn't leave me as I reached up, grabbing the fabric of his shirt in my hands.

He looked at me for a moment longer, then, as if finding an unspoken understanding, his hand extended toward my skin again. His touch, warm and tentative, slid under the fabric of my shirt, his fingers settling lightly at the small of my back.

I remained calm, and he exhaled a breath he seemed to be holding. His hand ventured further up, a faint smile playing at the corners of his mouth. The sensation of his touch, once alien, felt oddly comforting in that moment.

"How long was I asleep?" I blinked, trying to shake off the remnants of drowsiness.

"Not too long. I didn't want you to get cold," his words were gentle, carrying a sense of care that warmed me more than any blanket could. For the first time since my father was alive, I felt secure and cared for.

"Thank you." The words slipped out, gratitude flooding my heart. It was more than just the act of bringing me inside; it was the unexpected warmth and care that surrounded his actions.

"Just brought you inside, Sweetheart." The name hung in the air, a softness that seemed to catch him off guard. I smiled, feeling the tension ease from his posture.

"Not just for that." His gaze lingered on my face. "For showing me that it doesn't always have to be scary." I briefly brushed away the thoughts of the recent ordeal, finding solace in the present moment, within this protective bubble with him.

"I'm sorry I got angry earlier." I placed my palms against his chest, feeling the steady beat of his heart beneath my touch as he spoke.

"I just feel overly protective of you and seeing him …" his words faltered, carrying a weight of vulnerability. "He would take what matters to me just to make a point." My heart clenched, understanding he meant me. He closed his eyes briefly. "We have a complicated history."

Jace had given me a glimpse into his past, but I knew there was more to the story.

"You don't have to tell me." I reached up, my palm

cupping his cheek. His eyes met mine as they opened.

"But I want you to know everything. I don't want you to have questions when it comes to me." There was a depth of sincerity in his voice that touched me.

"How about you tell me when all of this is over?" I offered, feeling his hand on my back as his other hand covered mine against his cheek.

"He chose to go against me when I needed him most." Jesse's voice was laced with a mixture of regret and frustration as he began to recount the intricacies of their past, his eyes fixed on a distant point, lost in the shadows of memories that haunted him. I listened intently; my eyes fixed on Jesse as he recounted the story that had etched its mark on their lives.

"Years ago, there was an incident," he continued, his voice faltering momentarily. "A situation that tested our loyalty and trust in each other."

He paused, as if to gather his thoughts.

"Jace was faced with a choice between what he believed was right and our bond," Jesse explained, his voice tinged with an indescribable ache.

A heavy silence enveloped us as I grappled with the weight of those words.

"He fell from grace," Jesse continued, his expression etched with sorrow. "The choices he made led to a fracture in our relationship, a betrayal that I never thought possible."

The pain in his eyes spoke volumes, a testament to the depth of the rift that had torn through their bond.

I reached out, instinctively wanting to comfort him, to offer solace for the wounds that time hadn't healed.

"It's not your fault," I murmured, my voice a soft reassurance amid the turmoil of emotions.

Jesse's gaze met mine, gratitude and pain mingling in his eyes. We sat in the quiet aftermath of his revelation, two souls entwined in a story of shattered trust and the remnants of a bond that had once been unbreakable.

"Can I kiss you?" The words slipped out, surprising both of us. His face lit up with a wide smile.

"You don't have to ask." He stayed still knowing I would feel better if I was in control. "I would never do anything you didn't want me to. I would never do anything to hurt you." His eyes held a softness that reassured me, a gentleness that put me at ease.

I searched his eyes, looking for something I didn't find. All that was there was a sort of gentleness.

Pulling back slightly, I gauged his reaction. His breath had quickened, but he remained still, respecting my pace. Encouraged by his patience, I leaned in again, letting the moment linger. This time, I allowed myself to be pulled into the kiss as he deepened it. I tried my best to keep my mind clear, leaving only him and me, pushing everything else out of the way.

he shifted, rolling to place himself above me, ensuring his weight was supported. My body tensed slightly, a shiver coursing through me, but I tried to conceal it. As soon as he noticed something was off, he lifted his head, searching my eyes.

"Charlie?"

I pinched my eyes shut not wanting to see pity in his face.

"Please look at me." I opened my eyes, reaching up to try and pull him back down to me, but he didn't budge.

"Jess," I murmured. "Please."

"You're shaking," was all he said.

"It's different this time." I left my palms pressed to the side of his face. "It's not because I am afraid." He thought for a moment before the worry turned to relief and a small smile filled his eyes.

He leaned down, once again pressing a small kiss to my lips before rolling us over, pulling me onto his chest.

"Get some sleep." He pulled the blankets up around us, cocooning me against him, before leaving a kiss atop my head. "Thank you." His words warmed my skin. "For letting me in."

"I want to see you." His eyes searched my face. Trying to figure out the meaning behind my words. "All of you." I placed my finger in the hollow of his throat, feeling his pulse quicken beneath my touch, and the metal of the pendant.

"Are you sure?"

I nodded, swallowing hard. He leaned forward, placing a long, slow, kiss to my lips.

"Okay then." He guided me up from the bed, leading me across the hall by the hand. Behind a washer and dryer there was a staircase, concealed from view. "Downstairs."

"Downstairs?" He led the way downstairs, his hand warm and reassuring in mine. The basement, though dimly lit, appeared around half the size of the upper floor of the rental.

Jess switched on a small lamp beside a comfortable-looking couch, revealing a fireplace set into the wall. A smile spread across my face, and Jess let out a soft chuckle at my reaction.

"I didn't know this was down here." His arms wrapped around me, pulling me back against his chest.

"I don't use it often." His breath warmed my skin.

"We should."

"We?" he echoed. I felt the heat of embarrassment creep up my neck and into my checks.

"I'm sorry." He spun me to face him, eyes hard.

"Don't ever apologize to me." He took my face in his hands. "We," he emphasized the word, "I fucking love the sound of that." His fingers wound their way into my hair. "Are you ready?" He rested his forehead against mine.

"Yes." He stood back taking a deep breath before he reached down, pulling his shirt up and over his head, throwing it onto the armrest of the couch.

"Come here." He pulled me into his outstretched arms. "Now's your last chance to back out."

"Never." His bare skin was warm against me.

"Close your eyes." I did as he said feeling him cocoon me against his chest. "Keep them closed." I felt my body be enveloped in a soft silky warmth, brushing against my exposed skin. A soft glow visible through my eyelids.

"You can open them."

Slowly, I opened my eyes looking up. The glow came from the skin in the hollow of his throat fanning out into a ring around the base of his neck.

The warmth lifted from my body furling out on either side of us.

His wings were stunning.

Raven colored feathers spread from his back turning a stark white at the very tips.

I gasped, stepping back.

"You're beautiful." He chuckled "Can I touch them?" He nodded, taking his bottom lip into his mouth, watching as I raised my hand gently touching my fingers to the feathers exiting his back.

He shivered against my touch, closing his eyes. I slipped behind him running my fingers along where his wings exited his skin. His breath hitched and I pulled my hand back like someone had burned me.

"I'm sorry, does it hurt?" He brought them in spinning to face me.

"No." The pained look on his face fold me otherwise.

"What's wrong?" I pressed my palms to his chest, feeling his skin beneath my fingers. "Talk to me."

"I've never shared this," he admitted, his gaze fixated on his wings. "Not like this." His hands covered mine, still resting on his chest. "They remind me of the darkness, of all the bad things I've ever done." His head bowed. "They get darker with every sin I'm summoned to commit." The realization dawned on me, the reason behind the stark contrast in colors now unveiled. "I was afraid you would look at me differently." I shook my head stepping forward. "But you didn't."

"No," I affirmed, smiling gently. "I know who you are, Jess." His name on my lips seemed to affect him deeply.

Reaching out again, I touched the delicate feathers near his arm. "Look at me." With a quick movement, his wings retracted, encircling us, pulling me close against his chest. His warm breath brushed my face as he whispered, "Can it just be you and me for a while?"

"Just here and now, nothing else," he said, as I nodded feeling the relief enter his body. "You are my ember of light, Charlie." His words resonated with me, recalling the moment on the porch, but instead I was encased in the ring of white-tipped feathers.

"Here and now." I murmured. His fingers shook as he ran a hand along my cheek, coming down to cup the side of my jaw.

"I don't want to scare you." His breath danced over my lips, a hand sliding down to my neck. "But..." He hesitated, lips hovering close to mine. I reached for his arms.

"I want you," his words echoed, and my heart started to quicken. "I just want you close." His arms enveloped me, drawing me into the warmth of his chest. Held securely, he let out a deep breath, and my heartbeat steadied, understanding what he meant.

"You should get some sleep," his voice resonated from deep within his chest.

"Here and now," I murmured, meeting his gaze briefly before his lips captured mine, his hands pulling me closer.

I was slowly becoming more comfortable with his gentle touches, but my heart raced when he lifted my body, wrapping my legs around his waist. His wings retracted, leaving a tingling sensation where they had been.

Jess carried me up the stairs, never breaking our kiss as he pushed open the bedroom door. A shuddering breath escaped me, mingling with his fervent kisses.

"Jess." I gripped his arms tightly. He gently placed me on the bed, taking his place beside me. "Jess?" My voice quivered with a hint of panic, but he drew me close against his chest.

"Here and now," he whispered. "Forget your past, just be here with me."

"I can't," I murmured, feeling my lip quiver.

"Yes, you can."

"Jess."

"I'm not asking you to do anything." His lips pressed

tenderly against my forehead. "Just lay with me." I nodded, relief washing over me knowing he didn't expect anything more. His chest rose and fell in a soothing rhythm, the warmth of his body easing my tensions. "Sleep." I nestled closer, feeling a sense of foolishness for panicking earlier. I longed so desperately not to be afraid.

"Charlie." I slowly felt the fog lifting from my mind as my body woke up. "It's time to wake up."

My eyes focused in on my surroundings.

"Are you sure you still want to go to work?"

I lifted my head so I could look at him.

"I need to." His eyes fell.

"If this is about money, I can help."

I smiled sweetly at him.

"Yes, I need the money." I sat up in the bed. "But they need me too." I pulled my hair back from my face. "Miles can't do paperwork to save his life." I chuckled softly.

"What about the Stigmatophile?" I raised an eyebrow in question. "The tattooed wonder." Jesse's response carried a hint of tension that caught my attention.

"Mason?" Jesse shifted, sitting up beside me. "He started at the clinic almost a year ago. He's helped me through some of the times where I didn't have enough money to pay the bills." I felt a knot form in my throat, but I forced a smile and stood, gathering clothes, and heading to the bathroom. I heard Jesse stand.

"You should let me look at your leg so I can change the bandage." I stood in the bathroom waiting for him.

When he didn't walk in, I peeked back into the bedroom. He still stood by the edge of the bed; his arms crossed loosely across his chest.

He was waiting for my permission to follow me.

"Are you coming?" I invited him, watching as his hands fell to his sides before he followed.

He grabbed supplies from the drawer, arranging them on the counter. I pulled down my leggings on one side, giving him access to the bandage.

Jesse meticulously tended to my injured leg; his touch tender yet purposeful as he knelt in front of me. Each movement was deliberate, but it still made me wince as he carefully removed the bandage, revealing the reddened skin beneath. His focused expression softened slightly as he noticed my discomfort.

"Sorry, I'll be gentle," he assured me, his voice calm and soothing.

His gentle touch as he cleaned the area felt almost contradictory to the stinging sensation. I winced again as the cream was applied, offering relief but also a new kind of discomfort. I breathed through the pain, managing a grateful smile as he smoothed the fresh bandage over my skin before rising to his feet.

"Thank you," I murmured, trying to convey my gratitude despite the underlying unease.

"Don't thank me yet. There's another vial on the counter in the kitchen," Jesse mentioned, the faintest trace of concern in his voice.

My stomach twisted at the reminder of the vial. I took a deep breath, gathered my resolve, and left the room. I forced the contents of the vial down my throat before stepping outside. The cold air bit my cheeks, the chilly breeze providing an unwelcome contrast to the warmth of the indoors.

When I got into the car, Jesse was already waiting, his eyes fixed on the road ahead. The atmosphere inside the car felt heavier than usual. His features, usually relaxed, were taut with an underlying tension that I couldn't decipher. His shoulders were squared, his jaw clenched subtly, betraying the facade of calm he was trying to maintain.

"Ready?" his voice was measured, his eyes flickering briefly to mine through the rearview mirror.

"I'm going to be fine," I replied, trying to reassure myself as much as him. Despite my words, an uneasy feeling lingered in the pit of my stomach, a gnawing worry that refused to dissipate.

"I still don't like this," Jesse pulled the car into the clinic parking lot, stopping in a spot near the front door. I turned to face him.

"I will be fine." I reached over grabbing his hand. He rubbed his thumb along my skin.

"Wait for me to pick you up." Jesse leaned over, reaching into the center console. He took my hand and flipped it over, scrawling a string of numbers along my palm with a pen he had retrieved. I couldn't help but smile at his gesture.

"You know I have your number on file," I teased lightly.

"Yes, but now it's extra close in case you need it," he quipped back, a hint of a grin playing on his lips. I chuckled softly before unclipping my seatbelt and grabbing my work bag.

"Please be safe," he insisted as I prepared to step out of the car.

"I will." I nodded, opening the car door and making my way toward the clinic.

Before I could take another step, I heard the car door click open. In a swift motion, warm, arms encircled my waist, pulling me gently back against a solid chest. I felt a rush of warmth at his closeness.

"I mean it, Charlie," his voice, low and husky, resonated in my ear. "I have a few things to do today, but you're my priority."

Turning within his embrace, I met his gaze. He brushed a stray strand of hair from my face with a gentle touch, his fingers lingering for a moment.

"I'll be back to get you later." His eyes held a hint of concern as they searched my face. "I shouldn't be late, but if I'm going to be, I'll call."

I nodded softly in understanding.

"Five o'clock?" he confirmed, seeking my agreement. I met his gaze with a reassuring nod, feeling a sense of trust and reassurance in his words.

STOLEN SILENCE

By the time five o'clock arrived, I made sure everything was in order before I headed outside, scanning the street for Jesse's car. As minutes ticked by, I couldn't shake off a sense of restlessness, wondering if something had delayed him. I reassured myself that he had promised to call the clinic if there were any changes in his plans.

The minutes stretched into what felt like an eternity, and I couldn't help but feel a pang of worry. The knot of anxiety tightened in my stomach, and I began to pace slightly, trying to keep my unease at bay.

As the sky started to darken with the onset of evening, I decided to give Jesse a call, entering the clinic once again. The phone rang a few times before going to voicemail. I left a brief message, trying to sound nonchalant despite the tinge of concern in my voice before heading back out.

The sense of uncertainty clung to me. I couldn't help but wonder what could be keeping him, hoping fervently that he was all right. Minutes turned into an hour, and I found myself torn between staying put and taking action.

"I can drive you if you want." Mason paused, stepping out of the shelter. The late hours meant he had stayed behind to help. "I have time before my date."

"Date?" I smiled up at him. "The girl from the shelter?" His cheeks flushed.

"No," he hesitated again. "Her brother." I grinned, the pieces of Mason's personal life starting to click into place.

"I'm happy for you," I said, and he nodded, a persistent smile on his face.

I gathered my work bag, ready to leave.

Jesse had told me to wait for him, but I knew Mason and I didn't want to sit around and wait for another hour. I'd call and let him know from the landline, so he didn't worry.

Sitting in the car, I fastened my seatbelt, the cool click resonating as I waited for Mason to maneuver out of the parking spot. The amber hues of the setting sun cast elongated shadows, painting the ground with scattered leaves, a mosaic of autumn colors spread beneath the car's tires.

"Take the next right. It's the fastest," I instructed, my voice carrying a subtle urgency. The anticipation of reaching home and the comfort of familiar surroundings were the only thoughts circling in my mind.

As we approached the turn, Mason didn't slow down. "Here," I pointed, the edges of panic now creeping into my voice, but the car continued along its straight path, the streetlights flickering by in a blur.

"What are you doing?" My heart began to hammer in my

chest, a knot forming in the pit of my stomach, dread slowly clawing its way in. Mason's sympathetic expression only added to my growing anxiety.

"This really wasn't my idea," his voice held a tremor, betraying a mix of fear and helplessness. My grip on the seat tightened.

"Please. Stop the car.," my words came out strained, attempting to hide the fear edging my voice. I struggled to maintain composure, attempting to grasp the situation's escalating gravity.

"Charlotte, you know I can't do that," Mason's voice was steady, almost regretful, yet he kept his foot on the accelerator.

"Mason, please." My pleas fell on deaf ears as he stayed silent, a conflict stirring behind his eyes. "It's been you all along." The words hung heavily between us, a heavy weight of betrayal in the air.

"I'm just the errand boy." His admission was soaked in anguish, implying coercion or manipulation beyond his control.

Fear bubbled in my chest as I sat.

My words came out panicked, my gaze snapping to the window. The world outside blurred into a swirl of colors as a sharp pinch stung the left side of my neck. Shocked, I turned back to Mason, my eyes widening at the sight of the hypodermic syringe retracting from my skin. He wore a small, pitying look, his features shrouded in an unsettling calmness.

"I wasn't sure how much to give you," he murmured, his voice distant, detached. "I assumed about as much as a small golden retriever." A jolt of disbelief mingled with the buzzing sensation rapidly spreading from my arms, the sedative already seeping through my body. Did he just compare me to a dog? I tried to voice my shock, but my words slurred and tangled, lost in the fog already clouding my thoughts. My arms fell, limp weights at my sides, leaving me helplessly sinking into the seat.

We continued to drive, Mason steering the car, my consciousness slipping away bit by bit. As we headed through town, moving farther and farther north before veering east, the familiar streets became hazy, the edges blurring into obscurity. I struggled to keep my eyes open, but the sedative was an insistent force, coercing my eyelids to droop, the world around me slipping into a disoriented daze.

I fought the encroaching darkness, my eyelids heavy and uncooperative, only managing a slit of light filtering through. The effects of the sedative rendered me incapable of resistance, yet some sliver of consciousness persisted in this numbed state. Suddenly, I was yanked from the car, my arms dragged from my sides as I was pulled into a disorienting fall. My legs gave way, buckling beneath me, and my head snapped forward upon impact.

The voices around me echoed, creating a disorienting symphony of sounds. Two men hauled me out of the car, their rough hands gripping me, dragging my body across the rugged ground. Mason's presence loomed close behind, an unsettling shadow in the chaos. Every move sent rocks slicing into my knees, their sharp edges cutting through skin. I cried out in pain, but my voice was muffled, barely audible through the fog of sedation.

The effects of the sedative still lingered, blurring my vision and numbing my senses. The world swayed and spun as they dragged me through the dirt, my body rendered helpless against their force. The air grew colder with each passing moment, carrying the scent of damp soil and the earthy musk of the terrain.

Struggling against the sedative's grip, I attempted to lift my head, to make sense of my surroundings, but everything was enveloped in darkness. Eventually, I let my head drop back, the thud of it meeting the cold ground reverberating through my skull. Soon after, my arms were seized again, yanked roughly behind me. I winced as the rough fibers of a rope bit into my skin, securing my arms tightly to a nearby post.

I tipped my head back, feeling the relief of resting against the wooden post, a small comfort amid the commotion.

With a heavy effort, I pushed my eyelids open, straining to adjust to the surrounding darkness. A small carbide lamp cast a dim glow about five feet in front of me, reminiscent of the lamps once used by miners. I was in the old Hayzun mine, hidden behind the water tower.

Movement in the shadows drew my attention. A figure loomed, barely discernible. "Mason?" My words came out strained, and I coughed, my head rolling weakly to the side.

A mass sat huddled nearby, a few feet to my left. The outline of a person, the missing woman, lay on the ground, her body rising and falling with deep, labored breaths. Long strands of hair sprawled over the dirt, a disheveled halo around her head. She had been here the whole time, just out of reach.

I felt the urgency rise within me—I needed to help her, to get us out of this terrifying predicament.

"Mason?" Finally, his face emerged from the shadows, his expression strained, his features contorted with discomfort. A red flush crept up his neck, coloring his cheeks.

"I'm sorry, Charlotte," his voice held an undertone of regret as he took a hesitant step closer. "If it were up to me, I'd let you go."

"Mason, please?" My plea was feeble, almost a whisper. He shook his head, kneeling in front of me.

"You know I can't." A solitary tear traced a path down my cheek, glistening in the faint light.

"She needs to die by your hands," his words reverberated in the dark cavern, echoing like a sinister mantra.

"What?" I struggled to grasp his meaning, the confusion and fear etching deeper lines on my face. His voice continued, but my mind could only latch onto the final haunting phrase.

"Just like the others."

"Excuse me?" my voice trembled, a mixture of shock and disbelief shook through my words. He recoiled, fading into the shadows, leaving behind a chilling silence that rang in my ears. "I had nothing to do with their deaths."

The rough, fraying wood scraped against my skin as I rubbed my hands against it, feeling the sharpness prick at my flesh. His words echoed, intensifying the overwhelming sense of urgency. *She needs to die by your hand, just like the others.*

"My visions they—"

"They weren't visions, Charlotte. They were suppressed memories."

Memories? The thought sent shockwaves through my mind, cascading memories into vivid images, and I found myself reeling backward. My heart hammered erratically against my chest, anxiety churning my insides.

"I don't understand," I stuttered, trying to make sense of the fragments flooding my mind. The haunting dreams that felt so vividly real, all seemed to intertwine into an inexplicable maze. "What do you mean, memories?" my voice quivered, panic and uncertainty tightening its grip around my throat.

"For the ritual to work, you had to take the sacrifices." He stood, backing away.

His presence loomed, shadowed and haunting. "I'm not your enemy, Charlotte," he uttered, his voice laced with an odd mixture of sadness and frustration. His eyes, once familiar, now held an enigmatic intensity that froze me in place.

The chilling clarity began to pierce through the fog of confusion, my mind grappling to piece together the fragments that felt like shards of a shattered reality.

He remained silent, fading into the darkness, leaving behind a trail of unanswered questions and unsettling revelations. I was left alone, the echoes of his words reverberating in the chamber of my mind, setting off a relentless cycle of unanswered queries and a pressing urgency to make sense of it all.

The rope, thick and abrasive, bound my wrists tightly, causing my skin to itch and burn. I strained against the coarse bindings, the splintered beam adding to the discomfort. With persistent determination, I focused on freeing myself, feeling the fibers of the rope fray under the strain. My wrists were raw, but the desperation to survive propelled me forward. I refused to succumb in this desolate place, not while another soul lay helpless beside me.

With a final snap, my wrists broke free, the relief washing over me as I caught my breath. I cautiously scanned the shadows, ensuring no one lingered in the periphery, before slowly making my way to Piper. Her limp form lay in the dirt, her stillness unsettling. A piece of her scalp was missing, an awful wound crusted with dried blood. I shook the disturbing image from my mind and gently pressed my fingers to her neck. Her pulse, faint and feeble, whispered of life's fragile grip, but it was there—she was alive.

"Can you hear me?" my voice barely carried in the cavern's eerie silence. "Piper?" Her fluttering eyes gave no response, urging me to act swiftly. I positioned myself behind her, my fingers quickly assessing the knots of her bindings.

Desperation fueled my efforts as I fumbled with the knots, urging her silently to hold on, to wait just a little longer for rescue. Each knot I unraveled heightened my anxiety. How long had she been here? The final knot fell apart in my trembling hands, but before I could react, the rope was yanked away violently, pulled by an unseen force.

A sickening thud followed by the metallic sound of a spike embedding into wood jolted me backward. In the darkness, I rushed around the beam to reach the girl. As I grasped her arms, warmth oozed between my fingers, making my skin slick. The sight paralyzed me—a long metal spike protruded from her chest, fresh blood pooling around her lifeless form. She was gone. Dead. Just as Mason had ominously predicted.

Gathering my shattered resolve, I staggered to my feet, clutching the carbide lamp, my heart pounding in terror. I headed in the direction I hoped was the way out, the darkness pressing in around me. My legs wobbled under the weight of the sedative.

A sharp metallic click shattered the silence, reverberating off the tunnel walls. I froze, slowly turning to identify the source. A man emerged from the shadows, a gun aimed, its barrel pointing directly at me. Recognition dawned, mixed with horror, as I recognized the face behind the firearm.

"Mayor Montgomery," my voice quivered with fear and desperation as I stumbled toward him, my body shaking uncontrollably. "Please," I begged, tears streaming down my face. "Piper, the missing girl…" I struggled to speak through my sobs. "I found her, but…"

"You killed her." My Panic rose once again.

"No, when I untied her," I protested, my head shaking in disbelief.

"Go," the mayor gestured toward the way I came, his gun still pointed in my direction. "Now."

My chest constricted at the threat in his voice. I turned and headed deeper into the maze of the mine, his gun's cold gaze pressing into my back.

We returned to the small chamber. My broken bindings lay discarded, but Piper was nowhere to be seen.

"She was here, I swear," I pleaded desperately, scanning the shadows, but there was only the chilling silence and a pool of blood-soaked gravel.

"Tie yourself back up," his command sliced through the darkness.

"What?" My voice caught in my throat, a growing sense of terror taking hold.

He raised the gun again, aiming at my chest. "Now."

A new wave of fear surged through me. He was a part of this sinister plot.

"You?" The word slipped from my lips, disbelief mingling with horror as a sly smirk crawled across his face. My gaze darted between the gun, my bindings, and the exit behind the mayor. "Why?"

"I'm not here for pleasantries," he snapped, his tone chilling. "Quickly, please."

In a split-second decision, my legs moved. Noise erupted in the chamber, a searing pain shooting through my left thigh, forcing me down to my knees. My vision blurred, white spots clouding my sight.

"Running?" His voice echoed, distorted by the pain racking my body. "Now is that any way to treat your father?" His words sliced through the haze, stirring confusion. Father? I pressed my palms into my eyes, fighting against the agony and the disorienting revelation.

His chuckle resonated in the chamber, echoing against the cold, stone walls. The shock and confusion etched across my face only seemed to amuse him further.

"Andras Harper, nice to meet you," he declared, tucking his gun into his waistband. "Imagine my reaction when I learned the first void soul in centuries was my daughter." His admission sent shivers down my spine, disbelief mingling with the searing pain in my thigh. "A daughter I didn't even know I had."

I attempted to process his words, but before I could fully grasp their weight, two sets of calloused hands seized me, yanking me backward into the dirt. The same pair that had forcibly pulled me from Mason's car, I presumed. My arms were roughly bound, the ropes digging into my skin, as I watched a dark trail of dirt meet my leg, where it pooled beneath me, mingling with the crimson flow from the bullet wound.

My breaths came in frantic gasps, my pulse thundering in my ears as the reality of my circumstances sank in. The pain in my leg pulsed rhythmically, threatening to swallow me whole. Yet, the shock of Andras being my father gnawed at my mind, clashing with the immediate danger at hand.

Andras towered above me, a sinister smile spanning his face as he paced around, surveying his surroundings with a chilling calmness. The two figures restraining me remained silent, their presence heavy and menacing in the dimly lit chamber.

My consciousness fluttered back into focus, the world swimming hazily before my eyes. The sharp pang in my leg surged through me, dragging me back to the grim reality of the situation. I blinked hard, trying to clear my vision, and found Mason kneeling beside me, concern etched into his features.

"Mason," I rasped, his name catching in my dry throat. His hands gingerly hovered over the wound, assessing the damage.

His eyes met mine, a mix of determination and worry. "You've lost a lot of blood," he murmured, the gravity of the situation evident in his tone.

Without hesitation, he swiftly unfastened his belt, a makeshift tourniquet in his hands. My breath hitched as he looped it around my leg, cinching it tightly above the bullet hole. Agony seared through me, a guttural cry escaping my lips.

He tore my pant leg, revealing the gruesome wound left by the bullet. With practiced hands, he packed gauze into the cavity, pressing it firmly before binding it in place with torn fabric, creating a makeshift bandage.

"I bet you missed your date then, huh?" I managed a bitter chuckle through the pain, trying to mask my discomfort.

Mason's gaze softened, but he remained silent, his focus intent on staunching the blood flow.

"Are you even gay?" my words escaped before I could stop them, a futile attempt to divert my mind from the searing agony.

The question lingered in the air, but Mason didn't respond. Instead, his attention remained fixated on the injury, his silence permeating the tense atmosphere.

"I didn't lie about everything, Charlotte," Mason murmured, his fingers fidgeting with the makeshift bandage.

"Is that supposed to be comforting?" I grimaced, the throbbing in my head intensifying as I leaned back against the rough post. "Try not to fall asleep," I chuckled weakly, trying to mask the rising pain.

"Don't pretend to worry about me. Blood doesn't make family," I spat out before he could respond. He stood abruptly and strode deeper into the murky tunnels.

Alone, fatigue clawed at me. Staying awake became an insurmountable task, but I fought against the encroaching darkness. I couldn't afford to succumb to unconsciousness, fearing I might not wake up if I did.

Thoughts of escape flickered, but the memory of the unintended tragedy loomed large. Mason's warning about the frayed wood, the accidental death of Piper—it all weighed heavily on me. Nausea swirled in my stomach at the memory of the metallic sound as the spike pierced her chest.

My eyelids threatened to droop, but I willed them to stay

open. I couldn't afford to die here. Every heartbeat seemed to echo in the wound on my leg, a grim reminder of the blood I was losing. I felt the pulse intensify, signaling another drop seeping into the hastily-packed gauze.

23

TANGLED ROOTS

Hands seized me, jolting me from my stupor. My head spun, their voices blurring into incoherent chatter behind me. How much blood had I lost? My bindings loosened, but my exhausted body lacked the strength to resist when they yanked my arms, forcing me upright. My legs faltered beneath me, inciting a string of curses from my captors.

"Stand up!" the voice was gruff, jabbing me roughly in the stomach. My legs felt useless, my breaths ragged and loud. "Useless."

They hoisted me up, carrying me between them. Agonizing pain shot through my wounded leg.

I struggled to yell as they ferried me deeper into the mine. We must have taken the left tunnel; the right had collapsed long ago, entombing miners inside. The memorial plaque on the entrance testified to the lives lost. The mine's instability loomed, the threat of further collapse omnipresent.

The distant cawing of birds echoed—a haunting sound that signaled the depths of peril—Valing.

Thrown violently to the ground, a piercing scream erupted, shattering the air and sending shockwaves through my being. My head snapped back, meeting the cool earth with a sickening thud.

Fogged, sunken eyes stared back at me. Bloat had taken over the body, and given it in ungodly shade of blue, but I knew instantly who it was. My mother's decomposing body lying in the dirt beside me. Nausea surged as I confronted the sight. Fluids oozed from bloated tears in her skin, a grim testament to how long she had been dead.

"What did you do?" My eyes blurred with tears. We weren't on good terms, but I never wanted to see her dead.

"Oh that." Andras's face contorted. "She gave up your whereabouts pretty easy, but loose ends and all." He shrugged as if that was a good enough answer to my question. A foray of flies had taken up residence on her corpse.

I was yanked up once more, jostled around, and bound again. My eyelids fought against the weight, struggling to stay open. My blurred vision caught the unsettling gaze of a large Valing seated nearby, its eyes flicking over me in a jerky, mechanical manner.

"Lysander, that's no way to treat our guest," Andras's voice echoed through the cavern, his face illuminated by a scattered array of candles that cast eerie shadows on the walls. I met his gaze, a mix of defiance and unease taking over. There were countless questions clawing at the edges of my mind, but facing the truth felt like staring into an abyss. It was a reality I wasn't entirely prepared to confront, especially after the recent horrors I'd endured.

The oppressive darkness of the mine pressed in on me as I sat there, bound and vulnerable, at the mercy of a man I'd just discovered was my father. His features were etched with a cold resolve, the revelation of his identity a heavy weight upon my shoulders.

"Why?" my voice quivered with a blend of fear and anger, the emotions wrestling within me.

Andras approached with a calculated stride, his demeanor chillingly composed. He knelt beside me, his fingers tracing the ropes that bound me, a cold smile playing on his lips.

"Charlotte," his voice held a chilling calmness, void of any warmth. "You're the key to our plan. An anomaly born of the Sol and Ember bloodlines, a forbidden existence that should never have come to be, yet it's precisely what we need."

Dread coiled in my stomach, a nauseating mix of horror and disbelief clouding my thoughts.

"What do you need me for?" I demanded, though I already knew the answer, hoping to hear it confirmed. I wanted to hear him say it.

Andras's gaze remained averted as he answered, "The ritual to release Disias requires a void soul as a sacrifice. The blood of one born from both light and darkness is the final element needed."

His words struck me like a physical blow. I felt a chill crawl up my spine as I finally realized the full weight of his intentions. I was to be the sacrificial offering in a ritual that would unleash a God of Shadows upon the world.

"What happens after Disias is released?" I pressed, my

voice barely above a whisper, though I dreaded the answer.

Andras's tone took on a fanatical fervor, his eyes alight with fervent belief. "Once Disias is free, our order foresees a new world order, ruled by darkness. We will wield power beyond measure, and our influence will reign supreme."

Tears welled in my eyes, my voice trembling with fear and desperation. "And me? What happens to me?"

Andras's cold gaze finally met mine, devoid of any empathy. "You, my dear Charlotte, will become a martyr, remembered for making it all possible. Your sacrifice will be revered, your name etched in our annals." He let out a low chuckle. His mocking tone cut through the darkness, dripping with scorn. "Your little 'candle of protection' went out today," he sneered, making exaggerated air quotes. "Coincidence isn't it." His taunting words aimed at Hayzun's yearly tradition. I never put much thought into the candle and its ceremony, but the fact that its flame had been doused deepened the pit in my stomach.

The gravity of my impending sacrifice crashed over me, a cocktail of rage and despair bubbling within. The world I had known was crumbling, and the architect of this malevolent plot was none other than my own father.

As Andras filled in the gaps, a chilling realization dawned upon me—I was the only hope to stop The First Chosen and prevent the release of Disias.

24

CONJURING SHADOWS

Mason stood on the sidelines, his face pale. There was a look of reluctant obedience in his gaze, as though he was torn between loyalty and revulsion. My heart ached for him despite the hatred, for the brother who had been twisted by the darkness that surrounded him.

Andras stepped forward, a look of fervor in his eyes as he began to explain the ritual. His voice was alarmingly composed as he delved into the gruesome details. I listened in silent horror.

Mason brought forward a large dagger, the hilt and blade fashioned from human bones. It was a grotesque and chilling creation, a macabre instrument of death.

"In this ritual," Andras began, "the blade itself is a creation of darkness. Crafted from the bones of those who fell victim to our cause and adorned with the blood of the last innocent soul from the Chalice of Shadows, it possesses the power to bridge the chasm between this world and where Disias has been imprisoned."

The room seemed to grow colder as he spoke, his words reverberating with a sinister devotion. I shuddered, bound and helpless on the cold stone altar, as the enormity of the ritual's horror unfolded.

The roof of the mine revealed a small opening, through which the silvery glow of the moon pierced, casting a glow around the chamber.

Andras continued, his voice unrelenting, "When the eclipse aligns with the opening in the roof, it will serve as a bridge, and the ritual shall begin."

He raised the dagger. "This blade will be the key. As it pierces the heart of the one who embodies both light and dark the doorway shall be unlocked."

I could feel the impending darkness, the weight of destiny bearing down upon me. I knew that the ritual was inescapable, but I clung to the hope that there might be a way to thwart the ritual and prevent the release of Disias.

Jesse was supposed to help me through this, to make a plan. But right now, he had no idea where I was.

The atmosphere in the mine grew darker as a crowd of The First Chosen spilled into the room. The air seemed thick with energy.

Andras, stood at the center of the gathering. The dagger fashioned from human bones cradled in his hands. The moon began to redden as it fell into the earth's shadow. The blood moon was a fitting event.

As I lay bound on the altar, the anticipation in the air was intense. The members of The First Chosen had gathered around, their faces bathed in the light of the moon.

The components of the ritual were laid out before me, each more chilling than the last.

Beside the altar lay the Chalice of Shadows, filled with the blood of the third victim. The image of Piper's lifeless body flashed in my mind.

An Engraved Stone, an imposing ancient tablet etched with cryptic symbols served as the altar upon which I was bound.

My body was awash in the red glow of the moon as it was almost fully aligned.

A chant arose around me causing the hair on the nape of my neck to prickle. Their voices swirled together in an eerie chorus.

As the eclipse neared its peak, the room darkened further, and I knew the moment of reckoning had arrived.

Andras stepped forward, his hands trembled ever so slightly as he took hold of the Chalice of Shadows.

The chalice was ornate, its surface etched with intricate patterns.

With the chalice cradled in one hand, Andras turned to the bone dagger. The white tones causing nausea to roll.

Andras dipped the blade of the dagger into the chalice, its surface instantly stained with a mixture of blood, each drop representing the souls that had been claimed for this purpose.

Andras's voice, once wavering with anticipation, took on a steady tone as he began to chant. The words were ancient, cryptic, and spoke of a darkness that had slumbered for far too long. They echoed through the chamber, forming a chorus that seemed to reverberate through the very stones of the mine.

I fought against the bindings that held me. Hot wet tears running down the sides of my face. I wanted to scream, but my body was too tired, and the effort would be unyielding.

Andras's eyes never left the blade, as he chanted. It was a moment of unparalleled significance, the culmination of a plan that had spanned generations. As the chant continued, the alignment drew closer to its zenith, and the world held its breath, waiting for the ancient god to awaken.

The crowd watched, their expressions a mixture of reverence and awe. The weight of their collective belief had an unshakable force.

Andras raised the blade high, the moonlight gleaming on its blood-stained surface. The room seemed to hold its breath as he brought the dagger down, its tip aimed directly at my heart.

My heart pounded with frantic desperation. I pulled against the restraints, straining every muscle in a desperate attempt to break free. The air grew thick with the eerie chorus of incantations, echoing against the stone walls. Beads of sweat formed on my brow, a testament to the fear and anguish that enveloped me.

Andras's voice rose above the haunting chant, each word imbued with a chilling intensity. The dagger loomed over me; its gleaming surface poised to strike.

My thoughts raced, trying to conjure any shred of hope or escape. My breaths came in short, ragged gasps, my chest heaved with a mix of terror and defiance. I was determined not to surrender to the fate Andras and The First Chosen had planned.

As the blade descended, a deafening roar reverberated

through the mine. The air crackled with electric energy, sending tremors through the earth. The moon's reddish hue intensified, casting an ominous glow over the chamber.

25

THE FINAL EMBER

As the blade sank into my chest, a guttural scream tore through the air, reverberating in the cavernous space. Andras pressed the dagger deeper, its sharp bone edges scraping against my ribs as it slid between them almost meeting the resistance of the cold, unforgiving altar. The room quivered as if the very earth beneath us protested the heinous act.

With the dagger embedded in my heart, an intense burst of blinding light erupted from the wound, cascading through the cavern like a radiant shockwave. The brilliance of the light seemed to defy the shadows, casting them aside in an ephemeral dance. The air crackled with a surge of otherworldly energy, and the chants of The First Chosen reached a fevered pitch, their voices intertwining in a chaotic symphony of anticipation.

In that agonizing moment, the bone dagger, now coated

with my essence, rose again, catching the glint of the fractured moonlight. Suddenly, it shattered into a myriad of blinding shards, scattering in all directions. Each shard carried a fraction of the dark energy that had infused the dagger, creating a display of malevolent sparks.

The pain, though excruciating, was overshadowed by a profound disconnection from reality. My consciousness teetered on the precipice of oblivion, slipping away like sand through grasping fingers. However, amid the torment and chaos, a peculiar sensation emerged—a presence, subtle yet unmistakable, offering a strange comfort amid the maelstrom.

As the ritual persisted, The First Chosen pressed forward with unrestrained enthusiasm, determined to complete the dark invocation and unleash Disias upon the world. Their movements became more frenzied, an unholy dance of anticipation and fanaticism.

In the midst of the uproar, I clung to the thread of consciousness, aware that the outcome of this macabre ceremony could reshape the fate of the world. The blinding shards of the shattered dagger continued to linger in the air, pulsating with an ominous energy that mirrored the impending emergence of Disias.

The cavern seemed to echo with the clash of forces—the mystical currents of the ritual colliding with an opposing energy that defied the intent of The First Chosen. The fate of both worlds hung in precarious balance, and I, bound and battered, remained at the center of this cosmic struggle, a pawn in a game that transcended mortal comprehension.

As the ritual surged forward, the air thick with arcane energies, I steeled myself for whatever revelation or transformation awaited on the edge of this journey into the unknown.

A hushed awe settled over The First Chosen, their fanaticism giving way to uncertainty. I felt a shift within me, a connection to something ancient and incomprehensible.

In that moment, I ceased to be just Charlotte, a mere sacrifice in the ritual. I became something more, something far greater, a harmonious blend of light and darkness. The shadows responded, swirling around me as if they had found their rightful place.

The members of The First Chosen watched in both astonishment and trepidation, their grip on the ritual faltering. The balance between light and darkness was being redefined, and I was at the epicenter.

The Eclipse ritual continued, but the balance of power had shifted. The world teetered, and I was determined to protect it from being consumed by shadows.

The very essence of the cavern seemed to shift. The shadows, once menacing and foreboding, now appeared to be in harmony with me. Their intent had morphed into something altogether different, as if they recognized their true purpose.

The struggle for balance and the future of both light and darkness had taken an unforeseen turn, and the weight of the world's fate lied with me.

A fierce blast of wind and debris swept through, scattering the assembly and sending Andras staggering back.

The sudden chaos shattered the eerie serenity, and figures clad in dark attire burst into the room. It was a surge of unexpected intrusion, disrupting the ritual with forceful determination.

Among them, I caught a glimpse of Jesse as he fought through The First Chosen, aiming straight for Andras.

The sight of Jesse gave me a surge of hope, a flicker of light in the encroaching darkness. A renewed determination flooded through me as I strained against my bindings once more, fueled by the possibility of salvation.

The room devolved into pandemonium as a fierce confrontation unfolded, the air crackled.

Caught in the midst of the upheaval, I remained bound but emboldened, my gaze fixed on Jesse, willing him to succeed in stopping Andras and The First Chosen.

As the clash ensued, I clung to a glimmer of hope.

The air popped with anger, and I could feel the power emanating from him.

The ground beneath us began to tremble, stones dislodging from the cavern walls. My vision blurred, and I coughed, wheezing as blood trickled from the wound in my thigh. The pain was agonizing, but I couldn't take my eyes off Jesse, whose very presence seemed to be commanding the earth itself.

In that surreal moment, a shadow slipped behind Jesse, and a sudden gasp of surprise escaped both Andras and Mason. The bindings that held me in place dropped from my arms, and I tumbled heavily to the ground. I struggled to push myself up, my strength ebbing with each passing second.

Jesse reached out, his hand extending toward me, but before he could grasp me, Andras yanked me away. His grip was merciless, driven by the urgent need to complete the rite. The world around me blurred as I was forcibly pulled from Jesse's reach.

Mason, standing at the precipice of a heart-wrenching

decision, found himself torn between his loyalty to Andras, and his deep-seated feelings against him. His gaze darted between the two forces.

The pain from my gunshot wound in my thigh, compounded by the loss of blood, was becoming unbearable.

The figures I didn't recognize were led by one I did. Jace plunged a dagger into the chest of one of The First Chosen, pulling the life from the individual's body as he retrieved the dagger to swing again.

My eyes unfocused, and the world around me swayed like a mirage. The echoing sounds of the battle between light and darkness, love, and ambition, became distant and muffled. With a final, labored breath, I succumbed to the overwhelming exhaustion and the searing pain.

The darkness enveloped me, and I could no longer keep my eyes open. I felt myself slipping away, like a ship retreating into the fog, until everything faded into blackness.

26

WHISPERS IN THE WIND

My consciousness floated in a dark, timeless void. A sense of weightlessness surrounded me, a numbing detachment from reality. Images flashed sporadically, remnants of the chaotic battle, the clash between forces, and the faces etched with determination and conflict.

Moments passed—or perhaps hours, I couldn't discern—before a distant voice began to filter through the haze. It was a faint whisper at first, barely audible amid the darkness, yet growing steadily clearer.

"Charlie, can you hear me?"

The voice tugged at the fringes of my fading awareness. I struggled to respond, my words feeling like distant echoes in the abyss.

The voice, familiar and resolute, stirred something within me. I focused, clawing my way back. Shapes and sounds began to take form—a dim light piercing the darkness, muffled voices, gentle touch of hands on my skin.

I blinked, trying to orient myself. Gradually, the void loosened its grip, replaced by a dimly lit room that swam into view. Figures moved around me, their voices blending into a soothing murmur.

The world was a hazy blur around me as I lay in Jesse's arms, my vision obscured by a mix of pain and exhaustion. The ritual's wounds, had inexplicably healed, contrasted with the persistent agony of my broken arm and the gunshot wound in my thigh along with the cuts the broken vial had left.

Jesse's face, etched with worry and determination, hovered above me as he cradled me gently.

In the haze of pain and dizziness, the world felt like a disjointed patchwork, fleeting glimpses of reality interspersed with moments of oblivion. Jesse's unwavering presence was a beacon, his voice a soothing murmur amid the commotion.

We moved through the passageways, the echoes of Officer Gates and her team preparing to search the mine growing closer. The walls of the mine had been shaken to their very core by the ritual. Any sudden unwarranted movement would most likely cause a collapse.

As we emerged from the mine's oppressive darkness into the open air, a rush of frigid wind swept over me, sending shivers down my spine. The cool air cut through the adrenaline-fueled haze, momentarily sharpening my senses.

Jesse laid me gently on a waiting gurney, and the paramedics and first responders sprang into action, their voices a comforting hum in the background.

The world continued to spin around as I was loaded into

an ambulance, the flashing lights casting a surreal glow on the world around me. The sirens wailed, causing a throbbing ache to settle behind my temples. The darkness encroached once more; its pull irresistible against the backdrop of the chaotic scene. I surrendered to its embrace, the world fading into a dreamlike blur as the ambulance raced toward the distant promise of safety and solace.

HEARTWHISPER

"Sir, you'll have to come back tomorrow. Only family members are allowed in right now." There was a pause before a low growl.

"I am the only family she has right now."

"Sir—"

"I believe it would be in your best interest not to argue with me right now," the voice cut her off. It was angry, possessive. But it was a voice I knew.

I tried to call out, but my mouth was too dry. Pain surged in my body as I tried to move.

"Hey, hey, hey." Warm hands came gently up against the bruised skin on my arms. "Just relax, I'm here." I forced my eyes open, a harsh white light filling my senses. "I've got you, sweetheart." My eyes began to adjust, letting me open them wider Jesse's face came into view, as I felt wet, hot tears roll down my face, leaving a burning in their wake.

In the sterile room, the harsh light accentuated the clinical nature of the environment, casting an uninviting glow against the walls. The curtains, once vibrant, were now a faded powder blue, their edges slightly frayed from years of use. The tiled floor bore the marks of wear and tear, scuffed in patches that mirrored the years of footsteps it had endured. Scratchy white and gray striped sheets itched my skin.

My vision adjusted slowly, bringing Jesse's concerned face into focus. His eyes were a mix of relief and worry as his warm hands cradled my bruised arms gently.

I tried to speak, but my throat felt parched and raw, rendering my attempts futile. Pain surged through me as I attempted to move, a reminder of the ordeal I had just endured.

Jesse's voice, a soothing anchor in the disorienting haze, urged me to relax, his words laced with genuine concern. As I fought to keep my eyes open against the harsh light, the sight of blood soaking Jesse's shirt jolted me.

"It's not mine," he murmured, pulling a chair to the side of the bed. Sitting down he said, "It's yours." This time he was the one to cringe. My body felt heavy as I looked down at it.

In the dimly lit hospital room, the only sounds were the gentle hum of medical equipment and the soft whispers between Jesse and me. His touch, tracing the line of the intravenous needle, offered a sense of grounding amid the chaos that threatened to engulf me.

"They had to clean and close the bullet wound and set the bones in your arm," Jesse explained calmly, his voice a soothing balm to my frayed nerves. His eyes met mine, a silent reassurance that I sought desperately. "Neither Mason nor Andras were caught."

"Did the ritual work?" He adjusted his body.

"We're not really sure yet," his voice was strained. "But Jace was able to get rid of many of the members."

I knew instantly what he meant by get rid of. The image of Jace plunging a knife through flesh filled my vision.

I clenched my jaw, the weight of Mason and Andras's escape pressing heavily upon me. It was a harsh reminder of the danger that still lurked in the shadows, an unresolved threat that loomed over my life.

Is he really my father?" The question weighed on me. My heart twisted at the confirmation Jesse's gaze conveyed. The truth was as unwelcome as it was distressing.

"But that doesn't mean that everything he said was true," Jesse interjected, a glimmer of hope shining through his tired eyes. His attempt to ease the weight of my realizations was evident, yet his own unease was unmistakable.

I shifted uncomfortably, trying to navigate the complexity of my emotions.

"Is my mother still alive?" The memories of Andras's ruthless pursuit and the consequences it brought flooded my mind. "My birth mother."

Jesse hesitated, his demeanor reflecting the gravity of his words. His gentle touch on my hand felt both comforting and burdened.

"As far as I know, yes."

Relief flooded through me, the mere possibility of finding her a flicker of hope in the darkness.

"I want to find her," the determination in my voice was resolute, driven by a desire to unearth truths, regardless of their weight. But Jesse's expression darkened, and his words carried a solemn warning.

"Charlie, she may not be the person you're imagining," he cautioned. His words echoed with a truth I couldn't deny, a reminder that my hopes might not align with reality. "She's a trained liar. Her duty was to infiltrate The First Chosen and bear a child able to overthrow Disias."

The weight of his words settled heavily in my chest. I nodded in solemn acknowledgment, a mixture of disappointment and resignation coursing through me. Yet, a stubborn resolve simmered within, a determination to navigate the web of deception and still strive for a chance to stop Disias. I nodded knowing exactly what I was to her, a means to an end. maybe I could still help stop Disias if the ritual had been successful.

"I want to find her."

He nodded, looking me over. He reached up raking his fingers through his hair before taking my hand in both of his again. His fingers were gentle on my skin, soothing. I wanted nothing more in that moment than to be wrapped in his arms. Safe and secure. I felt another tear escape. He gently reached up and wiped it away.

"Don't cry." He tried to smile, but it fell from his handsome face.

"Jess?"

He hummed softly.

"Will you please just hold me?"

He sat still for a moment before standing. I tried to move over in the small hospital bed.

"Hey, don't move." A small smile formed on his lips. "I'll make it work." He sat on the edge of the bed, lifting his legs up beside mine. He raised his arm, draping it behind my shoulders.

"Come here, baby girl." He gently pulled me into his side. I winced letting out a cry of pain. "Shhh, I'm sorry,"

I adjusted against him. Pain raced up my leg and down my broken arm. "I'm so sorry." He reached over grabbing the hand of my broken arm, gently moving it. I hissed through my teeth, but when he settled it back against me It felt much better than it had, the pain dissipating.

"How do you do that?"

"Do what?"

"Get rid of the pain?" I noticed it first in the clinic, then at his rental when the alcohol he used to clean my cuts didn't sting. Now here.

"I'm not sure," he murmured. "I didn't know I could." His body tensed. "I'm used to inflicting pain not taking it away."

"Maybe it's a side of you that's always been there, just waiting," I encouraged. He adjusted his body leaning further back into the bed. I let my weight fall into him.

"Get some rest."

"Please don't leave." I felt fear inch its way back into my body.

"I'll still be here when you wake up."

I nestled my head deeper into his chest, breathing in his familiar scent, his heart beating beneath my cheek.

"Thank you," I murmured. "For finding me."

An angry growl vibrated in his chest.

"Not soon enough."

"I'm alive because of you," I affirmed, trying to reassure him. His embrace tightened, conveying both protectiveness and an unspoken apology. The hospital gown, abrasive against my skin, drew a groan from me.

"I am so sorry I wasn't there to pick you up from work on time," he confessed, regret thick in his voice. I nodded against his chest, acknowledging the impact of that moment.

"Where were you?" I prodded gently, seeking answers.

"I was getting reinforcements," he explained, the weight of his words carrying history and resolve. "Former members of The First Chosen. They wanted to take down Andras just as much as we did." The puzzle pieces clicked into place, understanding washing over me.

"What's wrong?" He noticed me wince, his concern immediate as I fidgeted with the rough hospital gown.

"It feels like sandpaper," I complained, feeling the discomfort grow. His response was instant. He chuckled softly, pulling his phone from his pocket, silently pressing a few buttons. He put it back into his pocket before adjusting the equally as itchy blanket around me. He leaned down pressing a soft kiss to my forehead.

"If I sleep, I'll dream, and I don't want to dream of that place," I confessed, seeking refuge from the horrors in my slumber.

"You're safe here. I've got you," he reassured me, his words a promise of protection. I allowed my heavy eyelids to flutter shut, trusting him to shield me from the nightmares that lurked in my subconscious.

As sleep threatened to envelop me, voices from the hallway sliced through the room, carrying an undertone of urgency and anger. It wasn't Jesse who roused me from the brink of sleep; instead, it was the discordant echoes of heated conversations, stirring me from the brink of sleep.

"Sir. Sir." The same nurse from before was silenced by a low almost animalistic growl out in the hallway.

"It really isn't up for debate."

The woman faded away as movement drew closer.

I pushed my eyes open to see a blond mop of hair saunter through the doorway. He gave me a sweet smile to which I returned.

"Errand boy," he quipped with that ever-present sweet smile, the gesture masking the underlying concern.

"He was worried about you," Jesse murmured, leaning in to plant a kiss on my temple before preparing to stand.

"Where are you going?" He smiled, standing and taking the bag from Jace. He pulled a shirt from the bag before looking to face Jace, who gave a slight nod, to which Jess went into the joining bathroom. Jace sat in the chair beside the bed.

"How are you doing?" Jace leaned forward in his chair, his eyes holding a mix of care and scrutiny. "And don't tell me fine, because I know you're not." His straightforwardness elicited a smile from me, just as Jesse returned, donning a clean shirt.

"Would you like to get changed?" Jace gestured to the bag of clothes, a small but meaningful gesture of consideration.

"Thank you."

Jace smiled, giving me a nod as a tried to sit.

"Easy," Jace murmured, standing to help me sit. Jesse was beside me in a second. Once I was seated, Jess looked at Jace.

"Can you give us a minute?"

Jace nodded, leaving the room, closing the door behind him. Jesse pulled the clothes from the bag: a loose pair of shorts and one of his T-shirts.

"This should be loose enough. It won't rub on your stitches," he assured me, stepping closer. With gentle movements, he reached behind me to untie the itchy hospital gown, preparing to help me change into more comfortable attire.

"Wait," I murmured. He turned the IV pump off before carefully disconnecting the tubing from my hand. His skills with medical equipment were surprising, but my immediate concern was to ensure I maintained my privacy while changing.

"I have nothing on underneath," I confessed quietly, feeling a surge of vulnerability. His hands paused, his focus shifting entirely to me.

"Sweetheart," he murmured softly, his eyes unwavering, "you can trust me." I nodded, acknowledging his reassurance.

"It's not that I don't trust you." I met his gaze, searching for understanding.

He stepped closer, cupping my chin with a gentle finger, encouraging me to look up at him. Leaning down, he pressed a tender kiss to my lips.

"I won't look," he promised, his attention solely on my eyes. With his guidance, he skillfully removed the hospital gown, being mindful of keeping me covered. He ensured my broken arm was comfortably placed in the loose sleeve of the shirt before gently handing it to me, maintaining my modesty as I readied it over my head. Despite his care, pain shot down my arm, and I winced.

"I'm sorry," he expressed, a furrow of concern raising his brow at my discomfort. I nodded, acknowledging the gesture. "The bottoms will be tricky," he contemplated, assessing the situation. He fetched the bottoms, sliding my feet into them cautiously. Any movement intensified the pain coursing down my injured leg. As he attempted to pull them up over my hips, a jolting pain made me cry out, causing him to grimace in response.

"Do you think it would be okay if we got Jace to help?" He looked at me, a silent plea in his eyes. I paused, contemplating the idea. His request stemmed from a genuine desire to alleviate my discomfort, and the growing bond between the brothers was evident. Slowly, I nodded in agreement.

His pleading eyes told me he didn't want to hurt me anymore, and I was happy to see the brothers getting along.

Within moments, Jace returned to the room, his gentle eyes immediately locking with mine, filled with concern. His presence brought a sense of calm, and I felt a touch more at ease despite the persistent ache.

"Hey," he greeted softly, glancing at Jesse, who had re-entered the room, joining us at my bedside.

"Can you lend a hand?" Jesse's voice was gentle, his eyes flickering with gratitude toward his brother. Jace nodded, moving closer.

"I'm going to help lift you, and Jesse will keep you covered, all right?" Jace's tone was reassuring, and his approach was cautious. I nodded, feeling a mix of gratitude and vulnerability.

With careful coordination between the two, they expertly lifted me, ensuring the least amount of strain on my injured leg and arm. Jesse shielded me with the blanket, his hands deftly securing it.

"Easy now," Jace murmured, gently adjusting the

bottoms over my hips, taking extra care to prevent any abrupt movements.

I cringed at the pain in my leg as I was sat back down. Jess threw the gown over the back of the chair before hooking the IV back up and turning the pump on again.

A moment later they both gently turned me and laid me back in the bed, pulling the blanket up around me.

"Are you hungry?"

My stomach growled at Jesse's words. The lack of food in my stomach was now very apparent. He smiled.

"What would you like?"

"Anything."

He nodded bending down to give me a kiss, soft and slow.

"I won't be long," he whispered against my lips before straightening up. "Stay with her, please."

Jace nodded, claiming the chair next to the bed once again. Jace's presence nearby was oddly comforting.

"And keep your hands and thoughts to yourself." Jesse pinched the bridge of his nose. His protectiveness of me gave me a sense of security.

"Don't worry, Boss." Jace raised a hand giving him a mocking salute.

As Jess left to get me food, I struggled to get comfortable against the stiff bed. Jace chuckled beside me watching me struggle. I grimaced at him.

"Can you get me more pillows?" I managed, feeling the strain in my voice. Jace's smirk softened, and he rose to help, acknowledging my discomfort. As he adjusted the pillows, a surge of pain shot through my leg due to the awkward angle, contorting my face in discomfort.

Jace noticed as he moved closer to the bed. He sat silently, kicking his legs up on the small bed raising his arm for me. I looked at him wearily.

"Come," he murmured softly, a playful smirk tugging at his lips. "I promised to keep my hands to myself, remember," his words carried a hint of humor, attempting to lighten the mood. The persistent pain in my leg urged me to accept the comfort he offered, and I leaned into his side, finding a small measure of relief in the adjusted position.

His arm dropped around me, cradling me into his side. His touch was gentle and caring, but it wasn't familiar like Jesse's. My stomach ached wishing he was here, but he would be back soon.

Jace hummed a soft tune, his head resting back against the scratchy hospital linens. I let out a small sigh, allowing my body to relax against his, feeling the fatigue weigh heavily on me. With a sense of gratitude for the temporary relief, I closed my eyes, seeking solace in the momentary respite.

A low growl jolted me back into consciousness.

"I told you to keep your hands to yourself," his voice was strained.

"She was uncomfortable and in pain. This way she could keep pressure off her leg," he stated calmly, his hands raised to show he wasn't touching me.

"You could have gotten pillows," it was low and guttural.

Jace's response had an edge of playful insolence, "She asked me to, but I liked this better."

I hesitated, unwilling to intervene, wanting to understand

more from the conversation.

"Let her go, please," the pained plea cut through the tension. Something told me he wasn't just talking about now.

"I will when she chooses, but not until then," Jace mused, his voice laden with an unspoken significance that left me wondering what he meant.

Moments later soft hands came against my back.

"Charlie?" I opened my eyes, turning my head to see Jesse. "Your food is here."

Jace took his sweet time getting up from beside me, resting his hand on my good leg.

"I should go," his voice barely above a murmur as he glanced toward Jesse, who remained silent, focused on arranging the food on the rolling tray he had pulled over.

"Thank you for coming," my words came out soft, but he smiled, giving a slight nod as he disappeared through the door. I focused back on Jesse as he busied himself with arranging the food. I tried to reach out to him, my fingers gently clasping his. He stiffened, a momentary pause settling over him. His eyes remained fixed on the food; his response delayed.

"Is everything okay?" I asked softly, sensing a disturbance in his demeanor. His hand slipped out of my grasp; his attention solely focused on the meal spread before us.

"You should eat," he said quietly, evading my question. "Before it gets cold." His words carried an unspoken weight, a subtle shift in his usual warmth. I nodded in acknowledgment, reaching for a french fry and savoring its familiar taste. My growling stomach urged me to consume more, and I continued, but as I attempted to grasp the burger,

I struggled, my weakened state making even simple tasks challenging.

"Here," Jesse murmured, cutting it up into quarters so I could manage it better. I mumbled another thank you as I grabbed one of the now smaller pieces. He nods. Panic rose in my throat.

"Did I do something wrong?" That soft look that I am so used to takes over his features as he brings his eyes up to mine.

"No, love, not you."

His words were warm, but there was a shadow, an unspoken weight behind them. I picked at the tray of food, the apprehension tightening in my chest until I was no longer hungry. Jesse tidied up the remnants, his movements controlled and precise, before settling back on the bed beside my injured leg. His eyes fixated on the area where the bullet had pierced my skin, as though searching for answers buried within the scars.

I swallowed hard, breaking the silence that wrapped around us. "Why did you tell Jace to 'let me go'?" His body stiffened, a sudden shift in his demeanor as his eyes snapped up to meet mine, a myriad of emotions dancing in their depths. There was a silent plea in his expression.

"You heard that?" his voice wavered, a tinge of desperation lacing his tone. I nodded, sensing there was more he wasn't telling me. His gaze darted around the sterile room.

"Are you sure you want to know?" He shifted closer, the air between us charged with anticipation. "Kiss me, first." His request was a mix of yearning and dread. I felt a pang of worry clawing at my chest. "Because once I say it, I can't take it back."

"Jess?" My voice quivered with anxiety. "What is it?" His eyes shimmered with unshed tears, a heaviness in his expression. I nodded, urging him to share. As he leaned in, his lips brushed mine gently, a tender, bittersweet moment before he drew back.

"You..." He halted, a frustrated curse escaping him. "You are my Heartwhisper."

"Heartwhisper." The word echoed in my mind, stirring up a whirlwind of emotions. It sounded profound, yet the weight of his distress indicated something else.

"It's like what you would call a soulmate. You're bound to me by fate."

My heart stuttered in my chest. Did he not want to be? Is that why he was so upset? What did this have to do with Jace?

"I don't understand."

He started again. "You're my Heartwhisper, but I'm not yours..." pausing, he let the words and their implications sink in. "Jace is."

The revelation hit me like a sudden, nauseating whirlpool. The room seemed to spin, my mind grappling with the implications.

"That is why I asked him to let you go." The sheen in his eyes had not left him. It only grew more apparent.

The more I thought about what he had said, the more my brain refused to comprehend it. This man in front of me had saved my life more times than I cared to count. He had quickly become my entire world. Yet here he was telling me that his brother was my 'Heartwhisper,' whatever that means. My heart ached.

"I would like to go home." My voice was barely a

whisper, carrying the weight of confusion and hurt. Jesse's searching gaze met mine, acknowledging my unspoken turmoil as he quietly left the room. The emptiness that lingered was suffocating, leaving me grappling with a truth that felt impossible to comprehend.

Minutes passed into what felt like an hour before Jesse returned with a doctor. Neither one looked happy.

"Miss. Lowrey." The nurse stepped up beside the bed.

"It is in my opinion that you should remain under our care for the next couple of days." She reached for the IV pump, turning it off. "Your friend here is very persistent." I looked to Jess where he stood in the doorway. The doctor removed the IV from my hand. "I have given him care instructions for your wounds and extra bandages."

I looked to his hand where a small plastic bag was in his grasp. I gave him an appreciative smile as he stepped out of the way as a nurse rolled a wheelchair in beside the bed. It was a blaze of different pain radiating through my body as I was jostled and lifted.

Soon I was seated in the passenger seat of Jesse's car.

Once locked in the silence with him I turned.

"Thank you."

He forced a soft smile, before pulling out of the parking lot. Amid the steady hum of the car, my mind raced, jumping between fragments of recent memories. Images of Mason and Andras clashed with thoughts of my estranged family ties, interspersed with the revelation Jesse had shared earlier. It was an entangled mess of emotions and realizations, each demanding its own space in my thoughts.

Lost in the whirlwind of my mind, I barely registered the familiar surroundings until the passenger door swung open.

The sight snapped me back to the present, revealing that we were parked outside the small rental.

The evening air was cool against my skin as Jesse knelt beside me, his expression wrought with an unspoken vulnerability. His hand rested on the car seat, and I could sense the weight of his emotions in the silent moments that passed between us.

"I think it's probably easier if I just carry you in, okay?" His voice held a subtle uncertainty, a hesitancy that hinted at his internal turmoil. I gazed at him, the flicker of concern in his eyes echoing the tumultuous thoughts in my mind.

"Jess," I murmured, a pang of guilt nudging at me for not reassuring him sooner.

"You don't have to say anything," he interrupted gently, shaking his head. "I see the way he looks at you." He paused, as if grappling with his own emotions. "I can take you to him if you'd rather?"

"Jesse, please take me inside," I requested, sensing his internal struggle. His movements were gentle yet deliberate as he slid an arm behind my back and the other beneath my knees. I winced in pain as he lifted me from the car, the door shut with a heavy thud behind us.

"I don't care," I whispered, my voice barely audible against the backdrop of the night. I nestled my head against his shoulder, feeling the steady rhythm of his heartbeat. "I don't care if you are not my 'Heartwhisper' and I don't care if Jace is." His movements stilled, the air thick with unspoken emotions.

"You are my angel," I confessed softly, feeling the warmth of his breath against my cheek as he nuzzled his face close to mine, a shared moment of understanding in the quiet night.

"Let's get you inside, yeah?" his voice was gentle, filled with an underlying current of concern. I nodded, urging him to move, but he seemed momentarily lost in his thoughts, his focus elsewhere until he guided us to the door, navigating carefully.

"Jess?" My voice tugged him from his reverie, prompting him to continue. He maneuvered me inside, handling the door with care before redirecting his attention to me.

"Let's get you into bed." His suggestion was met with a pause, my own request surfacing.

"Actually … can I have a shower?" His smile softened the melancholy in his eyes as he nodded in understanding, leading us into the bathroom. As he seated me on the countertop, a pang of pain shot through my leg.

The need for a shower was overwhelming, the sensation of dirt and grime clinging to my skin and hair. Jesse moved to start the shower, emphasizing the limitations about my stitches and bandages getting wet. I glanced at him, acknowledging the need for his assistance. A gentle kiss on my forehead reassured me before he stepped away momentarily, returning with the bag provided by the doctor.

He carefully tended to my arm first, wrapping a protective plastic covering around the cast, securing it in place. I watched him work in silence, his attention shifting to my leg. With delicate movements, he adjusted the bandages, applying a clear, protective layer that sealed around the edges.

"I'll replace the bandages when you're out of the shower." His reassuring gaze met mine as I looked up at him, grateful for his care and support in a moment filled with uncertainty.

His fingers brushed against the hem of my shirt, a simple gesture that triggered a sharp intake of breath. His eyes met mine, an unspoken promise of safety in them.

"Just let me help," his voice was gentle, and I nodded as I let him pull the fabric of his oversized shirt over my head, discarding it on the floor. I brought my eyes up to his to find he was already staring intently into mine. "Can you stand for just a second?" He grabbed my hand, helping me off the counter. He kept his eyes on mine as he rid me of the rest of any clothing before picking me up and lowering me onto the shower floor.

He grabbed a bottle of shampoo before kneeling beside me, wetting my hair, scrubbing it clean and rinsing the grime from my scalp. I sat letting his fingers gently clean my skin, getting lost in his touch.

All too soon the water stopped. and a soft towel was wrapped around my body. Seated back on the counter in another loose shirt and pair of shorts I watched as Jesse towel dried my hair.

"Thank you." These words should have been coming out of my mouth, but instead they came from him. I looked at him quizzically. "For trusting me." He moved his attention to the bandages on my leg, gently easing the edge of the water-resistant bandage from my skin.

"Thank you," I murmured, reiterating his words. "For everything." I hissed through my teeth grabbing his wrist as the bandage pulled.

"I'm sorry sweetheart." His jaw tensed.

"It's okay." He continued to gently ease the bandages off, taking the gauze with it. I winced as the gauze pulled from the tender area, around the stitches. Pain flared, and my breaths quickened, the sight of the exposed wound making my stomach churn. The torn, pink flesh and the stitches beneath felt like a raw reminder of the recent ordeal.

"Charlie." His hand cupped the side of my face redirecting my attention to his eyes. "Breathe."

I focused on him, trying to push the ripped angry looking skin out of my mind.

"Jess," my words came hoarse.

"Don't look." his soft kiss on my forehead accompanied the reassurance. "It'll be over soon, okay?" I complied, shutting my eyes tightly.

His careful touch moved around the wound, and a sharp intake of breath betrayed my discomfort. A cooling sensation followed as he applied some soothing ointment along the stitches.

"Just breathe," he coached, his voice a steady anchor in the midst of the discomfort. "Almost done."

I sensed the gentle wrapping of fresh gauze around my thigh, secured in place with delicate taping. Soft, tender kisses graced each of my eyelids before I slowly opened them.

"Tired?" His breath brushed against my lips.

I nodded weakly, meeting his gaze in the muted glow of the room. With a swift and effortless movement, I found myself enveloped in his sturdy embrace, being carefully settled into his bed.

"Stay," I found myself pleading softly, my gaze fixed on him, hoping against hope that he wouldn't refuse.

A smile danced in his eyes, soothing my fears. "Just let me shower first."

His words carried reassurance, but the prospect of him briefly leaving made my heart race with anxiety.

I closed my eyes, trying to pass the moments swiftly, my mind yearning for his presence and the comfort of his nearness. I didn't want to be away from him, even though I knew he wasn't going to be long.

In the semi-darkness of the room, the shadows began to gather, casting a familiar yet terrifying atmosphere. It wasn't long before the murky haze enveloped everything, pulling me back into the bleak, chilling depths of the mine. I felt the roughness of the post against my skin, the constricting bind of ropes, and the creeping sensation of blood soaking through my clothes. Panic took hold, and my voice tore through the oppressive silence, reverberating against the cold walls of the mine.

Suddenly, hands seized me, roughly releasing me from the post, but the relief was short-lived. I was yanked deeper into the abyss, my cries stifled by the inescapable darkness. Desperate screams echoed in the void, a chilling soundtrack to my terror. My body fought against the invisible hold, clawing at the air for any semblance of escape.

In a frantic blur, my eyes flew open, fighting the ghosts of that harrowing place. My fingers dug into flesh, a desperate attempt to break free from the haunting memory. Breathless and raw, my voice cracked as I pleaded for release, begging to be spared from the suffocating grip of that nightmare.

Strong arms enveloped me, drawing me close to a comforting warmth, and Jesse's soothing voice cut through the chaos. His words became an anchor, pulling me back to reality, back to safety. Tears streamed down my face, a mix of terror and relief as I buried myself in the sanctuary of his embrace.

"Jess," I sobbed, seeking solace in his presence.

"I know," he murmured, his fingers tangling in my hair, cradling me gently.

Visions flashed through my mind, haunting images of my mother's vacant, lifeless gaze, her eyes robbed of their usual stare. The memory pierced through me, a reminder of the painful losses I had endured.

My body shook in his grasp.

"Everyone's gone," the words escaped in a broken whisper, a haunting revelation of loss and guilt. I lifted my gaze to Jesse, my eyes clouded with fear of his response, afraid of the judgment that might reflect in his eyes. "And I'm responsible for those deaths," I confessed, the weight of my admission pressing upon me like a heavy burden. "All those girls, it was me."

He shook his head, running his thumb along my bottom lip.

"It wasn't you, not intentionally."

"But I still did it."

His eyes searched mine before he rested his forehead against me.

"You," he murmured. "Have the kindest heart of anyone I've ever met."

"You don't hate me?" He laughed, sitting back from me.

"Charlie," he said, taking my hands in his, his fingers gently intertwining with mine. He exposed the faint marks on his forearms. "Look at these." His voice was calm, reassuring. "Nothing you could ever do would change how I feel about you."

I dropped my head, feeling a wave of relief wash over me, tinged with disbelief. His words struck a chord deep within, carving out a fragment of hope amid the darkness of my thoughts.

"Would you do me a favor?" I met Jesse's gaze, hoping he'd understand. After a brief pause, he nodded. "Would you go to the bathroom and grab me the suture removal kit the doctor gave you?" He glanced at me, his concern evident, but he complied, returning with the sterile package.

I struggled to open it with my one functional hand. "I used these," I confessed, pulling out the scissors. "Bigger ones," I added, noting the slice marks on my exposed wrist. His expression shifted, but he remained quiet as I handed them to him. A reminder of what I was capable of.

He accepted them, his eyes reflecting a mix of emotions.

"I want to remember them," I admitted softly, extending my arm toward him. "The same way you do." The reminders on his arms danced across his skin. The people I killed, those innocent women. I needed a reminder of them that I would never be able to forget.

His eyes met mine, his discomfort obvious. "Where do you want them?" he asked gently. I scanned my arm, contemplating for a moment.

"Where did you start?" I inquired, tracing one line with my finger.

"Here," he said, running his thumb over the inside of my arm.

"Okay," I whispered, allowing him to guide my arm closer. His touch was delicate, his thumb caressing the unmarked skin. As he poised the small, pointed blade, my heart raced, but I held still, bracing for the bittersweet moment.

"Close your eyes," his voice was gentle yet determined. I complied, feeling the weight of his actions. "Ready?" I nodded, anticipation building within me. Pressure followed, the blade tracing a deliberate path on my skin. One. A sharp intake of breath escaped me. Two. The sensation of warm blood made me shudder. Three. The last cut, swift yet deliberate. I opened my eyes to see Jesse swiftly tending to the wounds, his movements deft and caring.

"Thank you," my voice carried gratitude but also the weight of the shared experience. His gaze fell to the marks on his own arms, a reflection of shared pain. I recognized the understanding in his eyes.

"You should get some rest," he suggested. But the restless thoughts lurking in my mind prevented any respite.

"I can't," I admitted, acknowledging the relentless pull of haunting dreams awaiting my slumber.

"I would like…" my words faltered briefly. "I'd like to go to the house and get a few things before the bank sells it." The memories and emotions tied to that place were complicated, a mix of loss and detachment.

"We can go now or in the morning if you'd like," Jesse offered, concern evident in his voice. "Either way, you should take more pain meds."

"Now," I decided firmly. "I'd like to get it over with."

28

WOVEN DESTINIES

The familiar silhouette of the house emerged on the horizon, casting long shadows across the overgrown lawn. My breath hitched at the sight, memories flooding back—the laughter in the kitchen, the echoes of arguments in the halls, the warmth of family dinners. But now, it stood silent, a hollow shell of what it used to be.

As Jesse parked the car, his hand hovered over the ignition, a silent pause before he turned toward me. "Are you ready?" his voice was soft, filled with empathy.

As we entered the house, I instinctively flipped on the lights, shaking my head when they didn't turn on.

Stepping in further my breath hitched in my throat when I saw the mass occupying one end of the couch.

Mason stood, taking a step closer.

In that moment, my world seemed to shatter into

fragments, each piece tinged with betrayal and confusion. Mason's presence, once threatening, now radiated an unsettling mixture of remorse and desperation. Jesse's protective stance behind me kept me grounded, his mere presence a lifeline in the midst of this unexpected encounter.

"Charlie." He grabbed my shoulder. "Get behind me."

"Charlotte please." Mason raised his hands level with his shoulders. "I'm so sorry." His face contorted. "I didn't want for any of this to happen."

Mason's eyes flickered between Jesse and me, his posture showing genuine remorse. "I didn't know the extent of Andras's plans. I came to Hayzun to reconnect with my sister, to bring you back home." His words held a genuine sincerity, yet they collided against the harsh reality of the past weeks.

My grip on my emotions wavered. How could I reconcile with this person in front of me. An individua who helped orchestrate my capture, the one I associated with terror and helplessness?

"Leave before I kill you." Came low growl from behind me.

Mason continued as though Jesse hadn't spoken. "Andras never told me he planned to liberate Disias." He shook his head. "I'd never have helped him if I'd known."

I felt my bottom lip quiver.

"You kidnapped me and tied me up. You let me kill those women."

"No," his voice came out loud and rushed. "I mean yes, I took you. But I didn't know he had you killing them."

"Charlie?" I raised my hand silencing Jesse, taking a step forward.

"I want to hear what he has to say."

Mason looked relived.

"Charlotte, I really am sorry."

I wanted to believe him, to see a glimmer of truth in his eyes, but the pain of betrayal was too raw. Then, something shifted in the room—a shadow lurked in my periphery.

My eyes widened as the figure emerged from the darkness, the features finally coming into focus. It wasn't a threat but rather someone who seemed to carry a silent plea for understanding. Their presence, unexpected and enigmatic, added another layer to the situation.

Confusion and dread mingled within me, my mind struggling to comprehend. As the figure stepped closer, my instinct warred with the vulnerability in their stance. All I knew was that the unraveling of the truth had only just begun. The recognition in my voice wavered, disbelief laced with a faint glimmer of hope as I pieced together the presence before me.

"Dad?" I breathed, barely daring to believe what I saw. His smile was familiar, comforting amid the chaos, a memory from a time when life was simpler. He had been here all along, watching over me in the shadows. His attempts to pull me from Hayzun flashed in my mind, his silent protectiveness evident even now.

But the moment shattered as I refocused on the grim reality unfolding before me. Mason, the brother I had only recently discovered, now held a weapon in his grasp. His features twisted in an unsettling blend of desperation and determination.

"Mason?" my voice quivered; eyes fixated on the glint of the blade. Fear surged through me. Jesse shifted protectively a solid presence ready to shield me from any threat.

The air thickened, every heartbeat pounding in my ears. The sight of the weapon in Mason's hand gnawed at the fragile peace hanging between us. Had his remorse been a façade all along? Or was there a more profound turmoil driving his actions?

A growl rumbled low in Jesse's chest; a warning as he braced himself to defend. The surrealness of the situation, the presence of my father after all this time, mingled with the imminent threat before me.

"Mason, please," my plea was barely a whisper, but the urgency in my voice echoed through the room. I pleaded with him to reconsider, to let go of the weapon, hoping against hope that the brother I thought I knew was still within reach.

The seconds stretched, a taut thread poised to snap, leaving the outcome hanging precariously in the balance. My heart raced, echoing the turmoil raging within me, torn between hope, fear, and an overwhelming need for resolution.

"I thought it only fitting." He raised the blade looking at it, the clocktower tolling twelve eerily in the background. His eyes raised to mine once more as he quickly brought the knife to the skin of his throat.

Before I could speak a large tear spread across his jugular, widening as the blade sliced further. The meaty sound of flesh tearing and ripping apart filled the gaps between the clocktower tolls.

Mason fell to the floor, a pool of crimson blood spilling from his throat with each gurgled breath.

In a heartbeat, a piercing scream tore from my throat, a guttural plea for help and a desperate rush to reach Masons side, overrode the searing pain in my leg. Every movement sent a jolt of agony through me, the stitches protesting with a sharp, biting sensation. But the urgency of the moment eclipsed my physical torment.

Kneeling beside him, I felt a surge of panic seize me, his labored breaths rattling through the thickening air. Blood gushed from a severe wound on his throat, a crimson stream that I tried futilely to contain with my trembling hand.

"Jesse," I gasped, my voice fraught with fear and urgency. My fingers pressed against the wound, but blood continued to slip through, coating my hand with its warmth. Panic surged through me like a rising tide, threatening to overwhelm my senses.

"Call nine-one-one," I pleaded, the words tumbled from my lips in a frantic rush. My gaze remained fixed on Jesse's face, hoping that help would arrive in time, that somehow my touch could stem the flow until the professionals took over. Every second felt like an eternity, each heartbeat hammered in my ears as I fought against the terror threatening to consume me.

THE RITUALS ECHO

Anger pulsed through my body, drowning me in a whirlpool of betrayal and resentment. Loud sobs racked my chest as tremors shook every inch of me.

As Jesse reached for his phone, a strange sensation washed over me. It began as a gentle warmth in my chest, coursing down my arms. I watched in awe as a soft glow emanated from my palms, slowly brightening and casting light across the room.

The energy surged within me, making the room vibrate with its intensity. Raising my hands, the light intensified, pushing back the shadows that enveloped me. Jesse stared at me, his eyes wide with wonder and concern, witnessing this inexplicable manifestation.

In the midst of the radiant glow, my body hummed with a mixture of awe and fear. My mind flashed back to the ritual, the blinding light, and the dagger shattering into shards. Disias. The ritual had worked, but not as anyone expected.

My journey was far from over, but I was ready to walk the path ahead, accompanied by the God of Shadows' light. I sensed an ancient and powerful energy pulsating through me, connecting me to something beyond comprehension. The weight of responsibility mingled with the exhilaration of newfound strength.

Jesse eyed me as he cautiously extended his hand toward the glowing energy emanating from my palms. The warmth responded to his touch, flickering like a living entity.

"What does this mean?" Jesse asked in a hushed voice.

"I think … I think I've become the vessel for Disias's power," I replied, still gaping at the vibrant glow. "The power that The First Chosen wanted to control."

The radiance intensified, forming a protective aura that extended beyond my hands. Confidence surged within me, recognizing the potential of this newfound ability.

"I think I can use it to bring balance," I said, my voice steadier. "To counter the darkness that The First Chosen wished to unleash."

Returning to the present, I felt my hands gravitate toward Mason's throat, the radiant glow penetrating his skin. Tears streamed down my face as I yearned for more time with him, for a chance to free him from our father's grasp.

Mason drew a gasping breath, his eyes springing open. The only remnants of his death remained in the pool of blood and a scar stretching across his neck.

I gasped, watching in disbelief as Mason drew a shaky breath, his eyes darting around in confusion. His body convulsed with ragged coughs as life seemed to flood back into him. The vivid scar across his throat served as a stark reminder of what had just occurred.

"Mason!" my voice broke, a mix of relief and shock echoing in the room. Tears cascaded down my cheeks, mingling with a flood of emotions. He blinked, disoriented, trying to comprehend his surroundings.

Jesse's hand found mine, a silent reassurance in the midst of this surreal moment. His gaze held astonishment, mirroring my own tumultuous feelings.

"Mason, it's okay," I whispered, reaching out hesitantly toward him. His eyes locked onto mine, a myriad of emotions swirling within them. Fear, confusion, and a hint of recognition flickered across his face.

I stumbled over my words, trying to grasp the inexplicable turn of events. "It's … You're alive." I gestured to the blood pooling beneath him. "We thought … you were gone."

Mason struggled to sit up, his hand instinctively going to his throat, feeling the jagged scar. His breaths came in short gasps as he tried to piece together what had just transpired.

"I-I saw you die," I stammered, my voice shaking with a blend of relief and disbelief. "But you're here."

He opened his mouth to speak, but no words emerged. Confusion and panic clouded his expression. The air in the room crackled with an inexplicable tension.

Jesse moved closer as we waited for Mason's explanation. I glanced at Jesse, a silent exchange passing between us. What had just happened was beyond our understanding, beyond anything we had ever encountered.

Mason's eyes flickered between us, his gaze finally settling on me.

"I don't know what happened," he managed to whisper hoarsely. "I felt, I felt like I was gone, but then..." His voice trailed off, lost in the surrealness of the moment.

A sudden rush of footsteps echoed down the hallway as the police arrived, summoned by the commotion. Jesse moved to intercept them, providing a hurried explanation, while I stayed close to Mason, grappling with the inexplicable miracle before us.

As the officers rushed in, their voices merged into a blur, and I felt a pang of guilt for not having the answers they sought. Mason's resurrection remained a baffling mystery, one that would need unraveling in the days to come. The room buzzed with frantic activity, yet amid the chaos, a sliver of hope emerged—hope that somehow, against all odds, life could triumph over death. That maybe, I was in fact, the ember of light in the shadows.

To be continued …

Bonus
Content

JACE'S REVELATION
Jace's POV

I've known from the moment I laid eyes on her. Charlotte, the woman who had captured my attention from the very first glance.

It wasn't her smile or her eyes, although those were part of it. No, it was something deeper, something that reached into my very being and whispered, "This is your heartwhisper."

As I watch her now, from a distance, my heart ached with the knowledge that we were intertwined in a way she could not yet comprehend.

She was happy, blissfully so, with Jesse. And even though it would be so satisfying to take her away from him, I can't bear the thought of causing her pain.

Being a Heartwhisper isn't just a matter of destiny and inevitability. It's a delicate dance between two souls, a choice that goes beyond the supernatural. Charlotte, being part human, holds a say in this matter. A choice she doesn't even know she has.

She deserves to make her own choices, to follow her heart, even if that heart leads her to another.

THE GATHERING
Andras's POV

The concealed chamber, a well-kept secret behind the bustling town of Hayzun, was a testament to the hidden history and arcane power that fueled The First Chosen. The stone walls, adorned with ancient symbols and etchings, seemed to pulse with an otherworldly energy. Torch sconces, their flames dancing in an eerie, golden hue, cast elongated shadows across the faces of the gathered members.

The Valing, our silent companions perched in the chamber's corners, their dark feathers ruffled around them as they cawed. They served as both witnesses and agents of our clandestine endeavors, ensuring that messages and information flowed seamlessly between us, and our secrets remained hidden from prying eyes.

I, Andras, stood at the head of the gathering,

"We gather tonight," I began, my voice echoing in the chamber's hallowed silence, "to fulfill our destiny, to release Disias from his ancient prison. The Sol bloodline has held him captive for far too long, and it is our sacred duty to set him free."

The members of The First Chosen nodded in agreement; their faces shrouded in determination.

But what they did not know, what I had concealed from them was my true motivation. As their leader, I had ambitions beyond their knowledge. I planned to harness the power of Disias for my own purposes, controlling it to attain my own desires.

I continued; my words designed to stoke the fires of their excitement. "Once Disias is released, his powers will be harnessed, and together we shall achieve greatness. The world will bend to our will, and we shall become the builders of a new era, where shadows and light shall be our instruments."

The Valing, those silent sentinels of our intentions, watched over us, their presence a silent affirmation of our purpose. The chamber crackled with an energy both ancient and deadly.

DICTIONARY

1. Valing: Raven-like creatures used by The First Chosen for spying and messaging.

2. Heartwhisper: A term for soulmates, individuals destined to be deeply connected and share a profound bond.

3. Void Soul: A person born of both Sol and Ember bloodlines, possessing the unique ability to balance light and darkness.

4. Sol Bloodline: An ancient lineage connected to the element of light, often associated with goodness and purity.

5. Ember Bloodline: An ancient lineage tied to the element of darkness, often associated with shadows and secrecy.

6. The First Chosen: An enigmatic organization with the goal of releasing Disias, The God of Shadows, and reshaping the balance of light and dark.

7. Disias: The God of Shadows, imprisoned to maintain the balance of good and evil in the world.

8. Eclipse of Shadows: An intricate ritual aimed at freeing Disias from his ancient prison, involving the sacrifice of a void soul and celestial alignment.

Dear Readers,

I'm so excited to have you on this journey with me. Your support means the world, and I would be grateful if you could take a moment to share your thoughts.

If you enjoyed the story, kindly consider leaving a review on Amazon and Goodreads. Your reviews not only offer valuable feedback, but also help other readers discover the book. Your words have the power to make a difference.

Also, I'd love to connect with you on Instagram. Follow me @hannahjacklinauthor for updates, behind-the-scenes glimpses, and more exciting content. Feel free to tag me in pictures with the book; I would love to see them.

Thank you for being a part of this journey.

Until next time,

Hannah Jacklin

ACKNOWLEDGMENTS

Writing a book is a journey, and it's one I didn't take alone. To my dearest friends Bethany Davis and Victoria McCauley, your creative minds sparked many of the ideas woven into these pages. Your inspiration lit the fire that kept this story alive.

To my love Joe, thank you for your unwavering support and the constant encouragement to see this dream through to the end. Your belief in me never wavered, and I'm forever grateful for your patience and motivation.

A huge shoutout to Getcover.com for bringing my vision to life with the incredible cover design. Your creativity gave my book the perfect face.

To the authors who paved the way with their exceptional storytelling: Alex Aster, Jennifer L. Armentrout, and Becca Fitzpatrick, your books were my guiding stars, illuminating the path when my writing journey hit rough patches.

A special mention to Charlotte Dobre, whose captivating videos provided a welcome escape and entertainment during the writing process. Thank you for inspiring me with your creativity.

Heartfelt thanks to my parents for their unwavering support and belief in my dreams. Your encouragement has been my guiding light.

Special gratitude to Nomi Palmer and Melissa Smith for their invaluable beta reading and Mekhala for your amazing editing skills. Your constructive feedback and insights have enhanced the story in ways I couldn't have achieved alone.

And last to everyone else who supported me along the way—friends, family, and fellow writers—your encouragement and belief in this project fueled my determination to bring these words to life.

Thank you, from the bottom of my heart.

Hannah Jacklin

ABOUT THE AUTHOR

Hannah Jacklin, a dedicated writer, has been weaving tales since she could hold a pencil. Her passion for storytelling ignited the creation of her debut novel, "Ember of Light." Residing in a serene Ontario town with her loyal canine companion and supportive fiancé, Hannah finds inspiration in the quietude of her surroundings.

An ardent animal lover, Hannah's days are infused with creativity and passion for the written word. When not engrossed in the enchanting world of writing, she indulges in her love for crafting and immerses herself in the captivating narratives of books.

Through her imaginative storytelling and love for the written art, Hannah aims to captivate readers' hearts and minds, inviting them into worlds crafted with vivid imagination and unwavering passion. "Ember of Light" is just the beginning of her literary journey, promising many more captivating tales to come.